D1451041

CPSIA information can be obtained at www.ICGtesting.com
Printed in the USA
BVOW010807030513

319806BV00005B/11/P

9 781921 919664

THE BANISHING STONES

by

ELIZABETH WARD

THE BANISHING STONES
Copyright © ELIZABETH WARD 2013

First published by Zeus Publications 2013
http://www.zeus-publications.com
P.O. Box 2554
Burleigh M.D.C.
QLD. 4220
Australia.

The National Library of Australia Cataloguing-in-Publication

Author: Ward, Elizabeth, 1970-

Title: The banishing stones.

ISBN: 978-1-921919-66-4 (pbk.)

Target Audience: For primary school age.

Subjects: Fantasy fiction.

Dewey Number: A823.4

ACKNOWLEDGEMENT

Special thanks to Peter Tyas, my youngest reviewer, and to Alison Roberts, for introducing me to some inspirational children's books.

DEDICATION

For my sister, an authority on dwiggles.

Contents

Chapter 1 – Above the Restaurant

It was around midnight by the time the mops finished scrubbing the restaurant floor.

'Nice work,' Stella told them as she ushered them back into the closet to join the brooms. 'Horribella's going to be pleased tomorrow.'

Stella felt sorry for the humble working brooms and mops because they never got taken for a fly. For all she knew, they might have forgotten *how* to fly.

With a weary sigh Stella hung up the damp tea-towel she had been using, and then snuffed out all but the shortest candle, which she used to light her way up two flights of stairs.

The attic smelled musty as usual, though a refreshing little breeze darted in through the open window.

Stella set the candle down in a sheltered nook by her bed (an old mattress on the floor), and made straight for the window. Apart from a cat in the shadows grooming its velvet black coat, the town square below was deserted, and hazy moonlight prowled the shops in silence. Perhaps the cat sensed Stella watching, for its head jerked up, its jade eyes flashing.

Resting her elbows on the sill, Stella gazed up at the bats that swirled in the dark sky. Tonight their ragged black wings and ghoulish red eyes showed up clearly, for the breeze had dispelled most of the smog that usually hung over Wartville.

As Stella continued to lean out the window, she could hear the baby bear, Horribella's latest prisoner, clawing at the solid bars of its cage. By hanging her head right out of the window and looking straight down, Stella could see the solitary cage beside the restaurant entrance. It was too dark to make out the cub inside the cage, but Stella already knew its fuzzy, sad face by heart. If only

1

she could think of a way to rescue it. But a bear cub would not be easy to conceal.

Then it whimpered, and a second later Horribella's head ducked out the first-floor window below. 'ENOUGH OF YOUR RACKET!' she bawled.

The cub quietened down, and Horribella pulled her head back inside.

As Stella turned away from the window, Horribella's nasally voice carried faintly. 'You really *mean* it? I've *won*? I *can't* believe it. I feel so overcome.' *Sniff! Sniff!* 'It's such an *honour* to have my cooking talent recognised. *Thank* you, thank you so much.'

Horribella was probably talking to her reflection again, practising her acceptance speech for the Fine Dining Award she expected to win for her Savoury Baby Bear Stew.

Stella changed into her nightgown.

'Don't you go out on me,' she warned the candle's feeble flame, before dropping onto the mattress.

Then she took up her storybook.

Most nights, Stella lacked the energy to even *lift* the weighty volume, let alone read it. But tonight she felt only a tiny bit sleepy.

The first story in her storybook Stella knew for a fact to be true. The rest? Well, she liked to *imagine* that Jack and the Beanstalk, Cinderella and Peter Pan might actually exist. Peter Pan frequently starred in Stella's dreams, flying through the attic window and whisking her away to Neverland. Sadly, he never put in an appearance outside her dreams.

The book fell open at the place marked with a ribbon, and Stella brushed her hand over the yellowing paper and old-fashioned writing. As usual, a delightful thrill coursed through her. Within moments, the lonely attic melted away and she lost herself in the narrative.

Stella was so worried for Jack, who didn't seem to be chopping down that beanstalk fast enough, that she was quite unconscious of the creak upon stairs.

2

Abruptly the trapdoor was thrown open, and sky-blue dreadlocks and a candle flame surfaced through the gap.

Stella slid down flat and folded the book protectively in her arms.

'Reading again and using up *my* candles,' Horribella said in an aggrieved tone. 'No wonder you fall asleep when you're supposed to be working.'

Stumbling over dented cauldrons and bursting trunks, Horribella bore down on Stella and snatched the book from her arms. With a quick intake of breath Stella sat up straight, anxious as to what Horribella might do.

Horribella deposited her candle on a battered hat box and flicked through *An Assortment of Tales*, tutting and humphing. Her habitual frown gave the impression that she had a chronic case of indigestion, which was rather unfortunate for a chef.

At last Horribella clapped the book shut like a bite.

'I don't imagine you've thought of studying something *useful* – like recipe books – instead of all this happily-ever-after nonsense?' she croaked. 'Spellfest is only three days away you know. There'll be dozens of covens flying in to Wartville, and I'm expecting *Wartalicious* to be packed every day for the entire –'

Just then, a small shadow slipped from the pages, spiralling lightly to the ground. Stella saw it and knew at once what it was.

Horribella saw it too. Candlelight illuminated her distrustful expression as she bent over to squint at the floorboards. Swiping a cockroach out of the way, her gnarled fingers closed upon a lock of curly brown hair.

'Well, well. What have we here? Where did you get this then?' she asked as she straightened up. 'It's *human* hair, or I'm much mistaken.' She seemed to be examining it with very great interest.

'Uh-huh,' Stella answered. 'A human boy's hair. The first story is all about him. It's my favourite story. He came from a world far, far away. You can read –'

Horribella's green eyes were bulging. 'From another *world?* Snakes and serpents! Don't you realise how *rare* this is? How *precious?*'

Stella just blinked in bafflement.

'You must be dopey as a giant,' Horribella declared. 'I'll be taking this book and these hairs to Morbidia first thing tomorrow.'

'But they're *mine!*' Stella protested. She could count on her fingers and toes the pitiful assortment of things she actually owned – the book, a broomstick, a wand, a black dress, a pair of worn shoes, a stained apron, undergarments, a comb … Everything else had been taken by Horribella to pay for her board.

Stella had spoken without thinking. Now Horribella swelled up in a rage, and Stella shrank back.

'You impertinent little wench! After all the kindness I've showered upon you, is it too much to expect a *little* gratitude?'

Here it comes, Stella thought. *Here comes the lecture.*

'Who rents you a *whole* attic and a bed all to yourself, tell me that now?'

'You do,' Stella acknowledged with a dubious glance at the clutter hemming her in.

'And who gives you two square meals a day?'

Stella took a moment to answer. It was true that the cold toast for breakfast was invariably a square, but the stale sandwich for lunch was usually four little triangles. She considered correcting Horribella, then thought better of it. 'You do.'

'And who gives you a job to keep you out of trouble?'

Stella knew what would happen if she tried to explain that she didn't like her job as chef's assistant one bit; that she didn't enjoy preparing dragon gizzard pâté with a drizzle of olive oil, or deep-fried robin-legs, hot and crunchy with mango-chilli dipping sauce. Horribella's eyes would narrow, and she would mutter, 'There's something *very* wrong with you. *Very* wrong,' and then she would compel Stella to swallow a generous spoonful of choc-snail jelly. That's what she always did when Stella didn't act 'normal'.

'You do,' said Stella.

'That's right. *I* do. Without *me*, you'd be sleeping with the wolves, and you'd do well to remember that.'

Horribella puffed out Stella's candle, which was about to drown in a pool of wax anyway, and barked, 'Go to sleep!'

Tucking the book under one arm, and taking up her candle in her other hand, the witch made for the exit. As she did so, her foot caught on a dusty rolled-up rug and she let out a grunt of frustration.

Horribella clomped down the stairs, pulling the trapdoor shut behind her and leaving the attic in darkness.

Stella's lower lip trembled as she sank down onto the mattress. Chances were she would never see her book again.

Chapter 2 – The Conch

Sarah Weaver propped herself up on her pillow and cast her eyes around the cabin in surprise. She must have fallen asleep in the car last night, for she had no recollection of arriving at the camping ground.

And now Sydney had been left far behind and two delicious weeks of holiday awaited.

Sarah bounded out of bed and padded towards the sunny window. The linoleum felt cool underfoot – not at all like the soft carpet at home.

There wasn't a cloud in the sky; only two pelicans.

Suddenly a round, chubby face materialised on the other side of the glass and poked out a tongue. It was a face she knew well; it belonged to her annoying little cousin Rufus.

Sarah treated him to a look of disdain, and twitched the curtains shut. She disappeared into the bathroom with a bundle of clothes, and emerged clean and tidy in denim shorts and a pink t-shirt, with her hair neatly braided.

Her brother was still asleep, sprawled across the top bunk. Much as Sarah was tempted to tickle his foot, which was flopping over the side of the mattress, she restrained herself, and climbed the ladder to shake his arm instead. 'Wakey wakey, eggs 'n bacy.'

Mitchell half-opened one eye, mumbled 'Go way', and closed his eye again.

Sarah shook him harder. 'Get up, lazybones. Check out the surf with me.'

He groaned. 'You're gonna keep bugging me, aren't you?'

'Yep.' By now she was tugging at his pillow.

'Alright! Alright!'

'Rufus and Aunt Al must've arrived last night too,' Sarah announced, descending the ladder victorious.

Mitchell pulled a face. 'Great.'

Across the other side of the cabin, their mother, Belinda Weaver, was stirring, and her eyes fluttered open. 'You're up early.'

'Tell me about it,' Mitchell grunted, dropping down from his bunk.

'Morning, Mum,' Sarah said, and stooped to plant a kiss on her mother's cheek. 'We're going for a swim.'

'Only if the lifeguards are on duty,' Mrs Weaver said firmly.

'Yeah, okay.'

While Sarah laced up her sneakers, Mitchell delved into his suitcase, flinging out items of clothing as he burrowed deeper. 'I can only find *one* thong,' he grumbled. 'I *know* I packed two.'

Sarah immediately thought of their dog. 'Fleabag probably stole it,' she guessed. 'It'll be in little chewed-up pieces all over the garden when we get home.'

It didn't take Mitchell long to throw on orange boardshorts, a red t-shirt and sneakers. He ran his fingers through his hair, and went in search of food.

Sarah just had time to smear sun cream on her face before he called, 'Sarah, catch!'

A muesli bar flew through the air, but Sarah missed it, distracted by a *rat-a-tat-tat!* on the cabin door.

'Yoohoo!' someone called out in a far-too-chirpy voice for that time of morning.

Sarah tugged the door open to find Aunt Alison's cherry lipstick grinning at her.

'Hey, munchkin,' Aunt Alison said, pinching Sarah's cheek. 'Just look how fast you're growing.'

Sarah rescued her cheek. 'Hi, Aunt Al. Mum's not up yet.'

Aunt Alison gave no sign of hearing as she brushed past into the cabin. 'Mitch, sweetie,' she said, mussing his hair, 'you've got the fashion sense of an egg cup, just like your father.'

And now Aunt Al parked herself on the bed beside Mrs Weaver, who sat up looking trapped.

7

'Hey, Bel! Isn't it great to be on hols again? So, Don didn't come then? Working as usual, is he? What are your plans this morning? I think I'll update my blog first thing – you know, take some family snaps to show everyone. I've bought a cute new cossie – found it on special, fifty percent off. I hope you haven't packed anything too dowdy, otherwise I'll have to Photoshop you into something trendy – no, it's really no hassle. I'll have to touch up my cellulite anyway.'

Mitchell jammed a yellow baseball cap on his head and took up his water bottle. 'C'mon,' he whispered to his sister, jabbing his thumb in the direction of the exit.

'Did I mention I've applied to go on *So You Think You Can Play the Ukulele?*' Aunt Alison rushed on, barely taking a breath.

Sarah, who was by now making towards the door, paused. 'I thought you wanted to be an *actor.*'

'I do, sweetie, but my big break hasn't broken yet, and reality TV might be fun. I've bought a ukulele and a book called *Ukulele for Dummies.*' Aunt Alison giggled. If her voice was jarring, her giggle was even more irritating: an octave higher than an ordinary person's. 'Oh, I know. I probably won't win,' she said coyly. She paused, and, when no one contradicted her, added, 'But music is its own reward.'

'Depends on the music,' Mitchell said doubtfully.

His mother shot him a don't-be-negative look, unseen by Aunt Alison who was already rabbiting on again.

'Come *on*,' he repeated to Sarah.

'Toodle-oo, kids. Keep an eye out for Rufy,' Aunt Alison called. 'And swim between the flags or the sea monster'll get you.'

As Mitchell and Sarah slipped outside, their aunt broke into her own unique brand of wheezing laughter. Sarah pulled the door shut, trapping the noise inside. They set off through the camping ground towards the beach, munching on their muesli bars.

'There's no one else here yet,' Mitchell remarked, looking up and down the rows of cabins and caravans as he trooped along.

As if to contradict him, an old man wandered into view with his scruffy little dog and said, 'G'day.'

'Hi,' Mitchell replied.

It only took a minute to reach the beach.

'Should've brought our sunnies,' Mitchell grunted, shielding his eyes against the sunlight glancing off the water.

'No lifeguards,' Sarah observed. Apart from a few fishermen waiting for a bite with the incoming tide, the two children had the long stretch of sand to themselves.

Mitchell trekked across seagull footprints towards the water; Sarah trailed a little way behind to step in his tracks, enjoying the feel of the salty breeze on her face.

A layer of foam hissed around Mitchell's sneakers. He squatted down and dipped his fingers in before it drained away.

'Is it cold?' Sarah asked.

'It's perfect,' he announced, straightening up. 'But we'll have to wait. Let's explore the rock pools.'

He led the way along the water's edge, scrunching on shells and stepping over strands of seaweed. Sarah counted six pelicans skimming low across the waves, then turned for a second to watch her footprints fill with water. That's when she spied her cousin Rufus mooching along some distance behind. She pretended she hadn't seen him.

'Race you to the rocks,' Mitchell said suddenly, and took off at a run.

Sarah tore after him, with no hope of overtaking him. She caught up with her brother on the broad rock platform, and together they pottered from one rock pool to another, examining little limpets and periwinkles and whelks. The rocks were slippery with green algae in places.

'See that tiny blue crab?' Sarah asked, pointing her sneaker at a Neptune's Necklace.

'Hey, I found a starfish.' Mitchell bent down to pick up the stubby five-armed creature.

'Oooh! Don't touch it. It could be poisonous.'

9

'Worrywart,' Mitchell scoffed, cushioning the sea star in his palms.

'What you got there?' came a squeaky voice from behind. Rufus had caught them up.

Mitchell held out the starfish to Rufus, and Sarah traipsed a little way ahead to where a beautiful spiral conch shell had grabbed her eye. It was smooth to touch, and shiny as if it had just been polished. Grandpa Traddle kept a similar shell in his lounge-room cabinet, and Sarah had often listened to its murmur of distant waves. How did that song of the sea get in there? It was almost like magic.

She raised the conch to her ear, but what she heard was so unexpected, she almost dropped the shell in surprise. She tapped her ear, convinced it wasn't working, and listened again.

Issuing from the centre of spiral was an awful, sinister chanting, quite tuneless – strange words repeated over and over, rising and falling in waves. There was something unhealthy, almost menacing, about the sound; something that chilled her blood and prickled her scalp.

'Mitch! Check this out!' she called.

With light strides Mitchell was beside her. 'Good find!' He took the shell from her hands and pressed it to his ear. His eyes widened.

'It's like Grandpa's, isn't it?' Rufus said in his high, piping voice.

Mitchell was listening intently. 'It's getting louder and faster,' he told Sarah.

'Let *me* have a turn,' Rufus squealed, prancing around Mitchell.

'In a jiffy.'

Sarah was feeling a little concerned, though she wasn't quite sure why. 'There's something … *bad* about that noise, don't you think?'

Mitchell didn't answer. He was too engrossed by the chanting noise.

'Why can't *I* have a turn?' Rufus whined, jumping up and down and bringing bright spots of colour to his chubby cheeks.

Sarah could hear the chanting quite distinctly now, as if someone had cranked up the volume. She could feel her concern escalating to fear. 'Toss it away, Mitch.'

Mitchell ignored her.

'I'm serious, Mitch. Put it *down!*'

Still he ignored her.

Sarah frowned. Very well, she would just have to take it off him. She clapped hold of the conch with both hands.

At that very moment, the chanting climaxed in a shriek ... and something quite extraordinary happened. Anyone with their eyes fixed on the rock shelf would have seen Mitchell and Sarah abruptly vanish.

Only Rufus, however, happened to be watching.

Chapter 3 – Morbidia's House

What transpired next was so fast and terrifying, Mitchell couldn't take it all in. A violent yank by his hair, followed by light so piercing he threw up his arms to shield his eyes, and after that, as if a thick blanket had been thrown over his head, he found himself enveloped in darkness accompanied by the sensation of falling. His flailing arms and legs encountered nothing but air; his insides seemed to be plummeting too.

And then his knees buckled slightly as his feet slammed into something solid.

Everything was still; everything, that is, except Mitchell himself, who was quivering all over.

What on earth had happened?

And what was that thin glow down on his left? Like light seeping through a chink under a door?

As his eyes adjusted to the dimness, shadowy shapes took on recognisable forms: shelves jammed with long-necked bottles, jars, bowls …

No … It can't be … I must be dreaming …

There were strange and varied smells: some stinky, some fusty, a few that seemed familiar – pickles perhaps, pepper, coffee?

This is mad, but I think I'm standing in a big pantry!

A shadow to his right suddenly shifted, and Mitchell froze like an ice sculpture, though his heart was going frantically. A moment later, a wave of relief washed over him. The dark blob was only Sarah; he could hear her quickened breathing.

And then a nasally voice spoke, and Mitchell jumped as if a vicious thorn had jabbed him.

'This is a *complete* waste of time, Morbidia. It's *clear* your incantation doesn't work.'

'Bat spleen. Course it works,' retorted a thin whining voice.

Never had Mitchell been more astounded. He stopped pulling at once, and Fyrddin released him.

'Gosh,' Sarah gulped, edging backwards, looking wholly and utterly staggered.

So what if it wasn't polite to stare? Whatever these beings were, they were definitely not human.

'Never met an elf before?' Warvel asked with an amused grin.

Elf?

If these were elves then they were not the cute, miniature, fairy-story variety. These were tall, lean warriors, dressed in grey military tunics, light chain-mail vests, and grey leggings. The hair visible beneath their peaked steel helmets was of the palest gold colour. But it was their faces that held Mitchell's gaze – oval faces with sharply tapered ears, and, most striking of all, slightly angled indigo eyes.

'We should have illuminated sooner,' said Fyrddin in a milder tone.

Illuminated?

Mitchell glanced up at what looked like a twinkling star floating above his head, the source of the light.

'Please listen,' Fyrddin went on. There was no missing the concern in his voice. 'Passing through that door will not take you home. The witches have whisked you into a completely different world.'

A different world?

The elf looked and sounded perfectly truthful, yet how could this be? Mitchell's mind was in turmoil. Of course he'd seen movies about other worlds before, but none of it was real …

'If we're in a different world, how come you can speak English?' Mitchell asked.

'We are speaking the common tongue,' Fyrddin answered. 'Everyone here speaks it. Our mother tongue is elvish, but I'm guessing you would not understand that?'

'Er …no.' Elvish was definitely not taught at Mitchell's school.

He studied his surroundings. No ordinary foodstuffs filled *this* pantry: the shelves were crammed with jars of coloured solutions, crystals and powders, and a hundred revolting things that gave him the willies. Now that he looked more closely he could read the labels – beetle paste, elbow grease, pickled eyes, toe jam, minced worms …

'Mind,' Warvel warned, and Mitchell saw that Sarah's foot had come into contact with brooms resting against the wall. 'That's noxie dust on the broom-heads. We didn't want any trouble from the broomsticks.'

Sarah appeared to barely register his words; clearly her shock was taking a while to fade.

'We're going to escort you out of Wartville to the safety of the Fragrant Forest,' Fyrddin informed them, keeping his voice as low as possible, 'but, for all our sakes, you must do *exactly* what we say.'

Sarah's eyes telegraphed Mitchell, 'What do we do now?'

The teaching Mitchell had received about 'Stranger Danger' echoed in his mind. These strangers had bows slung over their shoulders, swords hanging at their sides and daggers protruding from their ankle-boots, and the weapons didn't look to be just for decoration either. Sure, the elves' faces *seemed* honest, their manner frank, but still …

Warvel pulled two pocket-sized folds of shimmery green fabric from his rucksack and held them out with a disarming half-smile. 'Here, put these on.'

Mitchell had just started to extend his hand when Sarah clasped his forearm; he tensed and caught her warning headshake.

'What are they?' Sarah whispered. She looked small beside the elves – the top of her head only reached Warvel's waist.

'Dragon skins,' Warvel replied. His helmet brushed hemlock sprigs hanging from the beams. 'Drape one over you to make yourself invisible.'

Mitchell drew breath in wonderment.

Unreal!

He could feel the excitement flaring in his chest as he reached for a dragon skin again … and then Sarah's foot nudged him and he paused.

'Could you give us a demo?' Sarah asked timidly. 'You know, disappear then reappear?'

Fyrddin looked at Sarah approvingly. 'You're wise to be wary of magical objects. Very well.'

Drawing one of the skins around himself, Fyrddin vanished.

Although Mitchell should have expected this, it was still startling to watch, and he stifled a gasp, blinking stupidly at the place where Fyrddin had been.

'You can take it off now,' Sarah said.

In an instant Fyrddin was visible again.

'That's really cool,' said Mitchell. Eager to try this new trick for himself, he looked to Sarah, but she still didn't seem satisfied.

'If we all go out of here invisible, won't we get –'

'Separated? Lost?' Warvel finished. 'No, the skins won't hide us from one another once we have put them on.'

'We'd better get moving,' Fyrddin pressed.

Sarah glanced uneasily at her brother but offered no further objections.

The dragon skin was soft and silken to touch, weighed next to nothing, and tended to cling rather than billow. Looking out through the veil-like fabric, Mitchell saw that Sarah and the elves had a faint green tinge about them. 'Are we *really* invisible?' he asked.

'One hundred percent,' Warvel responded.

Mitchell could just imagine taking a dragon skin home with him and tricking his friends. He pictured their reactions in his mind. Wouldn't they be blown away!

'Right. Time to go,' Fyrddin said. 'And a word of advice – *don't* step on the unwelcome mat on the way out.'

'The *what*?' Mitchell asked.

'The front doormat,' Fyrddin replied.

'Don't step on the front doormat. Gotcha,' repeated Mitchell, and Sarah nodded to show she had heard.

'All set then? Follow me quietly,' Fyrddin instructed.

The hovering silver light shot towards the tip of Warvel's finger as if summoned, and was extinguished. Fyrddin tugged on the pantry door gently, and Sarah caught her breath as it yielded with a little creak.

A dreadful stench hit Mitchell's nostrils like a whack in the face. A salad of stewed cabbage, decaying fish and rotten eggs would have smelled appetising compared to this. He clamped his nose between his thumb and forefinger and tried not to retch.

'No sign of Morbidia,' Fyrddin reported in a whisper, stepping out first.

Filing out behind Sarah, Mitchell found himself in a kitchen-laboratory, a mess of tripods, egg-beaters, glass droppers, funnels, potato mashers and flasks.

A noise made him wheel around; there were two rats eating off dirty plates.

The source of the repugnant smell was a blackened pot suspended over the fire in the grate. For a crazy second Mitchell had the impression that the stick was stirring the plopping concoction all by itself. He looked again. The stick *was* stirring all by itself.

Fyrddin exited the kitchen, silent as a ghost. Sarah followed cautiously. Though Mitchell tip-toed after them with utmost care, the sagging, creaking floorboards seemed determined to expose his every step. The mangy black cat on the hearthrug appeared to be looking right at him.

Mitchell passed into a lounge room hung with cobwebs. On his left, daylight filtered weakly through a grime-streaked window, and a desk and a great cluttered bookcase took up most of the wall. On his right, a single armchair nestled close to an unlit fireplace. Two spluttering candles on the mantelpiece did nothing to dispel the gloom of the place.

Fyrddin was already halfway across the room, heading towards the doorway opposite, when a figure in black entered through it.

Fyrddin and Sarah backed up at once. Mitchell paused, ready to leap out of the way if need be; his pulse was racing.

The witch's frumpy gown brushed the floor as she shuffled towards the armchair. Both repulsed and fascinated, Mitchell stared at her. Surely the candlelight exaggerated the depth of her wrinkles, the hook of her nose, the length of her chin and the hideousness of the warts on her fingers. He presumed her eyebrows had been scorched by some kind of failed experiment.

And now she stopped before the cracked mirror over the mantelpiece, and began to address her reflection. 'Well dear, you've kept your radiant complexion yet; you're just as lovely as ever.'

Despite the tension, or perhaps because of it, Mitchell almost laughed out loud.

Then curiosity compelled him. Whereas Sarah proceeded smartly towards the exit after Fyrddin, Mitchell crept closer to the witch and paused directly behind her to peer into the glass.

Amazing! He saw Morbidia baring her gums in a toothless smile, but he himself had no reflection. It was reassuring – in an uncanny sort of way.

A hand fell on his shoulder, and Warvel steered him away, out of the lounge room and down the hallway, past spooky masks fastened to the wall. Fyrddin eased the front door open and stood aside to let the others pass.

Sarah exited first. Stepping out behind her, Mitchell found himself in a street filled with stone houses jammed together and leaning at alarming angles.

'Intruder! Intruder!' blared a gruff voice. 'Alert! Alert!'

'Good one,' Sarah hissed, and Mitchell realised he had managed to plant one foot directly on the doormat.

Warvel was out now too, and Fyrddin came last, pulling the front door shut behind him. 'Quiet!' he whispered.

In a flash the door was wrenched open again. 'Who goes there?' Morbidia challenged, wand poised.

'*Intruder! Intruder! Alert! Alert!*' The unwelcome mat was sounding more and more insistent. Morbidia was casting suspicious looks left and right.

Mitchell glanced around him, and in that glance he took in the number 13 painted on all the doors, bats hanging upside down from the eaves, winged gargoyles carved into the door lintels, and hideous faces peering out windows to see what had caused the ruckus. It all seemed like some fantastical movie set.

'INTRUDER!! INTRUDER!!' The unwelcome mat was by now screaming like a demented thing.

'Oh, give it a rest,' Morbidia snapped, stamping down hard.

The unwelcome mat fell silent, and Morbidia muttered something about 'kids' and 'pranks.'

Then she seemed to notice the neighbours watching, and barked, 'Busybodies!' before turning and stomping inside.

'Shrivelled turnip!' someone hollered back, just as the door slammed shut.

'Right. Follow me,' Fyrddin said quietly and started down the cobbled street.

Chapter 4 – Wartville

Mitchell could have sworn that the eyes of a sinister-looking gargoyle were following him. He glanced back over his shoulder. The stone creature had craned its neck and seemed primed to swoop and pounce.

'The gargoyles can see us,' Mitchell whispered.

'No, they can only sense our presence,' Fyrddin answered.

Very comforting, Mitchell thought grimly.

Beside him, Sarah gave a shudder as she stepped around cockroaches that scuttled underfoot.

A sallow-skinned witch with a hooked nose trotted past, laden with shopping bags. Her hair was a lime-green colour, and spiky like toothbrush bristles.

With hundreds of chimneypots spewing out foul green smoke, it was hardly surprising that the mellow morning sunlight struggled to reach pavement level.

'Where are we heading?' asked Sarah.

'The town square,' Fyrddin replied. 'It's not far. You can hear the noise from it now.'

'It's market day, so we'll have to dodge around the crowds,' Warvel added.

A hunched, shrunken witch with a protruding chin and a shock of orange hair like a pompom hobbled down a shadowy alleyway. Before long, the street opened up into a bustling market place where hagglers and hawkers were competing to be heard. Colourful striped awnings and street-stall umbrellas formed a bright backdrop for hundreds of witches dressed alike in black shapeless gowns and conical black hats.

'Check out the warts-and-wrinkles club,' Mitchell whispered in Sarah's ear.

All the witches had hairy warts and wrinkles upon wrinkles.

21

It seemed that the witches could not stand in line without shoving. 'I was here first,' one shrieked, raising her wand, but upon finding a score of wands raised back at her, she sloped away, muttering darkly. Mitchell saw that her lilac-tinted ponytail was tied with a small snake.

'Trained squinkles. Fifty percent off the marked-up price. One day only,' hollered a fleshy-faced vendor with crinkly green hair. 'Quality ink on tap.'

Mitchell edged closer to have a look. The stall was sinking beneath the weight of fish tanks squirming with squid. One of the squid, having flopped out of its tank, was dribbling ink into an ink well as if it were going to the toilet. Mitchell found himself fighting down another mad urge to laugh. Wartville sure was interesting, though he was mighty grateful for the dragon skin; he didn't fancy his chances without it.

'Hurry up,' Sarah urged in a whisper, drawing him away, and they hastened after Fyrddin who was weaving through the sea of black ahead.

Everything seemed to be going rather well until a plump rat scurried across Mitchell's path and his foot squished down on it.

'Ugh!' A loud gasp escaped him.

'Oi! Hold it right there!' came a shrill voice directly behind him.

Mitchell's heart lurched into his mouth and he whirled around on the spot to find himself face to face with a dreadful-looking witch whose scabby face and blackened teeth made his skin crawl. His feet took an automatic step backwards.

All around him, as if someone had hit the pause button, the babble of voices had ceased and the crowd was suddenly still, watching.

'So, Vulgetta, you dare to use *my* hair colour,' Scab-face said in a venomous tone.

Huh?

'I rather like raspberry tints,' rasped another voice behind him, and Mitchell spun back around to find himself looking up at a tall, weedy witch who was shaking out her long matted hair with the air of a supermodel. 'It suits my complexion better than yours, don't you think?'

Mitchell exhaled a breath of relief. Both witches were looking *through* him, not *at* him.

The audience was itching for a fight and it got one. Mitchell sidestepped just in time. Scab-face launched herself at Vulgetta in a flying tackle and brought her down, collapsing a stall into splinters under their weight.

'Can we stay and watch?' Mitchell asked Warvel who had suddenly appeared by his side.

Warvel flashed him a sharp look and herded him away.

Clearly not.

Outside the general store, Mitchell caught Sarah's eye and jerked his thumb towards the window display. Dragon lungs, bottled spider eggs, goat entrails floating in a milky fluid, griffin wings ... Sarah stopped gawping when a hairy spider on steroids bungy-jumped down beside her.

Further on, Mitchell paused outside a restaurant called *Wartalicious* where witches were eating and chatting around outdoor tables. He grabbed Sarah's arm and pulled her closer. 'What'll you have?' he whispered, indicating the blackboard specials. 'Frog flummery, maybe?'

'No!' gasped Sarah.

'I'm just kidding,' Mitchell said quickly, surprised she had taken him seriously.

'Look!'

Her finger pointed towards a single cage that stood beside the restaurant entrance against the wall. The saddest little baby bear imaginable was peeping out between the bars of the cage.

'Come on. We can't do anything,' Mitchell whispered. As he spoke, a scrawny witch girl stepped out of the restaurant; a witch girl with a pocked face and unwashed black hair.

'Wait,' Sarah muttered. 'What's *she* up to?'

The witch girl had dropped to one knee beside the cage. Casting fearful looks left and right, she pretended to fiddle with her shoe, while furtively slipping a slice of bread through the bars of the cage.

'What's the hold up?' Warvel whispered, coming alongside Sarah.

Sarah turned to him with pleading whispers. 'The baby bear. We have to free it.'

Warvel shook his head. 'Too risky.' His tone brooked no further discussion, and he paced away.

'Come on,' Mitchell whispered, tugging Sarah's plaits.

They hadn't progressed far before Mitchell stopped again. It took him a moment to work out that he was looking at a service station for broomsticks. There were broomsticks receiving an oil and balance, broomsticks being fitted with saddles – 'Hedgehog spine padding for the ultimate in comfort,' a saleswitch was saying – and broomstick ends being sharpened like pencils.

'Stop dawdling,' Warvel hissed.

Fyrddin navigated through a warren of snaking streets until at last the foursome came to a high city wall built of stone, upon which monstrous black ravens perched sentry-like, looking as if they'd relish the opportunity to peck out an eye or two. An arched gateway set into the wall was hung with wrought-iron gates topped with sharp spikes. Locked gates.

Mitchell and Sarah traded concerned looks.

'Dead end,' Sarah whispered.

'Gargoyle of the gates, let us pass,' Fyrddin said, addressing a fanged gargoyle that seemed to have frozen mid-leap out of the stonework.

The gargoyle's mouth stretched open in a conniving grin, and it began to speak in a crackly voice:

'The first is in haunted but not in fear.

The second is found in dagger and spear.'

A puzzle? This was not promising. If Mitchell been asked to hazard the answer to a knock knock joke he might have stood a chance, but …

'The third is in poison and also in pain.
The fourth is in bondage but not in chain.
The fifth is mirrored in serpent eyes
The sixth is echoed in terrified cries.
What am I?'

Mitchell shuddered at the images evoked in his mind. He sure hoped the elves could work the answer out.

Fyrddin slowly rubbed his clean-shaven chin. Warvel folded his arms, his face intent. Sarah appeared to be thinking hard too. She was smart, but not that smart …

The gargoyle drew its claws across the stonework with a scraping noise. 'Ten seconds to go,' it warned.

'Danger,' Fyrddin blurted.

The gargoyle gave a low chuckle. 'No.'

Fyrddin's brow creased. 'Surely there isn't *another* word that fits the clues. What's the answer then?'

A ghastly smirk overspread the gargoyle's face. 'I asked "What am I?" Can't you tell I'm a gargoyle?'

Faster than Mitchell's eyes could follow Warvel ripped a gleaming dagger from his boot. 'You evil-scheming fiend! Open the gates or I'll carve out your tongue.'

The gargoyle's smirk dissolved as the sharp blade scraped its cheek. 'You will have to answer another riddle.'

'Very well, but make it snappy,' grunted Warvel.

The gargoyle began to speak again. 'If the giant has double the honey of the pixie, and the genie has a quarter of the honey of the giant, how much of his honey does the giant have to give the genie so that the pixie and the genie have the same amount of honey?'

Tick, tick, tick went the second hand on Mitchell's watch. He was more optimistic this time. The riddle was an algebra problem. The elves were bound to work it out.

Sure enough, a light swiftly appeared in Warvel's eyes. 'The giant has to give one quarter of his honey to the pixie.'

The gargoyle frowned and a loud groaning noise made Mitchell jump.

Caw! Caw! Ravens croaked as the iron gates began to swing open, grating on rusty hinges.

Mitchell flashed a dubious look around – it seemed too good to be true that they should be allowed to exit the city like this.

The elves did not stop to marvel; they dashed through the widening gap before the gargoyle changed its mind. A moment later Mitchell and Sarah followed.

Chapter 5 – The Dead Wood

Tall, athletic, and in excellent physical condition, Fyrddin set a brisk pace. Sarah, whose legs were substantially shorter, had to trot to keep up. She thought he might have shown a little more consideration.

Passing through the gates of Wartville had brought them into a dead wood – a graveyard of leafless, crooked trees. There were no birds perched in the bare branches, no butterflies flitting about, no insects scurrying over the ground. Absolutely nothing stirred.

'This place is totally creepy,' Mitchell whispered.

Warvel, who was bringing up the rear, must have overheard for he said, 'This forest was vibrant and flourishing just a decade ago. Tragically, the ghastly fumes that mushroom Wartville have choked the trees to death.'

'Fyrddin! Warvel!' shouted a childish voice. Pausing mid-step, Sarah swung around and saw a human boy cloaked in dragon skin hurrying after them. 'Wait up.'

'Give me patience,' Fyrddin groaned.

Sarah studied the boy as he jogged up to join them – his friendly open face, his tumbled mop of auburn curls. He was shorter than her, about eight years old, Sarah guessed.

'Why is it you can never do as you're told?' Fyrddin berated the boy. 'Your reckless disobedience will get you killed before long. You should have learned more sense by now.'

Completely disregarding Fyrddin, the boy's eyes flickered alternately between Mitchell and Sarah, scrutinising them. 'You must be brother and sister,' he said.

Sarah nodded. It was a logical guess, because both she and Mitchell had hazel eyes, wavy brown hair, and lightly freckled faces.

'Why are you wearing those funny clothes?' the boy asked.

Funny clothes? To Sarah's mind that was a bit rich coming from a boy decked out in tights, a tunic gathered around the waist with a belt, and turned-up ankle boots.

'We're not here to discuss fashions, Brodin,' Fyrddin said severely. 'Come along. By my side so I can keep an eye on you. And I don't want to hear a single word out of you.'

'What if I need to take a leak? Can I say "leak"?' the boy asked, with a hint of humour about his mouth.

'No.'

'What if I spot a meteor crashing towards us? Can I say "meteor"?'

'*No!*'

'What if –'

'STOP TALKING AND START MOVING!'

Brodin fell into step beside Fyrddin who called backwards, 'Keep up.'

Mitchell and Sarah shrugged at each other. Maybe they'd learn more about Brodin later – if he was ever allowed to speak.

There was something singular about the way the elves moved, straight-backed like soldiers yet graceful like dancers, feet barely touching the ground. They left no footprints in the dirt, at least none that Sarah could see. Sarah, by contrast, felt as clumsy as a clown in oversized shoes. She kept stumping her toes on rocks and catching her feet on trailing tree roots.

'Fyrddin, can you tell us *how* the witches brought us into your world?' Mitchell asked.

Fyrddin did not slow his strapping pace as he replied, 'Horribella got hold of some hairs from your head.'

Mitchell and Sarah exchanged baffled looks and waited for more, but Fyrddin obviously thought his answer sufficient.

Warvel jumped in to fill the breach. 'It's vitally important never to let a witch come into possession of even one strand of your hair, or they can cast a spell on you even when you're not present,' he explained. 'Once Morbidia had a sample of your hair, she was able to pop it into a brew, chant an incantation over it, and drag you into our world. Sarah was probably touching you at the time?' He looked to Sarah for confirmation, and she nodded, wide-eyed. 'That's why Sarah turned up here with you. The spell was only designed to fetch one *boy*. Of course, when Morbidia didn't see you appear, she assumed the spell had failed.'

'How did Morbidia get my hair?' Mitchell asked, holding his hands over his head as if he feared she might drop from a tree and pluck another strand.

'You have never travelled to our world before?'

'No.'

'Then, it's a mystery,' declared Warvel.

Mitchell was scratching his head. 'Maybe the witches came into *our* world,' he speculated.

'Very unlikely,' Fyrddin said. 'If witches had the means to travel to *your* world, they would have snatched lots of children.'

'I'll bet Mrs Wozniak next door stole my hair. I'll bet she's a witch. She's got two black cats and she's always spying on us through the fence and she never returns my cricket balls and she goes about muttering –'

'That's ridiculous, Mitch,' Sarah exclaimed. 'Mrs Wozniak is old, and Mum says she's got dementia, but that's all. She's not a witch.'

Mitchell stomped on a twig, and it splintered into pieces. 'It's not fair! Out of the millions of kids in our world, *I'm* the one who gets their hair nicked.'

'Lucky we ended up in the pantry and not the kitchen,' Sarah reflected out loud.

'You didn't end up in the pantry by chance,' Fyrddin corrected her. 'Our army's been spying in Wartville for a long time, so we've learnt a little about foiling spells. You were *supposed* to appear in a circle Morbidia had chalked on the kitchen floor, but Warvel rubbed out tiny cracks in her circle and drew another in the pantry.'

Sarah wished Fyrddin would slow down. As she struggled to keep up he kept shooting glances over his shoulder, and at first she

29

fancied he was checking on *her*, but after a while she perceived that his gaze was actually travelling *past* her, as if he expected to see someone following.

'What's the potion the witches wanted to make with our blood?' Mitchell asked.

'Anti-ageing syrup,' Fyrddin responded. 'Human blood from *our* world is unsuitable, apparently. Something about the DNA being different. Witches are the vainest creatures in the world and are prepared to do anything to look good.'

Sarah arched her eyebrows. Clearly, whatever they were doing was having the reverse effect.

'Er, I guess they didn't just want a *small* blood donation either?' Mitchell inquired. 'I mean, I wouldn't mind making a *small* donation if the witches really, *really* wanted some of my blood.'

'Let's just say that they would have taken more than you could spare,' Fyrddin answered.

Just when Sarah was on the verge of asking Fyrddin to ease up a little, he increased his stride. 'We're being followed.'

A vivid picture of witches creeping through the trees came into Sarah's mind, and a shiver ran down her spine.

'*I* can't hear anything,' Mitchell said.

'Naturally,' Fyrddin responded. 'You are human. But elven ears can detect the faintest whisper of a ladybird's wings in flight. I can hear the padding feet of at least three wolves.'

'*Wolves?*' Sarah yelped.

'Packs of wolves roam right across the country – introduced by the witches,' Warvel put in.

Unfortunately, the stark, blighted landscape offered nowhere to hide, leaving the elves and the children no choice but to keep moving along briskly. Sarah's nerves only increased with time. What would happen if the wolves caught up? Most probably they would enjoy a little picnic in the woods.

Half an hour later, Mitchell started muttering about blisters. Warvel was so silent behind her that Sarah checked over her shoulder to make sure he was still following.

Shadows shortened as the sun mounted higher in the sky. Sarah could feel herself drooping. Her eyelids started to sag, and a tree branch slashed her face.

'Look where you're going,' Mitchell told her.

She could have hit him.

Hardly anyone talked now, except Warvel who kept saying cheery little things like, 'That's the way,' and 'Keep it up,' and 'You're doing great.'

The more Sarah dragged her feet, the more she tripped. Warvel steadied her as she stumbled yet again.

Seizing hold of an arthritic-looking branch, the last of her strength left her. 'Can't – go – on,' she said in a breathless voice, and slid down the trunk of a tree into a sitting position.

Everyone stopped. Mitchell flopped down on her left, and Brodin on her right.

Warvel forced a water flask into her hands, and she drank deeply. Then he produced tempting little cakes from his satchel and handed them around.

Sarah had never tasted cake so light and fluffy. With every mouthful, she could feel her tiredness falling away from her.

'Mmmm. Thesearefablus,' Mitchell mumbled, cramming a second cake into his mouth.

Apart from the elves, now deep in murmured conversation a few paces away, the wood was perfectly silent.

'I think we've lost the wolves,' Brodin said, licking his fingers clean.

Seizing her opportunity while Fyrddin and Warvel were distracted, Sarah asked him, 'Where did *you* come from?'

'Fragrant Forest. Same as Fyrddin and Warvel.' The boy extracted from his pocket a brown paper bag full of blue lollies. 'Have a fizz drop,' he offered.

Sarah declined but Mitchell said, 'Sure, thanks.'

31

Moments later the lolly shot from Mitchell's mouth – 'Eeeeuw!' – and he was on his knees, heaving.

'Not a flavour you like then?' Brodin enquired. He seemed unsurprised.

'*Like?*' Mitchell almost shouted. 'They're re*volting*! I've never tasted anything so disgusting, not even medicine.' Even when he stopped heaving and sat up he kept attempting to spit out the taste. 'Yuk yuk yuk! What are they made of?'

'Bat poo probably … Don't look at me like that, I'm only guessing. It's best not to know really. Oh well.' Brodin crammed the sweets back into his pocket. 'Shame. I stole them from Wartville. Thought I'd be safe if I kept away from mud mints and maggot munchies. Don't you hate that? When the things you go to the trouble of stealing turn out bad?'

'*We* don't steal things,' Sarah returned, a bit primly.

'I steal from the witches on principle,' Brodin retorted, equally primly. 'They deserve it. Hey, want a gumball instead?'

'No thanks,' both Mitchell and Sarah answered promptly.

'Suit yourselves,' Brodin said with a shrug, and popped a good-sized red ball in his mouth.

'The wolves are getting close,' Fyrddin announced abruptly. 'We have to move.'

Mitchell, Sarah and Brodin jumped to their feet and started to jog after the elves.

For the first ten minutes, Sarah felt like someone had popped new batteries into her.

'D'you think the elves are paranoid?' Mitchell whispered to Sarah.

As if in answer, a blood-curdling howl cut through the surrounding tranquillity.

'They're getting excited,' Warvel said quietly to Fyrddin.

It wasn't too hard to guess the reason. *What's the time, Mister Wolf? Dinner time!*

'Faster,' Fyrddin ordered.

Sarah wasn't used to jogging. It was becoming hard work.

32

'Ow!' Sarah turned her foot on a stone, and though she gritted her teeth and gamely pushed on, she fell a little way behind.

Brodin took her place beside Mitchell. The boys' breathing was laboured, like her own.

'So, what's *your* world like then?' Brodin panted.

'Can we chat later … when hungry wolves … aren't chasing us?' Mitchell gasped.

'Oh, sure.'

Scanning the skeletal trees to her left Sarah glimpsed a flicker of movement – a grey shadow skulking between distant trunks. Her heart battered her ribcage and she quickened her pace until she was almost treading on Mitchell's heels. Mitchell appeared to be clutching a stitch in his side.

Just when Sarah was wondering if the wood would ever end, it did. She groaned inwardly. Fyrddin had brought them to the foot of a hill covered in loose pebbles and sprinkled with heavy boulders. Not a welcome sight after a long march.

A deep growl sounded, and as one, the elves and the children whirled around.

Sarah's blood ran cold. Two – no, three – no, *four* huge wolves, not twenty metres away, were bounding directly towards them through the trees. It was as if they could see –

'Mitch!' Sarah squealed.

His dragon skin had slipped, exposing an arm and shoulder.

'You three, up the hill,' Warvel said tersely, spinning Mitchell around and shunting him towards the hill.

Fyrddin stepped around Sarah to stand beside Warvel, facing the wolves. The elves flung off their dragon skins, and Fyrddin's sword came singing from its sheath. With a thrill of horror Sarah realised the elves were readying for a fight.

'Quick, Sarah, follow me,' Mitchell said, and he and Brodin took off.

Sarah was too scared to move. She kept watching from where she stood a little way behind Fyrddin and Warvel.

Warvel whipped a leaf from his pocket to blow a piercing note that filled the air. The wolves skidded to a stop three metres inside the tree line, hackles raised, and lifted their muzzles to sniff the air. The whistle had to be some kind of signal. But for whom?

Meanwhile, Warvel had unsheathed his sword.

'Be off, before you get hurt!' Fyrddin told the wolves, just as if they could understand. His even tone of voice, his confident stance, spoke calm certainty that the elves would be the victors.

In response, the wolves curled their lips in snarls that revealed glistening white fangs, and fanned out between the trees, angling to attack from different sides.

Sarah stared into a pair of amber eyes and found herself mesmerised …

Mitchell's anguished 'SAAARAAAAH!' barely registered with her.

She only snapped back to herself when Mitchell seized her hand. He dragged her, slipping and sliding on pebbles, a little way up the hill to where Brodin had positioned himself on a boulder.

'Take off your dragon skins,' Brodin said. As he spoke he was shrugging off his own dragon skin.

'Are you *nuts*?' Mitchell returned directly. He still had Sarah by the hand and was eyeing the incline further up. 'Sarah, wanna go higher? The wolves will smell us. They can leap –'

'Be off!' Fyrddin repeated more forcefully. 'This will not end well for you.'

Sarah's hand was trembling as she drew it away from her brother's. She wanted to watch what would happen to the elves.

For a long, anxious minute nothing happened.

Then a blur of grey and white burst into the open and sprang at Warvel; there was a whizzing noise and something flashed down from the sky. Warvel was knocked over backwards, and the wolf let out a yelp as it landed on top of him.

Sarah stared, blinked, and stared again. The wolf's body was stuck with arrows. Blood was welling from its wounds. It gave a funny twitch and moved no more.

'We're invisible! We'll get shot!' Mitchell spluttered. He was tearing off his dragon skin.

Where did the arrows come from? Sarah wondered as she wrestled off her own dragon skin.

Warvel had already rolled the wolf off himself and sprung to his feet. His sword was buried to the hilt in fur and flesh. He pulled it free, the blade dripping with blood.

While all this was going on, Fyrddin had continued brandishing his sword and staring down the other three wolves. 'Leave now,' he commanded, 'before we kill *you* as we have your leader.'

'They'll all attack together, you'll see,' Mitchell predicted.

But he was wrong. The wolves threw a glance up the hill, then one by one, turned tail and slunk away.

'Woo hoo!' Brodin cried.

'Crikey, that was close,' Mitchell breathed.

Sarah was too deeply shaken to say anything. What was it that the wolves had seen that had scared them away? Craning her neck around, she saw a handful of elves standing on the crest of the hill above her. Lean and fair, and dressed in military attire, they carried an arsenal of weapons that winked in the sunlight.

Brodin hailed them and scrambled up the slope, scattering pebbles as he went.

'Are you okay?' Sarah asked Warvel, starting down the pebbly incline towards him.

'I'm covered in wolf hairs,' Warvel said with a swift smile.

Sarah's eyes moved to the wolf. Mitchell had dropped to a crouch beside it, examining it with interest. Each of its paws was the size of a dinner plate and its pink tongue lolled out the side of its mouth.

'Its fur's beautiful, isn't it?' Warvel said, dusting himself down.

'You sound like you're sorry it's dead,' Mitchell exclaimed.

'I *am* sorry, in a way,' Warvel returned.

Mitchell snorted. 'Better it that us.'

Warvel gave a short laugh. 'That's true.' He opened up his rucksack. 'Pop your dragon skins in here. You won't need them now.'

Sarah would much rather have held onto her dragon skin, but she handed it over without protest. Mitchell threw Sarah a regretful look as he followed her example.

Chapter 6 – Happiest Time of Life

Bubbling cauldrons and sizzling ovens had conspired to make the *Wartalicious* kitchen uncomfortably warm. It was *so* warm, in fact, that Horribella's brow was sheened with sweat as she stood before the stove, and Stella, who sat peeling her way through a pile of carrots, half expected to start melting like butter.

Horribella was cooking rissoles again. With a flick of her wand, one, two, three rissoles obediently flipped themselves over in the pan. Stella had an uncomfortable feeling about those rissoles, and a quick glance at the folded newspaper on the workbench deepened her discomfort. The headline ran: 'Wartville's Elusive Catnapper Strikes Again – 7 Kittens Mysteriously Disappear'.

Poor little kitties, Stella thought with an inward sigh.

'Hurry up with those vegies,' Horribella barked, giving Stella an annoyed look before turning her attention to eight bowls of chilled avocado soup ranged along the serving counter. 'In you go,' she said, sprinkling a handful of crickets into each bowl in turn. 'No, don't try and swim your way out.'

Five minutes later, when the last carrot had been peeled, Horribella clonked a plate down before Stella and grunted, 'There, I've made you a mothbutter sandwich, though you don't deserve it. Now eat.'

Making every effort to look pleased and grateful, Stella raised one of the sandwich triangles to her mouth and chomped hard. Her teeth made no impression in the bread at all, not even the tiniest indentation. It was always the same – Horribella deemed that stale bread not fit to be served to customers was quite suitable for Stella.

With a sigh Stella set the sandwich back down and watched Horribella waving her wand gracefully, orchestrating the movement of plates in and out of the kitchen. Heaped plates rose up from the counter and went soaring out through the doorway into the restaurant; likewise, used plates came whizzing back in to stack up in the sink.

Three minutes ticked by, and still Stella sat at the workbench toying with her impossible lunch, more indigestible than a griffin claw.

'I said *EAT!*' Horribella squawked, rapping Stella over the head with a salami sausage.

Stella looked up and met Horribella's glare. 'May I sit outside, Horribella? *Please?*'

Horribella's eyes narrowed with suspicion, and she thrust her face very close to Stella's. 'Why?'

'Only because it's cooler out there.'

Horribella drew herself up straight again and wiped a filthy sleeve across her forehead. 'Hmmm. The windows *are* rather steamed up …'

Stella jiggled hopefully in her seat.

'Oh, very well,' Horribella huffed. 'Be back in fifteen minutes, mind, and not a second later.'

'Thank you, Horribella.'

Stella levered herself off the stool, scooped up the plate and crossed the sticky tiles out of the kitchen.

The restaurant was packed as usual, serving up crowd-pleasers like smoked newt quiche and earwig crunch ice cream. A hubbub of conversation and clinking cutlery filled the room.

Stella began to weave around first one table, then another, ducking as a bottle of sparkling bog-water floated past her cheek on its way to replenish an empty glass.

Before she had taken a dozen steps, a customer whose bobbed hair was dyed a vivid pink toppled from her chair and began thrashing about at Stella's feet, wheezing and gasping and clutching her throat, clearly choking on something.

Stella lost no time. She planted her plate on the table, squatted down and proceeded to thump Pink-bob's back over and over. 'Cough it up. Come on. Cough it up.'

But whatever was wedged in Pink-bob's windpipe seemed determined to stay there, and Pink-bob continued right on making rasping noises.

'Anyone know the anti-choking spell?' Stella appealed to the customers who had swivelled around in their chairs to look.

'Unusual plum colour she's turning,' remarked the waitwitch, appearing at Stella's side.

Stella jumped up at once. 'Quick! What's the anti-choking spell?'

The waitwitch shrugged. '*Un-Stopper*? No, wait, that's to open a genie bottle.'

Pink-bob's eyes were bulging now. There was a loud scraping of chairs and dozens of patrons hemmed Stella in, pushing and elbowing for a better view.

Surely *someone* would step forward to offer assistance?

But no, a quick glance around the circle of onlookers showed only delighted expressions and goggling eyes. Meanwhile, Pink-bob was progressing to a peculiar shade of blue.

'*HORRI-BELLA!*' Stella screamed with all her lungs. '*HORRI-BELLA!*'

And then, just when it seemed Pink-bob would not make it, Horribella rushed from the kitchen, knocking chairs and patrons aside, and raised her wand. '*Un-Block!*'

The effect was instantaneous. A stubborn lump of gristle flew out of Pink-bob's mouth high into the air and splashed with a *plop!* into a tumbler of cactus juice.

'Good shot!' someone exclaimed, and the suspenseful moment was over.

'I knew it was *un*-something,' said the waitwitch.

Feeling faint with relief, Stella assisted Pink-bob back into her seat.

'Carry on, everyone!' Horribella said, smiling broadly.

'You there!' A customer was waving a spoon at the waitwitch. 'Why aren't there crickets in my soup?'

'And mine?' another customer called.

'You must've let them escape,' the waitwitch grunted. 'I'll fetch some more.' She set off towards the kitchen.

'You should know the *Un-Block* spell, you ninny,' Horribella snarled in Stella's ear.

'Sorry, Horribella,' Stella murmured.

Horribella had a point. This wasn't the first choking episode at *Wartalicious*. One time the culprit had been a bone of some clumsy rat that had tumbled into the stew. Another time it was a fur-ball the cat had coughed into the custard.

Stella took a deep breath, caught up her plate and hurried outside, hoping for a little peace and quiet.

It was not meant to be.

Two witch girls happened to be seated in the outdoor dining area, and though expanding black bubbles of spidergum obscured their faces, Stella recognised the girls at once. Before she could slip back inside – *pop! pop!* – the bubbles burst, and the girls sucked the gum noisily into their mouths.

'Why, look who's here,' said Grotchetta, with every appearance of friendliness.

Stella shifted the plate to her left hand and rested her right hand on the wand in her deep apron pocket – just in case.

'Stella! How delightful! Come join us,' Sleazilla said, as if she actually liked Stella.

Stella was on the verge of making some excuse when Horribella's figure filled the doorway.

'Good afternoon, Horribella,' Grotchetta said sweetly. 'We're just practising for the spelling bee. See?' She held up a wand in one hand and a twitching toad in the other.

Horribella looked impressed. 'You couldn't give Stella a few pointers, could you? – No, don't sneak away Stella – I'll shout lunch. What about fresh prawn-head cocktails?'

Grotchetta's mouth split into a smile, exhibiting her crooked grey teeth to the fullest extent. 'Oooh, delicious. Thank you, Horribella.'

Sleazilla, who was chewing her gum with gusto, nodded in support.

'Coming right up,' Horribella said, and withdrew inside the restaurant.

'Don't look so worried, Stella,' Grotchetta said with false sympathy. 'We'll start with a simple spell. Just turn this toad into slime.'

Stella rested her eyes on the toad. It gulped and venom oozed from its skin.

'I don't want to,' she answered.

'Oh, dear. Don't you know *how*?' Grotchetta asked with a smirk.

Sleazilla tittered, and Stella squared her shoulders. 'Course I know how.'

'Then *do* it, you dunderhead!'

Before Stella could think of a smart reply, Sleazilla was on her feet, wand raised.

Instinctively Stella whipped out her own wand, ready to defend herself.

But Sleazilla's wand wasn't pointing at her at all; it was pointing at a saggy-bellied rat in the doorway.

The rat stood no chance.

'*Stun!*' cried Sleazilla.

Still as a carving, unable to move its limbs, only the rat's fearful eyes shifted left and right.

'Nice ratty rat,' Sleazilla said, squatting to collect the stiff animal in her arms.

Stella, meanwhile, was spinning her wand like a baton, trying to make out she had just drawn it to play with.

'I heard about your book,' Grotchetta said, looking keenly at Stella. 'Your storybook with the human hairs in it. Morbidia used the hairs in a spell.'

'What spell?' Stella asked.

'She used the hairs to bring the book boy out of his own world into our world.'

Stella stopped twirling her wand and frowned at Grotchetta in disbelief. Surely that wasn't possible?

'Well, not the same boy *exactly*,' Grotchetta clarified, 'because the boy in your story would have grown old by now, and you can't make a beauty potion from *old* blood, can you? Morbidia had to fiddle with the spell a bit to make it work on a boy with similar DNA. First time it's ever been done. Morbidia will probably get a medal.'

Stella felt sickened. 'Where … where are they keeping the boy?' Perhaps there was something she could do …

'They're not keeping him anywhere. The gargoyles told us he escaped with some elves. A girl was with him too. Morbidia's rounding up volunteers to go after them. The bats will be joining the hunt as well.'

'Oh.'

'Aren't we supposed to be *teaching* Stella some spells?' Sleazilla demanded. 'Here, Stella, give the rat a tail. Simplest spell of all.'

'It already has a tail,' Grotchetta reminded her.

'Oh … yes. Well then, give it feelers or a pair of antlers,' Sleazilla said between ferocious chomps on her gum.

Grotchetta drilled her dirty fingernails on the tabletop expectantly and Sleazilla tugged the hairs on her designer wart.

But Stella shook her head. 'I don't want to.'

'I don't want to, I don't want to –' Sleazilla began in a singsong voice.

Grotchetta picked up the chant, repeating it over and over. 'I don't want to, I don't want to.'

Stella flicked back her greasy tangle of hair, lifted her head with the most disdainful air she could muster and strode away, wand in one hand, plate in the other.

'Your mother was a thief and your clothes are hand-me-downs,' Grotchetta called.

Pretending not to have heard, Stella proceeded to pick her way across the town square over fruit scraps blackened with fruit-fly and stinking cheese rinds. (There was no such thing as a garbage disposal service in Wartville.)

Then –

Whump! Stella's legs refused to hold her up and she fell, grazing her knee; the plate smashed to the ground.

Grotchetta lowered her wand, crowing with laughter, and a mother and daughter paused in their shopping to watch. 'Ah, childhood. Happiest time of life,' sighed the mother. The daughter gave a nasty giggle.

Stella reversed Grotchetta's *Floppylegs* spell and collected herself together, trying to look as dignified as a ripped skirt and cockroaches converging on her mothbutter sandwich would allow.

Grotchetta struck up a new chant: 'Misfit nitwit! Misfit nitwit!'

Fixing her eyes on the smoke-stained buildings and churning chimneys ahead, Stella kept walking. The chanting followed until she turned down a side street.

Today the teasing did not bother Stella as much as usual, for she was thinking about what Grotchetta had said about the hairs from her book and Morbidia's spell.

'I wonder if Horribella will let me join the hunt for the human children,' she muttered to herself.

The bats would find the children, Stella had no doubt. But she had a secret weapon that could be used against bats.

Some time ago, Stella had found a two-pronged, steel tuning fork in the attic. When she struck the tuning fork against the wooden window sill, it produced a high, clear note that sent the bats into a crazy, screeching panic.

'Bat ears are sensitive, you ninny,' Horribella had growled at Stella. 'Don't touch that tuning fork again, if you know what's good for you.'

Stella had not touched the tuning fork again, though it was sorely tempting, for she didn't like the bats.

If only she could get the tuning fork to the children, then at least they would stand a chance against the bats.

Chapter 7 – Nessie

By the time Mitchell and Sarah reached the brow of the hill, Brodin was trying to palm off fizz drops (without success) on the elves.

'Well done, team,' Fyrddin commended his soldiers. 'Brodin, put those rubbishy sweets away and come here, please.'

Brodin rolled his eyes and sloped towards Fyrddin.

Glad to stand still and catch her breath, Sarah gazed around. In one direction she could see miles of Dead Wood spread out below and Wartville leaching a sickly fog in the distance. In the opposite direction the slope fell away towards an expansive green valley set with a glassy lake, beyond which loomed a rugged chain of snow-capped mountains.

'The forest we're heading for is across the Midway Mountains and further south,' Warvel said, coming alongside Sarah.

Sarah's heart sank and she was tempted to plonk down on the ground and cry. Tired to her bones, how could she possibly climb a mountain?

Warvel ushered her towards the other elves. 'Mitch, Sarah, let me present to you our Special Recovery Team.'

The elf soldiers dipped their heads as Warvel ran through their names: Celedur, Belvere, Gwynia, Rhenyd, Rorthan. They all had blemish-free pale skin, slim clever faces, ears with pointed tips, and stunning violet-blue eyes.

'It's not safe to dawdle here,' Belvere cautioned. 'I chased off a centaur a short while ago, but I sense he hasn't retreated far.'

So down the slope everyone went, into the valley where Sarah found herself wading through knee-deep grass in the direction of the lake.

A little way ahead of her, Mitchell was chatting with Rorthan. Mitchell had left a trail of trodden grass in his wake, but the grass had sprung straight up again where Rorthan's feet passed. Sarah hurried to catch up with them.

'Dragon nests are usually impossible to get near, but the wizard Vanrod has been keeping the dragons busy, and busy dragons leave their nests unguarded,' Rorthan was saying as he strode along.

'Do you eat the eggs scrambled?' Mitchell inquired.

Brodin paused from chasing butterflies to hoot loudly.

'No indeed,' Rorthan answered with an amused smile. 'We hope to raise good and useful dragons to help us defend the forest. See here.'

It was only as Rorthan adjusted the travel cloak he was carrying that Sarah realised it held a lime-green dragon egg. And now that she was paying attention, she saw that each member of the Special Recovery Team was cradling a similar bundle in their arms.

But Sarah wasn't interested in dragon eggs. She had a burning question that needed answering. Gradually edging closer to Fyrddin, Sarah shot him a sidelong peek. The lines of strain that had made his face look severe back in Wartville had relaxed now that everyone was out of danger, and she plucked up courage to speak. 'Excuse me, Fyrddin.'

'Yes, Sarah?'

'Um, when do you think you'll be able to send us home?'

Fyrddin and Warvel traded rueful glances, and Fyrddin sighed. 'The magic of elves is extremely limited, Sarah. We do not possess the kind of *deep* magic that could transport you back to your world.'

'Oh.' Sarah tried to ignore the downward spiralling feeling in her stomach. 'Well, if *you* can't help us, who *does* have the power to send us back?'

Mitchell, who had now joined them, gazed searchingly at the elf, waiting for him to answer.

Fyrddin seemed to drag the words out of himself. 'There is a wizard who has the power to send you back to your world – but he is not a friend of the elves. He *may* choose to help, but more likely he will not.'

Sarah fastened imploring eyes on Fyrddin. 'Will you take us to him?'

Fyrddin hesitated. 'We'll discuss that another time.'

Sarah was about to mount a plaintive appeal when she realised the party had come to a standstill on a flat slab of rock at the lake's edge. At least two kilometres of glinting water separated them from the opposite shore. The water that lapped against the rocky ledge was so deep it was impossible to make out the bottom.

'Gwynia, did you retrieve the nightingales' song?' Fyrddin inquired of the only female elf present.

Sarah looked admiringly at the glossy golden hair tumbling over Gwynia's shoulders.

'I did,' Gwynia answered. 'Here, hold onto this egg for me.' And now that her hands were free she produced a small glass bottle containing a mercury-like substance. 'I found it in *Bubble Potions*, in a cabinet with other banned substances.'

'Well done,' Fyrddin said. He and the rest of the elves were looking delighted. 'Let's release it and hope the witches don't steal it again.'

The moment Gwynia unplugged the stopper, a lovely sound, a chirruping trilling song, exploded into the air. Mitchell and Sarah ducked as silver drops cascaded around them like firework sparks.

Suddenly a dozen birds floating on the lake flapped into the air, screeching. Something was stirring in the centre of the lake.

Sarah strained to see what it was. Mitchell, Brodin and the elves had fallen silent, watching too.

A lizard-like head snaked slowly out of water, on a long slim neck. Sarah clutched her brother's arm.

'It's just some kind of big eel,' Mitchell said bracingly.

'Are you *blind?*' Sarah hissed, for the neck was immediately followed by a grey body so bulky it caused a wave to swell and lap loudly against the shore, swaying the reeds.

'Strike!' exclaimed Mitchell. 'It's a monster!'

Sarah could feel the adrenalin pumping through her veins, readying her body to flee. She looked to the elves, who held themselves perfectly still, their eyes pinned on the monster. Why weren't they taking off?

'Nessie,' Gwynia whispered reverently. 'What luck to see her.'

Nessie? This great ugly thing is called Nessie?

Water streaked off the creature's hide as it gazed lazily around.

Discussing it later, Mitchell told Sarah he didn't think the monster appeared terribly menacing. He said it reminded him of something, though he couldn't think what.

As the creature rotated its head, it saw that it had company, and its neutral expression changed to one of unmistakeable disappointment. Without further ado it quietly sank until it was fully submerged, causing some of the elves to make sounds of disappointment. Only ripples suggested it had ever been there.

'Nessie's such a shy creature, she spends most of her time hiding,' Warvel told Mitchell and Sarah. 'It's a real treat to catch a glimpse of her.'

'She would have stayed up longer if we hadn't been here,' said Rorthan. 'It's a pity we weren't wearing our dragon skins.'

The wobbly reflection of the mountains returned to the water's surface and birds felt safe enough to congregate around the floating lilies.

Meanwhile, Celedur had deposited his dragon egg on the ground by his feet and dug a little wooden pipe – the sort you play music on – from his tunic pocket. Raising the pipe to his lips, he struck up a wild, dreamy tune, moving his fingers deftly over the holes.

Mitchell elbowed his sister. 'Look.'

Something was agitating the water in a tiny whirlpool close to where they were standing. Was some *other* creature going to show itself? Struggling to remain calm, Sarah watched.

Celedur's piping gathered speed and intensity, and, at the same time, the whirlpool was expanding, spinning faster and faster, forming a churning vortex as big as a truck tyre.

'Off you go then,' Fyddin said to Brodin.

Brodin turned to Mitchell and Sarah. 'I'll see you around,' he said, then stepped right up to the edge of the rocky ledge and dived into the blackness at the centre of the spinning water. To Sarah's horror, it sucked him under, like he was being washed down a giant plug hole.

'Why did he jump?' Sarah cried.

'Why isn't he coming up for air?' Mitchell appealed to Fyrddin.

'Don't be alarmed. Elven magic enables us to hydrochute from place to place this way,' Fyrddin answered. 'Brodin has been sent back to Penangalus, the island where all the elf children live.'

The tune Celedur was piping had changed now, and Sarah watched distractedly as Rhenyd, holding his dragon egg firmly, jumped and disappeared. And now Belvere was jumping, clasping *his* dragon egg. And now Rorthan.

'Your turn. Go ahead,' Fyrddin said to Mitchell. 'You'll be transported to the heart of the Fragrant Forest.'

'Er, okay then.'

Before Sarah could issue any warnings, Mitchell had followed Rorthan into the black hole.

Sarah's stomach lurched as the black hole swallowed up her brother.

Idiot! Idiot! Idiot! She could have killed him.

Fyrddin placed a hand on Sarah's shoulder, lightly pressing her forward. 'Just leap in, Sarah.'

Sarah shrugged his hand off and backed away from the water.

'Don't be scared. It's quite safe,' Gwynia encouraged.

'We travel this way all the time,' Warvel added, and he too jumped into the whirlpool and disappeared.

Fyrddin and Gwynia were looking at her; she could feel the pressure on her mounting.

Still Sarah did not move.

'You'll be in the Fragrant Forest before you can say catawampus,' Gwynia said earnestly, and then she too leapt into the water with her dragon egg.

'You can do it, Sarah,' Fyrddin said firmly.

Could she jump?

Could she *not* jump?

Sarah definitely didn't want to be left alone with Nessie.

She *had* to believe the elves. She *had* to believe her brother was okay.

She shuffled forward and stood overlooking the whirlpool, shoring herself up, then sucked in an enormous breath and leapt.

Chapter 8 – The Fragrant Forest

Mitchell gazed about in wonder.

Nessie's lake, the snow-capped mountains, and the grassy plain – these things had been left far behind. In their place flowed a gentle river, wide as a six-lane freeway, flanked by monolithic trees. Mitchell measured the trees with his eyes; he hadn't known a tree could grow to such a size.

Mitchell himself was treading water in the middle of the river, and moments later, Sarah's head broke the surface nearby.

'Thank goodness!' she gasped when she spotted him.

'This way,' Mitchell said, swimming after the elves, who were making for the shore.

The first thing he did, once he had helped Sarah to clamber up the slippery bank, was strip off his squelchy shoes and socks to give his blisters an airing.

Sarah, meanwhile, just stood there with water pouring off her, tilting her head right back. 'These trees are gigantic,' she marvelled.

'The merrin trees are centuries old,' Belvere told her.

Mitchell ducked to avoid a dragonfly and looked at the trees more carefully: the wide-spreading branches with leaves that shimmered so far overhead, the crimson flowers, and the knots in the trunks that bore an unsettling resemblance to staring eyes.

But more astonishing than the giant trees was the neat line of water rats standing upright on their hind legs. The dozen or so rats saluted Fyrddin with one paw across their chests, and Fyrddin acknowledged the little creatures with a nod. Mitchell was just about to point them out to Sarah when she said, 'Hey, Mitch. Is that an otter?'

Mitchell swung around and squinted at a sleek brown head bobbing in the water with a fish dangling between its jaws.

'I think it could –'

He broke off abruptly. The river had swum out of focus. The ground wouldn't stay still. The trees began tipping sideways. His head felt all light and whirly, and he reached out for something to steady himself, but his limbs seemed all wonky. And then he tumbled into a well of black fog.

Some time afterwards, Mitchell became of aware a faint, far-off voice calling his name.

'Mitch, wake up!'

He resisted the call. He wanted to lie in a little longer ...

'Open your eyes, Mitch. Look at me.' The voice was louder now, closer.

Someone was patting his cheek.

Reluctantly, Mitchell opened his eyes.

'That's the way.'

As the fog lifted from his mind, he realised he was slumped on the ground with Sarah and Warvel leaning over him. Sarah's face was screwed up with anxiety, Warvel's expression was slightly amused.

'Whahappen?' He could hear his words slurring as he propped himself unsteadily on one elbow.

'You fainted,' Warvel told him.

Mitchell stared at the elf. 'Fainted? I've never fainted before.'

'Your toe touched a noxie – see here.' Warvel pointed to what looked like a plain brown mushroom with a squat stalk and a wide cap.

Mitchell frowned. 'Isn't it just a mushroom?'

'No-o-o-o,' Warvel said with a chuckle. 'Watch.' He gave the noxie a prod with a stick, and Sarah squealed as the 'mushroom' hopped three centimetres to the left, releasing a puff of powder, like yellow icing sugar.

'Noxie dust. It's what we used on Morbidia's broomsticks. Makes you faint if it contacts your skin,' Warvel said. And then, as if he sensed that Mitchell was feeling like an idiot, he added, 'It's

51

happened to all of us at some time or other. Up you get. You've got more colour now.' He hoisted Mitchell to his feet.

'Ready, troops?' Fyrddin called, and plunged down a dirt path heading away from the river. His soldiers followed, blending so perfectly with the earthy colours of the forest that they almost seemed to disappear.

Mitchell was about to fall in behind when Sarah held him back.

'Did you notice Fyrddin acted funny when I asked if he could take us to the wizard?' she whispered.

'I noticed,' Mitchell responded. 'But we can't *force* the elves to help us, can we?'

'If the *elves* won't help, who else *is* there? What if we can't get home again?'

Sarah lips quivered; she was trying not to cry. Mitchell gave her a quick, damp hug. 'It'll be all right,' he said in his most confident voice. 'We'll work something out. At least we're safe here. Come on.'

They started off down the track at a jog, stirring up drifts of leaves that crunched underfoot and fallen petals that released subtle perfumes.

'Ewwww! Repulsive!'

The cry had broken from Sarah's lips just after she rounded a crook in the path.

A robin stopped preening its feathers to look, and insects paused in their chirruping.

There, to one side of the track, sat the largest pile of dung Mitchell had ever seen – easily sufficient to fill a washing basket.

'Yucko! I guess an elephant's been through here,' he said, skirting around the mess. 'Looks fresh too.'

At that moment, a movement in the overhanging branches caught his eye – monkeys running along the broad branches overhead. No, not monkeys. Animals with twitching whiskers, perky ears that stood straight up, and copper-speckled fur.

Rorthan stood waiting some way down the track, and Mitchell asked him about the tree-creatures.

'They're dwiggles,' Rorthan said, then addressed the animals directly. 'Hey, you lot. Got any merrin-nuts to spare?'

'Eee – eee – eee!' Three dwiggles descended bearing nuts the size of golf balls and capered about, as full of energy as if they had been guzzling red cordial.

'Their faces are a bit like squirrels, don't you think?' Sarah said.

'Lightfingers!' Rorthan said sternly. 'Give it back, you bandit.'

Mitchell tried to see what the dwiggle was brandishing in its hand.

'My muesli bar wrapper!' Sarah exclaimed. 'You took that from my pocket!'

'Eee – eee – eee!' The dwiggle danced towards Sarah and returned its prize.

Within twenty minutes the procession of elven soldiers and two humans reached a clearing the size of a football field, and a score of elves in russet tunics and leggings came forward to greet the returning travellers. Sarah dropped to the ground to massage her legs, and Mitchell made towards a stream that he had spotted cutting across the corner of the clearing.

The water was clear and fast flowing, chattering along over polished pebbles, and prettily flecked with sunlight. Mitchell had squatted down and scooped it up, cold in his hands, and was on the point of taking a sip, when he glimpsed a giant cat through the trees.

Mitchell stared first in disbelief, then dawning terror.

The cat, easily five metres long from nose to tail, was slinking directly towards him. Merely twenty paces separated them.

The water dribbled away between Mitchell's fingers. Had he eluded a pack of wolves only to be savaged by a ... by a *what*? Its fur was cream coloured. Could it be a white tiger?

Don't move. Don't move, Mitchell told his legs, which desperately wanted to run. Maybe the tiger had already eaten. Maybe it didn't hunt until dark.

Glancing around, it was evident to Mitchell that none of the elves had detected the danger. Warvel, the closest, appeared to be extracting a splinter from the palm of a dwiggle.

The tiger was closing in on Mitchell, barely ten paces away, its body low to the ground, its yellow eyes fixed right on him. Mitchell scanned the ground for a stick, a rock, anything to defend himself. *Like it's going to help,* he thought grimly.

Then an idea struck him. *Elves can hear a ladybird in flight, right?*

'Warvel!' Mitchell said in a barely audible voice. 'Help! Tiger!'

Warvel straightened up and looked Mitchell's way at once. 'There's nothing to fear,' he called out, striding closer.

That's all very well for you *to say …*

The tiger was leaping the stream, coming right at him.

Mitchell tucked himself into a protective ball. He heard the light thud of the tiger's paws, felt its fur against his skin.

But there was no painful mauling. The big padding paws continued on.

Mitchell let go a breath he hadn't realised he was holding. When he dared to uncurl himself and peek behind him, he saw Warvel fondling the tiger like a cuddly kitten.

After a minute, Mitchell shut his gaping mouth.

He decided to creep closer to Warvel, to watch. He could still feel his nerves all tense.

The tiger was actually purring …

'Hello, Mitch,' said a voice in his ear.

'Aaah!' Mitchell cried, leaping a foot off the ground.

A willowy elf with silky hair drawn back at the nape of her neck had come up unheard beside him. 'Sorry,' she said with an apologetic smile. 'I didn't mean to startle you. I am Fyrddin's wife, Jevelle. I was thinking you might like to change into dry clothes.'

Mitchell nodded. 'That'd be good.'

Collecting Sarah on the way, they came to a merrin tree at the edge of the clearing. Stooping through an opening, much like a doorway, in the trunk, Mitchell found himself in a simply furnished room that housed a pair of single beds.

Jevelle began to light some candles. 'You can sleep here tonight.'

Sarah poked her head through a doorway off to one side. 'There's a bathroom,' she exclaimed.

Mitchell and Sarah washed and pulled on the tunics Jevelle supplied.

'I wish I had a camera,' Sarah said, looking at Mitchell with something that was almost a smile.

'If you did, I'd break it,' Mitchell retorted. 'I mean, tights? Honestly!'

Sarah chuckled. 'It's not *that* bad. You look like a bit like Robin Hood. And these boots would be okay if the toes didn't curl up.'

'Yeah, well … Let's go and see if whatever's cooking in that fire-pit outside's ready. Did you get a whiff? It smelled delicious.'

Dinner turned out to be fish stuffed with nuts and herbs, and mushroom pasties. The elves were eating picnic-style on the ground, and following their example Mitchell and Sarah settled on a soft patch of grass and tucked in, keeping an eye on the noxies, which kept hop-shuffling closer when they weren't being observed.

'It's like they're playing red light, green light,' Sarah said.

The setting sun had turned the sky over the treetops to molten gold, and somewhere nearby a robin was whistling blithely.

'If you're not going to eat that, I'll have it,' Mitchell offered, reaching for Sarah's pasty.

She swotted at him. 'Hands off!'

Jevelle was approaching with a plate in her hand. 'May I join you?'

'SCOOT!' Mitchell yelled. 'Oh … sorry … not you, Jevelle … the noxies.'

'They don't see many humans, apart from Brodin, so I'm afraid you're a bit of a novelty,' she said, depositing herself on the grass.

Sarah suddenly stiffened, her pasty slipping through her fingers onto the grass. 'What's *that*?'

Following the direction of her gaze, Mitchell caught sight of something not-quite-solid drifting between the trees. His eyes locked onto it. It had the shape of a girl with leaves instead of hair growing out of her head.

'A tree spirit – a dryad,' Jevelle answered. 'They're perfectly harmless.'

Both Mitchell and Sarah followed the dryad with their eyes until she abruptly vanished.

Seated close by, Fyrddin and Warvel were conferring in undertones. Mitchell couldn't help overhearing snippets of the conversation.

'The gargoyle can hardly be trusted to keep its mouth shut,' Fyrddin said darkly.

'Indeed,' Warvel agreed, 'and the witches will be restless until blood is spilled. I have a foreboding they will attack the forest before dawn.'

Witches attack the forest?

Mitchell promptly decided he had misheard. After all, Wartville was miles and miles away ... wasn't it?

It was pleasant just to sit there and chill out. Colours softened into evening shades, and two half-moons – the larger twice the size of the smaller – rose majestically over the trees, bathing the clearing in silvery light.

'The moons aren't friends tonight,' Jevelle said. 'See their frosty expressions?'

Before Mitchell could determine whether Jevelle was a little crazy or being poetic, Sarah burst out, 'Over there! The poo source! The big-and-woollies!'

Sure enough, there were two elephant-sized creatures lumbering around the perimeter of the clearing, swishing long flowing tails.

'The big-and-woollies are snufflelumps,' Jevelle said with a twinkle in her eye. 'We shear them twice a year.'

Mitchell watched the creatures for a while as they munched on merrin leaves. They were draped in thick long fleece, and each had a single ivory horn jutting from its snout.

The sky grew blacker and a pageantry of stars began to glimmer.

'Unreal!' Sarah breathed.

The stars were not sprinkled at random over the sky. They were clustered into constellations so precise and detailed they might have been drawn by an artist's hand: an archer aiming an arrow, a sailing ship, a boot, an octopus …

Mitchell had only looked at a dozen or so when a prodigious yawn escaped him.

'You've both had a long day. Time to turn in,' Jevelle said in a motherly tone.

Neither Mitchell nor Sarah had the energy to argue. It *had* been a long day.

Inside the tree-house, Jevelle had laid out two nightgowns.

'No *way* am I wearing that!' Mitchell said, hurling his nightgown across the tree-house. He kicked off his boots, blew out his candle and sank onto one of the beds. 'G'night, Sarah,' he mumbled.

'Night,' she replied.

Exhausted though Mitchell was, sleep did not steal over him at once. There were scuffling, rustling sounds outside – probably small animals foraging. He heard Sarah's breathing settle. Somewhere close a tiger growled. There was no grumble of traffic, no rowdy party down the street, no barking dogs, no Mrs Wozniak calling in the cats. And it suddenly dawned on Mitchell how topsy-turvy everything felt.

Up until this point Mitchell had avoided thinking of his parents; he had blocked out his fears, telling himself everything would work out in the end; he had put on a brave face for Sarah's sake. But now his heart grew heavy as a dozen worrisome thoughts crowded in on him: *Mum will be going out of her mind. The police will have scoured the beach and found nothing. Maybe Dad's driven down from Sydney and joined the search. Grandma will be crying, thinking we've drowned or something. What if we really can't get back to our own world ...?*

A great aching lump began to build in his throat.

Chapter 9 – Battle in the Night

A long horn blast woke Mitchell – a high note, followed by a low note, then another high, then another low, like a siren.

It was still dark, and he turned over in bed, hoping to drift back to sleep.

Seconds later the same soaring, swooping sequence could be heard being relayed further, fading off into the distance. And there seemed to be a great commotion outside in the clearing.

'What's going on?' Sarah whispered.

Mitchell dragged his eyes open. 'No idea, but this better be good,' he grumbled as he shed his blanket and stumbled out through the moonlit doorway.

An elf came running towards him, yelling something, but Mitchell was too bleary-eyed and fuddled to take it in.

'The forest's under attack. Get back inside,' Warvel repeated. 'Stay hidden.'

By the time Mitchell finished rubbing his eyes, Warvel had sprinted away.

Now that Mitchell was waking up properly he spotted half a dozen elves high in the branches of the trees that encircled the clearing. He watched an elf flex the string of her bow, testing the tension, and a moment later an arrow was nocked, drawn and ready to fire. Lifting his gaze, Mitchell saw a witch astride a broomstick in sharp relief against the starry sky.

'Hooley Dooley!'

He turned back to the tree house, and found Sarah huddled in a blanket just inside the entrance, peering out. 'Unbelievable! The witches are still after us,' she said.

Mitchell dropped down beside her. 'Seems like it.'

The assault was fierce and sudden. Hundreds of airborne witches rained down jinxes and hexes in jets of light that split the sky like lightning and lit up the clearing dramatically. The elves returned fire, releasing arrow after arrow in unremitting waves.

'Please tell me that's not a fire,' Sarah said suddenly.

'Course not,' Mitchell said impatiently. 'It's just the – far out!'

Directly opposite, across the clearing, he saw what Sarah had seen: orange flames in the tree tops.

'How are the elves going to put it out?' Sarah asked, chewing her nails.

More branches caught and flared up.

'Dunno. Maybe we should run now, before we're trapped,' Mitchell replied. He began weighing up the relative merits of death by burning, or death in a cross-fire of arrows and spells. 'There's no wind to fan the fire …'

Even so, across the clearing the flames were spreading, leaping hungrily from branch to branch, devouring a merrin tree. A dryad wafted speedily away from the burning tree, her leafy hair streaming behind her.

Suddenly, much closer, a witch tumbled to the ground with three arrows in her chest. Her broomstick sped off, riderless.

'That's not … she's not …' Sarah couldn't get the word out.

'Dead,' said Mitchell. He could hardly absorb it himself. The sight was shocking, overwhelming, too real, too close. In his experience, dying was something a goldfish did before being flushed down the toilet.

Sarah screwed her eyes shut and put her hands over her ears to shut out the singing of arrows and agonised screams.

And so it came about that Mitchell witnessed something that Sarah did not. With a cold thrill, he saw an exposed merrin root snake around the dead witch and suck her into the soil. He decided not to tell Sarah – she looked scared enough already.

***

A human boy clambered up the bank of the Crystal River not far from where Mitchell and Sarah had entered the forest only hours before. He brushed the wet curls out of his eyes and stood there dripping for a moment, taking in the not-so-distant roar of raging flames, fitful bolts of green light playing across the sky, and the smell of burning merrin trees.

'Brodin!' An elf slipped out of the shadows and stood before him, looking more agitated than he had ever seen her. 'You really are a nuisance!'

Brodin put on his best surprised look and said, 'Hi, Aolyn. I must've been sleepwalking.'

Aolyn frowned, clearly unimpressed. 'Who piped you here?'

'I only wanted to see a bit of the fighting,' Brodin said pleadingly. There was no way he was going to dob in his best friend Tristor, who had hydrochuted him from Penangalus.

Aolyn let out a groan of frustration. 'I don't have time for this nonsense. Don't move a step. I'm about to send up the birds. Then you're going straight back to Penangalus.'

Brodin had other ideas about that, but he kept his mouth shut.

Aolyn swung her rucksack off her shoulder and opened it. 'Robins first,' she called to the birds flitting impatiently from branch to branch overhead. One by one, each of the robins collected a little bundle Aolyn extracted from her rucksack. 'You've got confusalus,' she told them. 'Go really high before you make the drop.'

Brodin followed with his eyes as the birds took to the smoky orange sky. As anticipated, the witches paid them no heed.

Moments later, Brodin was clapping his hands and five broomsticks were idling over the treetops in an intoxicated fashion. It was too dark to see, but he knew from past experience that the witches aboard the broomsticks would be looking pleasantly dazed.

'Quiet!' Aolyn said, giving Brodin a sharp look.

Brodin stopped clapping.

An eager beak poked Aolyn's shoulder. 'Okay, your turn now,' she said to the nightingales. 'I've put noxie powder in your packs. Off you go then.'

61

The nightingales leapt into the air, flapping hard and gaining height.

Brodin clenched his fists. 'Now!'

All of a sudden a passing broomstick veered into a tree, then another abruptly corkscrewed to earth, and a third nose-dived straight into the river. Brodin let out a series of whoops.

'Hush, Brodin! Don't you realise the danger? I'm going to pipe you back right – oh, what happened to *you*?'

The last question was addressed to a skunk, which had emerged from the undergrowth making pitiful squeaking noises, dragging its rear leg.

Brodin, sensing this might be his only opportunity to sneak away, did so at once. He followed the burbling river, walking as quietly as he knew how. Ten minutes later he spied a mottled frog at the water's edge. Brodin quite enjoyed daring elf girls to kiss frogs. He made a grab for it, but the frog plopped into the water with a croak and scissor-kicked away.

'I wasn't going to hurt you,' Brodin called.

Then he pulled himself up short.

Something dark as pitch had rounded the curve of the river. What could it be?

Brodin scooted behind a kipberry bush, squinting through the foliage to see.

It turned out to be a string of six canoes, creeping single-file through the water, propelled by magic. The moons came out of hiding from behind clouds of smoke and revealed a witch sitting stiffly in each boat. The sight almost took Brodin's breath away. Who could have anticipated that witches would enter the forest in *boats* when it was common knowledge that they feared water?

'You filthy, stinking rotters,' Brodin muttered.

His eyes scanned the blank burrow entrances along the opposite riverbank.

Come on, otters! Where are you?

Three agonising minutes later the canoes were gliding past Brodin's hiding spot.

He couldn't wait any longer. He plucked a merrin leaf – shiny green on top, with a silvery underside – and blew a piercing note that would reach even the deepest places of the river.

One whistle was all it took. Gleaming heads shot out of the water; dark holes in the riverbank suddenly possessed, first, blinking eyes, then faces.

'Get 'em!' Brodin whispered, hopping up and down on the spot as the otters converged on the canoes like hungry sharks and water rats swarmed down the muddy bank.

Then a few things happened simultaneously. The canoes tossed wildly. Frightened cries filled the air. Two of the witches had the presence of mind to shape-shift; Brodin saw a flicker as they shape-shifted into ravens and sprang into the air. The other four witches decided to fight, brandishing wands and muttering spells. It was hopeless; they lost balance, arms windmilling wildly. Wands plopped into the river and canoes capsized.

'Help! Save us!' they shrieked in panic.

'I don't think so,' Brodin whispered gleefully. If it didn't occur to them to shape-shift into a fish or a duck, then that was their problem.

The witches beat the water with their arms until, one by one, they disappeared beneath the surface.

Brodin did a little victory jig, and crept back into the trees.

'Eee – eee – eee!' Dwiggles in the tree-tops were screeching warnings everywhere. The clamour made Brodin tense and edgy. Could something *else* besides witches be infiltrating the forest?

Just then a loud snarl sounded and Brodin's stomach did a somersault as he spun around. A wolf had sprung out of nowhere.

Brodin and the wolf sized each other up, circling around opposite sides of the spindly sapling that stood between them. The wolf's amber eyes burned into him through the branches. Brodin wished he had brought his sword.

Then the wolf bared its fangs in a malicious grin.

Brodin turned and bolted. He made a wild grab for a low merrin branch and swung up onto it. The wolf jumped up, snapping at his heels with hot panting breath.

'You can't get me!' Brodin taunted. 'AAAARGH!'

The wolf had leapt up beside him.

Brodin scrabbled to the next branch, then the next, higher and higher. Surely the wolf couldn't follow? Surely …

All of a sudden there was the most blood-chilling yelp and the sound of smashing branches. Had the wolf fallen?

Brodin stopped his frantic climbing – he just *had* to look down. And what he saw eased his fear a little: streaks of white, streaks of grey, tumbling, snarling, in the dirt, a writhing jumble of claws and fangs, flying tufts of bloody fur. A white tiger had taken on the wolf.

It was hard to tell who was winning, and Brodin didn't plan on staying to find out. A snufflelump rumbled past below and Brodin dropped recklessly from the tree, expecting to land neatly on its broad back. Unfortunately his jump was wide, and he only arrested his fall by clasping the thick wool on the snufflelump's flank. His dangling feet had nothing to grip.

The snufflelump let out a startled bellow and surged into a gallop, and Brodin's arms were almost jerked from their sockets as he clung on for dear life.

Brodin had been taught at school that, with the right motivation, a snufflelump can travel as fast as a hippogriff. Now he was finding out that an unknown something bumping and flopping at its side was the right motivation.

'It's – just – me – I – need – a – ride,' Brodin finally managed to yell.

The snufflelump slowed abruptly and Brodin heaved himself up.

'Thanks,' he panted, settling down into the cushioned shagpile.

The snufflelump plodded along in a slow, regular way now, and from Brodin's high vantage point he glimpsed more grey shadows slinking through a dense bank of ferns to his right.

'Eee – eee – eee!' the dwiggles screeched as they pelted the wolves with merrin nuts.

'USE *ROCKS*, YOU PEA BRAINS!' Brodin bawled.

And now something was crashing its way through the trees on his left, something screened by hanging vines.

Closer, louder.

Then a massive bear burst into the open, and Brodin felt a rush of relief.

'Wolf meat this way,' Brodin called, directing the bear towards the ferns.

The bear reared up on its hind legs, taller than any elf, and let out a ferocious roar, before dropping down on all fours and charging straight across the snufflelump's path. Wolves swiftly surrounded the bear, who lashed out with furious swipes of his terrible paws. Brodin lost sight of the battle as the snufflelump bore him away down the track.

***

Blood-curdling screams. Terrified howls. Angry bellows. Shrill screeches. The din seemed to build as the night progressed.

From just inside the doorway of their tree-house, Mitchell kept his eyes riveted on the action and Sarah peeked through her fingers from time to time.

'The fire's getting worse,' Sarah said, a concerned frown hovering over her features. 'Don't you think we should move?'

Mitchell broke into a cough as a trail of smoke stung his airways.

The moons had been blotted out by black smoke. Streaks of burning green light hailed down faster and faster, and all the while deadly arrows cut through the air – *Twang! Hisss! Twang! Hisss!*

Completely unexpectedly, a figure loomed phantom-like through the smoky haze and dived through the doorway. Sarah gave a yelp and Mitchell drew in a breath …

'It's only me,' Brodin said brightly. 'It's a bit crazy out there, isn't it?'

'You nearly gave me a fit!' Sarah exclaimed, resting her hands over her chest.

Brodin planted himself beside Mitchell. 'Seen any bats with red eyes?' he asked.

'Nope,' Mitchell answered.

'I saw *one*,' Sarah said. 'Why?'

'They're the witches' spies. They're looking for you. Did it see you?'

'I don't think so,' Sarah answered uncertainly.

'Good,' Brodin said. 'So, when are you going to come and live on Penangalus?'

Mitchell would have liked to quiz Sarah further about the bat, but not wishing to appear over-anxious, he held his tongue.

'What's Pen – that thing you just said?' Sarah enquired.

'Penangalus? It's an island just off the coast. It's safer there. The Fragrant Forest's pretty big, you know – it goes all the way to the sea – and it's not easy to defend. Anyone can sneak into the forest. The island is harder to get onto; it's got high cliffs all the way around, so it's easier to protect. Fyrddin won't let you stay here for long. He doesn't like kids running around the forest unless they're supervised.'

'We're not planning on staying long,' Mitchell replied. 'We're gonna go home, back to our own world.'

Brodin's eyebrows shot up. 'How can you do that?

'We're gonna ask a wizard to send us home.'

'A wizard? … You mean *Vanrod*? … You're going to talk to *Vanrod*?' He collapsed with laughter, rolling around holding his belly.

Mitchell and Sarah looked at him.

'What's so funny?' Sarah demanded at last.

Brodin brought his laughter under control and suddenly became quite serious. 'Tell me, would you go and visit a *werewolf*?'

Sarah tossed her head. 'Course not.'

66

'Well, Vanrod's *much* more dangerous.' Brodin put a lot of emphasis on the word 'much' and Mitchell couldn't repress a sudden shiver.

Across the clearing, another witch plummeted from the sky, and Brodin hooted loudly.

Barely a second later an elf toppled from the branches of Mitchell and Sarah's tree-house, and thumped to the ground a stone's throw away. There was something abnormal about the way the elf lay – in a crouching position, with bow and arrow poised.

'He's hurt bad,' Mitchell said, moving to go to the elf's rescue.

'Leave him,' Brodin said quickly.

Mitchell looked at Brodin. 'But he's –'

'There's nothing you can do,' Brodin said. 'He's been petrified.'

'Petrified?' Mitchell repeated.

'You know, turned to stone.'

Sarah gasped and her hands flew to her mouth, her face ashen.

Shocked and sobered, Mitchell stared at the elf.

'Kelem has two children. They're going to be devastated,' Brodin said heavily.

Mitchell nudged up closer to Sarah and drew a comforting arm around her, in part to comfort himself.

And now a dappled fawn hopped into view on three legs, holding up an injured hoof.

'It's limping,' Sarah cried, crawling forward.

Mitchell yanked her roughly back and demanded in a fierce whisper, 'D'you wanna be statufied too?'

Then they both turned still as waxworks. Not even Brodin moved.

A small, slight figure had emerged out of the darkness, wand in hand, stalking the fawn. It was a witch girl, and her greasy hair shone as it caught flashes of firelight.

Closer, closer she crept to the fawn. Mitchell wanted to shout out a warning.

And now he could hear the witch girl whispering. The fawn stopped.

Run! Run! Mitchell's brain yelled, as if somehow the fawn might hear. But instead of bolting into the trees, the fawn waited for her to catch up.

This is not going to end well!

The witch girl was doing something – ripping a long strip of material from the hem of her apron.

It came as an anti-climax to realise –

'She's actually *helping* it,' Sarah said in the lowest of tones. 'Making a bandage.'

Once the bandage was secure, the fawn licked the witch girl's face, gave a little skip and bounded away.

Abruptly, the little witch girl turned her head directly towards the tree-house from which Mitchell, Sarah and Brodin were peeking out at her.

'*There* you are,' she said in a low voice, stepping closer. 'If the bats find you, scare them away with this.'

A silvery glint arced through the air. Mitchell instinctively extended his hands to catch it.

'Don't! It's a trick!' Brodin warned, and Mitchell dropped his catch like a hot potato.

Mitchell, Sarah and Brodin peered at the object now lying on the ground before them.

'What is it?' Brodin asked, warily.

'Looks like a tuning fork,' Sarah answered. 'My music teacher's got one. You have to hit it against something to make a noise.'

Mitchell's eyes followed the witch girl as she stole away into the trees. 'Do you think it *really* scares bats away?' he asked.

'You can't trust a witch,' Brodin answered definitely.

'But that's the same witch girl we saw in Wartville,' Sarah said. 'The one we saw feeding the bear. I think she might be a *nice* witch.'

Just then, a bone-chilling screech seemed to rip the night in two.

'Yikes! What's *that*?' Sarah whispered, shrinking back from the doorway.

Mitchell could feel the fear fluttering in his chest.

'Bats,' Brodin said. 'Quick. Under the beds.'

But there was no time to hide. There wasn't even time to scream.

With a whirring of wings, a colony of bats stormed the tree house, and Mitchell found himself knocked backwards by the force of their assault. Before his mind could even register what was happening, his head, his chest, his arms were seething with smelly bat fur and ghastly red eyes. The rustling of wings filled his ears, and nasty sharp claws pierced his clothes, plucking at his collar, yanking his sleeves.

'Scat!' yelled Brodin. 'Scat!'

Mitchell tried to swipe the bats off his face. He beat at the bats with his fists. The more he fought them, the tighter they clung, the heavier they pressed, until he was struggling even to breathe. It made him feel queasy.

Sarah's muffled calls were unintelligible through Brodin's stream of yells, and then claws sank into Mitchell's skin and he heard himself cry out in pain. He hit out harder; the claws dug in deeper. 'Ow! Getoff! Owww!'

'Take that!' yelled Brodin.

'Chooniork,' screamed Sarah.

'Get – off – me!' Mitchell gasped, sure that a chunk had been bitten out of his arm.

Sarah's frantic scream cut through the rasping of wings. 'Chooniork.'

And finally her cry made sense. *Tuning fork!*

It seemed pretty desperate, but Mitchell *was* desperate. Blindly, he groped on the ground with one arm, while making good use of the other arm to fend off the bats. 'Ouch!' Were they planning to eat him alive? In all probability he would suffocate first, smothered in a warm cocoon of bats clinging to his clothes and hair.

The bats were thrashing their wings; Mitchell had never supposed wings could make so much noise.

Where was the stupid tuning fork? Would it even work? He stretched his arm further, his fingers scrabbling in the dirt for endless seconds. He couldn't even tell which direction he was facing anymore. The stink of the bats clogged his throat, and he started to gag.

Finally! His finger tips encountered something cold and solid; stretching a little further, he snatched up the tuning fork.

'Aaagh!' Was his hair to be ripped from his scalp? 'Ow! Stop!' He tried to beat off the claws that had hold of his hair. The pain was so severe, Mitchell was not immediately aware that he had been lifted off the ground. When he eventually *did* realise, he went cold. The bats intended to carry him away, to deliver him to the witches.

Mitchell kicked and struck out violently, the panic unfurling in his chest.

'Tuning fork!' Sarah screamed again.

It was a timely reminder. Mitchell thrashed his arm about, hoping the tuning fork in his fist might bump against wood. A bed. A chair. Anything.

The bats were carrying him outside …

The tuning fork connected with the doorway as Mitchell was dragged, struggling and grunting, through it.

Abruptly he hit the ground and piercing screeches tore at his eardrums; bewildered, he cowered, covering his ears, while a stream of flapping shadows rushed over and around him, brushing against him. He took a deep breath, then another, without smelly fur invading his nose and mouth. By some miracle, the bats had dropped him. His mind flew to Sarah. Had she been so lucky?

Mitchell lifted his head, half afraid of what he might see. Bats were clamouring to escape the tree-house, wrestling through the doorway and scattering, all the while screeching like tortured creatures. Mitchell raised his eyes to the smoky skies. Sarah was not with the bats.

Go. All of you. Go.

The bats were definitely going, pursued by elven arrows … and by something else: owls.

Relief. Amazed relief. Mitchell let it flow right through him.

And now, as he uncovered his ears, the din had subsided enough to hear the fading note from the tuning fork.

'You okay, Mitch?' Sarah called breathlessly from the tree-house.

Mitchell touched his scalp. It felt tender, but he still had hair. His tunic felt damp with sweat. 'Yeah.'

'Keep hold of that tuning fork,' she warned.

He didn't need telling.

He went to stand up, but his legs felt rubbery, so, on hands and knees, Mitchell crawled back inside the tree-house.

He found Brodin lighting a candle and Sarah urging Brodin to blow it out. Their arms and faces were badly scratched, and their hair stuck out in all directions.

'I've lost three buttons,' Brodin told Sarah.

'Who cares about buttons?' Sarah protested. 'There are witches outside, remember?'

'Jevelle cares. She'll be mad at me.' He was scanning the ground, sweeping his hands across the floor.

'I really don't think she's … *EEK*!' Sarah slapped at something black that had alighted on her arm.

'It's just ash,' Mitchell said, waving aside what appeared to be fluttering moths in the air.

A new noise drew his gaze back to the doorway.

'Unbelievable!' he burst out.

It was raining. And not just a dribble; a serious soaking downpour.

'Finally!' Brodin exclaimed, as if he had been expecting rain all along. He jumped to his feet. 'I've gotta go.' He blew out the candle. 'See you later.'

'You can't go out there,' Sarah objected.

But he already had.

Never in his life had Mitchell felt so delighted to see rain, but the poor dead elf was being pelted with it, and Mitchell fought against looking at the miserable sight. Sarah buried her head in her arms.

Now that the witches could no longer set the trees alight, they found new ways to wreak havoc. One landed not ten metres away, clutching an arrow impaled in her arm. The pain didn't stop her sketching a symbol in the air with her wand and blasting first an elf and then a dwiggle; both her victims keeled over and her eyes glittered with triumph.

But her gloating was short-lived, for a snufflelump came galloping onto the scene, lowered its horn and tossed the witch into the air. Mitchell could hardly believe what happened next. With one almighty swipe, a merrin branch batted the witch with such force that she sailed quite a distance through the air before smashing into the ground.

'Far out!' Mitchell gasped. The witch's wand spat sparks of green light as it was trampled to pieces.

Sarah's head snapped up. 'What?'

Mitchell tried to relate what he had seen.

'Yes, well, the rain's making everything blurry,' Sarah said dismissively.

'I didn't imagine it,' Mitchell argued. 'It *really* happened.'

'Get real, Mitch! Trees don't *whack* people,' Sarah said, with a tut. Even as she was speaking, another exposed root was writhing like a serpent, twining itself around the dead witch.

'Wanna bet?' Mitchell shot back. 'Look! See that root dragging the witch into the ground?'

'Knock it off, Mitch!' Sarah said sharply.

There seemed no point arguing. Sarah refused to believe what she hadn't witnessed.

And now the snufflelump was charging towards another witch who had marched into the clearing. The witch seemed to lose her nerve; her wand hit the ground, and Mitchell cheered inwardly as the snufflelump bore down on her.

He was totally unprepared for what he saw next.

The witch's shape rippled; the witch was gone, and in her place there arose a white tiger, which sprang out of the path of the oncoming snufflelump.

For a second, Mitchell didn't take in what he was seeing. Then he rubbed his eyes.

Now I really am *imagining things...*

'What in the world –?' Sarah was saying.

A second white tiger came flying out of the trees, ears laid back, and next moment there was the a vicious, yowling cat fight in progress.

Witches can shape-shift! The realisation crashed sickeningly over Mitchell. 'How do we know what's real and what's a witch?' he whispered. 'How do we know who to trust?'

'It looks like the animals can tell a fake,' Sarah answered.

Mitchell hardly noticed when, by and by, the deluge stopped as suddenly as if a hose had been turned off, leaving the air fresher and cleaner. Neither did he notice the darkness thinning and the sky turning a pale slate colour.

Would the battle never end? The prolonged suspense was terrible. Who would win? Who would be injured – or worse?

Chapter 10 – Magic Medicine

It wasn't until the sun's early rays dispelled the darkness that the witches rocketed away on their broomsticks, the wolves retreated, and a mighty cheer resounded around the forest.

Sarah did not feel at all like cheering as she peered through the doorway at the fallen elf. The colour had drained from his skin – and not just his skin, his clothes too. He was completely grey. A stone carving.

There was a sudden desolate cry, and Sarah saw a female elf approaching, wet through and bleeding from a cut to the arm. Sarah could not bear to look at her eyes – tragic, stricken eyes – fixed upon the stone elf. Sinking to her knees beside him, she broke into a wailing song that spoke of terrible loss and heartbreak.

'This is horrible,' Sarah said numbly.

Other mourners began to gather, silent, respectful.

Sarah roused herself. 'Let's move,' she said in a hushed voice.

'Why?' Mitchell asked.

'Do you think they want us watching?' Sarah hissed.

And so, after Sarah had changed out of her nightgown, she and Mitchell took themselves away from the tree-house, across the clearing.

'What's this?' Mitchell asked, stopping before what Sarah on first glance assumed to be a clock, which was mounted on a granite pedestal. It stood as tall as she did. The brass clock face had two rotatable hands, but in place of numerals, the circumference was etched with symbols that resembled the sun and clouds.

'It's a sundial,' said Warvel who had come striding out of the trees, soot-blackened and dishevelled.

'A sundial?' Sarah repeated doubtfully.

74

'Genuine product of the Goblin Emirates, see?' Warvel traced a finger over the letters G E etched into the brass. 'Depending on what weather you want, you can swing the large dial around from dazzling sunshine to dark clouds, and the smaller dial from drought to torrential rain to snow.'

Sarah sensed the seriousness in Warvel's voice, but Mitchell must have thought Warvel was joking for he started to grin.

'This is how we made it rain when the witches attacked,' Warvel went on. 'Believe me, it's saved the forest many a time, though it *is* a bit slow. Cost a fortune, too.'

Sarah put out a hopeful hand. 'Can I play with it? Make it hail or something?'

'Not unless you want to shovel up snufflelump dung for weeks. That was Brodin's punishment when he created a hailstorm.'

Sarah pulled her hand back.

At that moment, a leafy-haired dryad glided up to them, holding a basket filled with fruit buns.

'Anyone hungry?' she inquired in a light, airy voice.

'Always,' Mitchell answered, helping himself to three buns at once. 'Thanks.'

Warvel, Mitchell and Sarah sat on a log to eat. And while water droplets pattered onto their heads from the rustling branches overhead, Sarah's gaze followed the dwiggles scooting about the tree tops. She almost choked on her bun in surprise. Her eyes had picked out a tiny head protruding from a pouch at its mother's belly.

'Look, Mitch! Some of the dwiggles have –'

'Eurgh! Get it off me! Get it off me!' Mitchell shrieked, springing to his feet.

'What's up?' Sarah cried, jumping to her feet to help, yet not daring to go near as Mitchell danced about slapping his shoulder.

'It's moving! I can feel it!'

'Come here and stop still,' Warvel ordered.

'Eugh! It's crawling lower!' Mitchell was wincing and squirming.

Warvel thrust a hand down Mitchell's collar at the back.

'Got you!' Warvel said after a moment. 'There you go, little fellow.' Grinning, he lowered a lizard to the ground, where it scurried away with all haste.

Sarah rolled her eyes. 'All that fuss over a lizard.'

'Yeah, well, I didn't *know* it was a lizard, did I? It could've been a spider,' Mitchell said.

'You've got to watch our tree-climbing friends,' Warvel cautioned. 'They're always playing tricks.'

Mitchell glared up the dwiggle seated on an overhanging branch. 'Don't drop lizards on me again or I'll climb up there and – OUCH!' An unripened merrin fruit collided hard with his forehead.

Mitchell's glare was even more pronounced now, and Sarah could tell he was tempted to yank hard on the dwiggle's dangling tail. 'You little –'

'I have to go now, to help with the work, to treat the injured,' Warvel said apologetically. 'There will be graves to dig, too – at least nine elves fell during the battle.'

'Can *we* do anything to help?' Sarah offered.

'If you like,' Warvel responded. 'Certain plants can be ground into a paste and applied to a wound for rapid healing. I can show you how to collect and administer this medicine.'

Sarah nodded. Mitchell was rubbing his temple, which seemed to be coming out in a lump.

As the sun continued rising, the threesome wended their way along muddy forest trails, trudging over mounds of soggy leaves, gathering a spray of herbs here, a sprinkling of lichen there, a scraping of tree moss. All kinds of slugs were out in force.

Though the forest was charred and fire-blackened in patches, and softly drip-drip-dripping, it was still a thing of beauty. Everywhere Sarah looked there were pleasing sights: a shaggy brown bear foraging for tubers; a rainbow of butterflies; water droplets quivering on a spider's web; a stag bounding over a log.

Once Warvel had crushed the ingredients in a bowl, he sent Mitchell and Sarah off to work.

The first patient they encountered was a grounded robin toddling around in circles dragging one wing.

'Hold it still,' Mitchell instructed Sarah, and he dabbed Warvel's medicine over the injured wing. 'There you go.'

Sarah squealed in surprise as the robin took off from her hands, flapping strongly into the air.

'Boy! That was quick!' Mitchell exclaimed, following the robin with astounded eyes as it gained height.

'Come on, Mitch,' Sarah urged. 'Let's find some more patients.'

Leafy ferns beckoned the children further, until Mitchell stopped abruptly.

'This isn't good,' he said. 'Wolf attack, probably.'

They had stumbled across the prone figure of an elf who had been badly mauled.

'It's Belvere, from the Special Recovery Team,' Sarah said in a voice that quavered.

The glazed look in Belvere's eyes told her that even Warvel's magic medicine could not save him. She crouched down and took his clammy hand in hers.

This was dreadful. First the petrified elf. Now Belvere.

'White as a ghost,' Mitchell whispered.

'He's lost heaps of blood, that's why,' Sarah said.

'Not Belvere. That!' Mitchell sounded panicky, and Sarah lifted her head at once.

'What? Where?'

'There.' Mitchell pointed.

Something white, half-obscured by a veil of vines ten metres away, seemed to be moving closer. Sarah's skin prickled. *Did ghosts come to collect the dying?*

Then her ears caught the *clip-clop* of trotting hoofs on damp soil. Surely *that* was no ghost.

And then, as the vines parted, the most majestic creature Sarah had ever seen stepped into view, sending a thrill right through her.

'A unicorn!' she said in a hushed voice.

The unicorn kept coming, picking up its feet in a stately manner, head held high. It must have been at least seventeen hands tall. Sarah watched, spellbound, as it shook its magnificent mane and nickered.

'I think it wants to say goodbye to Belvere,' Mitchell said in a low voice, drawing Sarah off to one side.

Still Sarah couldn't take her eyes off the unicorn. It stooped its head over Belvere, sunlight glinting off its silver horn. The unicorn's eyes started to water.

'It's crying,' Sarah whispered. She dashed away the tears welling up in her own eyes.

A single glittering tear trickled down the unicorn's face and splashed straight into the elf's mouth.

An immediate change came over Belvere; his deathly pallor lifted and his eyes brightened.

'Thank you, friend,' Belvere murmured, raising a hand to stroke the unicorn's nose.

'Unbelievable!' Mitchell breathed.

Sarah wanted to laugh and cry at once.

The unicorn nuzzled the elf briefly before lifting its head and turning away. As it departed, Belvere called Mitchell and Sarah over. 'Your ointment should work now,' he told them in a voice that rang with life.

Applying ointment to Belvere's wounds was tricky and unpleasant – 'You wouldn't want a weak stomach,' Mitchell said with a grimace, and Belvere gave a flicker of a smile – but the healing mixture did not let them down. Sarah watched, dizzy with wonder, as flesh grew over exposed bone and torn skin knitted together, right before her eyes.

'Good work,' Belvere said warmly, bounding to his feet.

Sarah couldn't help staring at him. What a transformation!

By mid-afternoon, all that *could* be done for the injured *had* been done. With flagging footsteps, Mitchell and Sarah followed a nightingale back towards the elves' assembly ground, passing dozens of dwiggles curled up asleep in the forks of trees.

'I quite like the dwiggles when they're asleep,' Mitchell mumbled through a yawn.

'Do me a favour?' a voice said behind them.

Turning, Mitchell and Sarah found themselves face to face with an elf cupping a tiny bird in one hand and dangling an empty basket in the other hand.

'Would you gather some kipberries for me?' the elf asked, indicating a tangle of bushes with glossy leaves and blue berries. 'I was going to collect them myself except I stumbled on this orphaned little owl chick.'

'Sure,' Sarah said at once, taking the basket.

While Sarah set to work breaking off great clumps of berries, the elf introduced herself to Mitchell. 'I'm Warvel's sister, Aolyn,' Sarah heard her say. 'You've met Warvel, right? Deputy commander of the army?'

Something soft brushed Sarah's leg. A bird that seemed mostly beak, neck and legs was gobbling the berries she had collected.

'Hey!' Sarah objected, lifting the basket high. 'Get your own.'

Aolyn gave a short laugh. 'Got to watch the tivers,' she said.

The tiver strutted away, and barely had its green and crimson plumage disappeared through a gap in the undergrowth, when an elf girl pounced, light as vapour, from a tree, and landed in a nimble crouch. With a quickness that caught them all off-guard she sprang forward and threw Mitchell a mighty punch.

'Ooof!' He buckled over, clutching his stomach.

'Elteace!' Aolyn exclaimed in a horrified tone, restraining the elf girl – one-armed, because she was still holding the chick. 'Stop this at once!'

'Let – me – go! – Take your – hands – off me!' the elf girl shrieked, twisting and pulling, her hair flying into her mouth as she tried to free herself from Aolyn's grip.

Sarah had by this time backed away, quite shocked.

'They killed – my dad!' the elf girl said in a burst of passionate bitterness as she struggled. 'They – *killed* – him!'

'Calm down, Elteace!' Aolyn said harshly. 'You know that's not fair. A *witch* killed your dad.' She gave the girl's arm a rough shake. 'Stop this nonsense!'

The elf girl stopped tugging. Breathing hard, she pierced Sarah with a hateful look, tears of rage starting down her cheeks. 'The witches only came to the forest because of these *humans*!'

Mitchell and Sarah exchanged an awkward glance.

'Elteace, the humans never wanted your dad to get hurt,' Aolyn said, speaking more gently now.

'I'm so, so sorry about your dad,' Sarah said. 'I really am.' The words sounded completely inadequate.

'I don't want your pity!' Elteace shot back fiercely.

'It's not like we *planned* for this to happen,' Mitchell tried to reason. 'How were *we* supposed to know that witches would come after us here?'

Elteace wrenched herself free from Aolyn.

'Touch them again and I'll speak to your mother,' Aolyn cautioned.

Elteace gave her a stony glare. 'Fine. But I won't forget.' She turned sharply and stormed into the trees, her long, lustrous hair swinging behind her.

Sarah followed Elteace with her eyes, wishing she could undo what had happened. She could hardly begin to imagine how the elf girl must feel losing her dad.

Aolyn, who was soothing the ruffled chick, said, 'Hey, cheer up. It's not your fault the witches attacked the forest – they'll find any excuse. Mostly they come to steal animals and plants for use in their potions. Now, how about getting those berries for me, and you can help me bake a pie if you like.'

'And eat it?' Mitchell queried.

'Why, of course.'

Chapter 11 – Reeks

That night, Stella slumped wearily onto her mattress and scrunched her eyes shut, hoping to fall into oblivion, to escape the disturbing memories of the battle in the forest. But there was no escape. A succession of images flashed through her mind: images of witches shot down from the sky, elves turned to stone, and animals attacked by wolves. It had been so violent, so horrifying, so tragic. Tears began to tickle her cheeks, soaking into her folded apron which doubled as a pillow.

Though Stella had bandaged what wounds she could, she had really achieved very little. Her only consolation was that the human children had not been taken captive.

Stella was quite convinced she was dreaming when, moments later, a warm golden glow suffused the attic.

'What's the problem?' demanded a shrill, business-like voice.

Stella bolted upright in shock.

Fluttering in mid-air an arm's length away was a fairy, no taller than her pinkie.

Stella could not have been more surprised or delighted. She hastily mopped her tears.

The fairy was dressed in a neat beige business suit, had a pair of glasses perched on her turned-up nose, and carried a briefcase in her hand.

'Tinkerbell?' Stella whispered, staring at the shimmering blur of delicate wings and the sparkles of floating fairy dust.

'Speak up and articulate clearly.'

'Are … are you Tinkerbell?' Stella repeated, half bold, half shy.

The fairy tossed her blonde curls indignantly. 'If I was called anything as nonsensical as Twinklebell I'd change my name pronto. Name's Reeks, R-E-E-K-S. Administrative Assistant, International Association of Fairy Godmothers.'

'Fairy Godmothers?'

'Yes, yes. I know what you're thinking. I'm no fairy godmother. Any fool can see that. But a backlog of work's been piling up in the Save-a-Life Division with fairy godmothers going off on stress leave like you wouldn't believe. Not surprising, given the number of countries they have to take care of. Consequently, *I've* been dragged out from behind my desk and posted on tear alert. Can't say I'm enjoying field work so far. Too emotional. An assignment in the Grant-a-Wish Division would have suited me better. But, no use complaining. One should be grateful to have a job at all these days, hey?'

'I, um, –'

'Just let me make myself comfortable before we begin.' The fairy alighted daintily on the bare mattress and, after a moment fiddling around with her briefcase, sat down brandishing a notepad and quill. 'Now, first things first. You haven't had a visitation before, have you?'

'Pardon me?'

'You haven't had a fairy godmother visitation before?'

'Er … no.'

'Good. That means our records are accurate. And if you haven't had a visitation, you haven't had an intervention. Mustn't have more than one. Contravenes rule six hundred and forty-seven.'

Stella struggled to come up with a response, but it seemed no response was required.

'Right then, let's get down to business, shall we? Why are you crying?'

All at once Stella recognised that here was someone who might be able to help the human children escape to somewhere safer than the forest. After all, hadn't a fairy godmother once helped Cinderella escape from a wicked stepmother? With quickening excitement, Stella began to speak.

'Well, you see, it all started a long, long time ago, when my grandmother met a human boy from another world. She was only a little girl then. They became friends and he told her lots of stories.

Before he went back to his world he gave her a curl from his head to remember him by. When she got a bit older, my grandmother wrote down all his stories in a book, and she kept his curl inside the back cover of the book. Probably she read the stories to my mother when my mother was little. And now my grandmother is dead and my mother is dead and so the book's mine...'

The entire time Stella was talking, Reeks kept her head bent over the notepad, taking notes with a scratchy quill.

'... at least, the book *was* mine until Horribella took it a few days ago. I didn't know *why* she wanted it. I thought she was just being mean. I didn't know that she could use the hair in a spell. Maybe if Horribella let me go to school more often I would have known. Grotchetta goes to school and *she* knew. But Horribella makes me work in the restaurant most days. And now ...'

Stella paused and let out a sigh.

'Whinging ... and ... whining,' Reeks muttered softly as she wrote. Then, stabbing a full stop into the paper, the fairy looked up wearing a tight smile. 'Regrettably this isn't a life-threatening emergency, so there's not much I can do –'

'But I haven't finished telling you everything,' Stella interjected. She hadn't got to the part about the boy and girl yet.

'No need to say any more,' Reeks said, with an impatient wave of the hand. 'I've got the picture. And I'm going to be perfectly frank with you, Stella, for your own edification.'

Stella nodded uncertainly.

'I don't suppose you have too many friends, do you?'

Stella shook her head.

'Always find yourself on the fringe, never one of the crowd?'

Stella nodded.

'Just as I suspected, and I'll tell you what your problem is: you need to be a little less selfish. I mean, really, would it *kill* you to share your toys and books with others? Now that Horribella has borrowed *your* storybook, you may find she'll lend you one of *hers*. You'd like that, wouldn't you? Remember, to *have* a friend, you've got to *be* a friend.'

Stella was completely thrown. 'You ... no ... but you've missed the ...'

'Oh, I know,' Reeks persisted. 'Not what you expected to hear? Truth a little unpleasant, eh?'

'But, you don't understand ...'

'Enough. I've heard enough.' Reeks packed her pad and quill into her briefcase. She terminated the interview with a few choice words of wisdom. 'Cultivate a generous spirit, Stella. A generous spirit.' And, looking rather satisfied with herself, Reeks departed in a blink, and the attic fell into blackness once more.

Stella sat there stunned for a few moments. Then she gritted her teeth. 'Stupid fairy!'

She threw herself back on the lumpy mattress in disgust.

Tinkerbell would have listened, she told herself.

And then, quite suddenly, completely out of the blue, an idea for rescuing the baby bear popped into Stella's brain.

She stared into the darkness, turning it over in her mind.

Would it work?

Could she carry it out?

Did she dare?

Chapter 12 – The Wizard and the Stones

The next day, Mitchell and Sarah saw an elf sitting under a merrin tree fletching arrows.

'It's Gwynia, from the Special Recovery Team,' Sarah whispered. 'Remember? She had the nightingale's song.'

Mitchell nodded, and together they approached the elf.

'Need a hand?' Mitchell inquired.

'I'd love a hand. Just take care not to cut yourselves on the arrow heads,' Gwynia replied.

And so Mitchell and Sarah made themselves useful, while skunk kittens frisked among the leaf-litter at their feet.

Mitchell took the opportunity to bombarded Gwynia with question after question.

'What happens when dwiggle mums are dangling upside down? Do their babies fall out of their pouches?'

Gwynia laughed, a delightful, ringing laugh. 'No. I've never seen a dwiggle-bub fall out of its mother's pouch.'

'How do you get running water in the tree-houses? I didn't see any pipes.'

'The merrin roots draw water up from reservoirs deep underground,' Gwynia answered.

'Are any of the spiders in this forest poisonous?'

'The spiders won't hurt you, but don't pick the little blue flowers.'

Odd, Sarah thought, but she had scarcely a second to reflect on this when a white tiger cub leapt into view with a joyous bound, and pounced on a skunk kitten that had popped up from its burrow.

'Drop it!' Gwynia said in a firm voice.

The cub looked at her appealingly, dangling the skunk from its mouth.

'Now.'

The cub released the skunk, and with a whisk of its tail dashed away.

'What do the tigers eat?' Mitchell asked.

'They hunt outside the forest,' Gwynia answered. 'Wild goat chiefly, sometimes wild boar, the occasional hare.'

Only half of Sarah's mind was following the conversation. The other half was worrying about her parents, and her heart ached with longing for home. With a heavy sigh Sarah looked up at the green light streaming through the tossing leaves. She could see birds repairing damaged nests and dwiggles stockpiling merrin-nuts.

'Our photos will be plastered all over the news, you know,' Mitchell said, quite out of the blue.

Sarah looked at him in surprise. For all of his outward composure, he was worrying too. She turned to Gwynia. 'Gwynia, can you tell us about the wizard that can send us back to our own world?'

'You'd best ask Fyrddin. His tree-house is that way,' she said, pointing through the trees.

'Okay, thanks,' Sarah replied.

Fyrddin happened to be perched on a log outside his tree-house, whetting the blade of his sword, when Mitchell and Sarah found him.

'Er, excuse me, Fyrddin,' Mitchell said.

The elf looked up, his eyebrows raised. 'Mitch?'

'Um, Fyrddin, could you tell us how to find the wizard – you know, the one with the power to send us back to our world?'

Fyrddin set aside his sword and gestured for Mitchell and Sarah to join him on the grass. As they did so, the breeze purring in the treetops sent leaves and petals floating down onto their heads.

When the elf began to speak, his words were circumspect, measured. 'Before you stumble like flies into a spider web, may I tell you a little about this wizard? Then you'll be better placed to decide whether or not it's *wise* to approach him.'

Not exactly encouraging, Sarah thought.

Mitchell nodded his willingness to hear Fyrddin out.

'Good,' Fyrddin said with a hint of relief in his voice. 'Good.' He stretched out his legs and began.

'Since the dawn of time, this country, Wystovia, has been protected by four magical gemstones with remarkable power: a diamond, a ruby, an emerald and a sapphire. We call them the Banishing Stones because they give us power to expel anyone we want from our borders: bad-intentioned intruders, invading armies, evil influences. At our command the stones will send them packing, back to wherever they came from.'

Just then a baby skunk pattered up to Mitchell and rolled onto its back, entreating Mitchell to tickle its tummy. Mitchell leaned away nervously.

A grin tweaked Fyrddin's features. 'Relax, Mitch. The skunks in this forest don't smell.'

'How come?'

'Witches stole *Essence of Skunk* from us some time ago, and we don't seem to be able to recover it,' Fyrddin said with a sly wink.

Mitchell put out a ginger hand towards the skunk and began to pat it.

'Anyway,' Fyrddin continued, 'for centuries the Banishing Stones provided Wystovia with unsurpassed protection, and custody of the stones was rotated annually between elves, dwarves and genies. Everyone seemed happy with that arrangement.

'Then we allowed witches to settle in Wystovia, in Wartville, secure in the knowledge that we could banish them if they put one toe out of line. Very slyly, over decades in fact, the witches stirred up trouble. They kept asking the giants, the merpeople, and the sprites, *Why doesn't anyone trust* you *with the Banishing Stones?*'

'In the end, giants, merpeople and sprites began to hotly demand that they too should be included in the rotation.'

'That sounds fair,' Sarah piped up. She was keeping one eye on Fyrddin and the other on a noxie inching its way closer.

'Fair yes, but wise no. Giants are slow and dull-witted. Merpeople and sprites are clever but untrustworthy.'

Mitchell leaned forward attentively.

'Sad to say, roughly a decade ago, tensions escalated into civil war, a gruesome battle that came to a head when a genie seized the Banishing Stones and attempted to expel all the giants.'

Mitchell's jaw dropped.

'The stones were never intended to be used by one Wystovian against another, and the magic in the stones backfired. Every single genie was ejected from our borders, and worse still, the Banishing Stones were scattered to secret places across the land and have never been brought together since. Lamentably, without the stones to protect Wystovia, the witches started having a grand old time, and a wizard promptly established a base for himself in the Midway Mountains.'

'Vanrod?' the children queried in unison.

'Just so,' Fyrddin nodded.

Sarah sat up straight. *At last!* Fyrddin was getting to the point.

'Wystovia lies sandwiched between Vanrod's vast territories to the north and to the south – the Dark Lands, as they are called – and Vanrod is hungry to gobble up Wystovia too, so that his armies might move freely across the country. But he is mindful that there are other wizards, other armies, which also look upon our land with greedy eyes, and he is worried they might challenge him. Therefore, his entire energy is riveted on finding the Banishing Stones so that he might one day rule Wystovia *un*challenged.'

'But he hasn't found any of the Banishing Stones, right?' Mitchell cut in.

Fyrddin shook his head soberly. 'A few years ago in Stompton, the giant town up north, a dog tumbled down an old forgotten well, and the rescued animal came up gripping the magic ruby in its jaws. Instead of keeping quiet about their find, the brainless giants boasted far and wide. Vanrod offered gold in return for the ruby, the giants refused to sell, so Vanrod took the ruby by force, turning many giants to stone in the process.'

'Oh no!' cried Sarah.

'Now that Vanrod has *one* of the gemstones, even if we were to find the other three we could not use them to oust him. All *four* are needed to work together. Some of my best soldiers have died trying to discover where Vanrod keeps the ruby.'

'So the other three stones are still hidden?' Mitchell checked.

'Three are still hidden, but for how long, we do not know. Vanrod's spies scour the land, watching and listening for any clue as to where the Banishing Stones might be. You might have noticed Vanrod's spies already. He is master of all the eagles in Wystovia.'

Sarah's eyes slid rapidly skywards; bright patches of blue were visible between the rustling branches ...

'Vanrod seems convinced that one of the Banishing Stones is lodged deep within the Midway Mountains – perhaps a crystal ball has shown him so, I don't know – and for the past three years, he has enslaved over one hundred dwarves inside the caves to dig for the jewel.'

'What a creep!' Sarah cried indignantly.

'Fire-breathing dragons guard the exits and ensure the dwarves work tirelessly,' Fyrddin went on. 'Vanrod pays the dragons with all the treasure that the dwarves dig out.'

'Wow!' Mitchell's eyes were flashing. 'I'd love to see a dragon.'

Fyrddin swatted away a fly. 'We would rescue the dwarves if we could, but Vanrod has all the advantage. His powers greatly exceed ours and, more importantly, he wears a protective ring which wards off arrows, bullets, daggers, poison – even magical attacks.'

'Gosh, wouldn't you want a ring like that?' Mitchell exclaimed.

'With his ring to protect him, only two things may harm Vanrod: another wizard or a white tiger.'

'A white tiger?' Mitchell echoed, a puzzled crease appearing between his eyebrows.

'Indeed. White tigers are the only beasts impervious to wizard spells and enchantments; they have a natural resistance to wizardry. More than that, their claws and teeth can rip through the magical shield provided by a wizard ring. They can claw and bite a wizard to death. Which, my friends, is why Vanrod tends to keep well away from the Fragrant Forest.'

'Does he ever take the ring off?' Sarah asked, her mind fully engaged in rescuing the dwarves.

'Would *you*?'

Sarah's shoulders slackened despondently.

'Anyway, back to the point. I don't mean to dampen your spirits, but I must be honest. I don't hold high hopes that Vanrod will grant your request for help. More likely you'll be placing yourselves in danger.'

Mitchell stroked the skunk for a minute, while Sarah stared into the distance through the trees, letting Fyrddin's warning sink in. She had to acknowledge that paying Vanrod a visit seemed as safe as treading in a snake's nest. She could feel a pricking behind her eyelids as she inquired chokily, 'Are there any *other* wizards who might help us?'

'I know of several other wizards who live in distant lands, but they all make Vanrod look like a good fairy,' Fyrddin answered.

Sarah dashed the tears from her eyes. The idea of never seeing her parents again was too awful to contemplate.

'You *do* know you're welcome stay with us in the Fragrant Forest, don't you?' Fyrddin said, almost tenderly. 'I'm sure Brodin would be delighted to have some human company for a change.'

'Oh, we really like it here,' Mitchell said earnestly, 'and we're grateful for everything you've done, aren't we Sarah?' Sarah nodded. 'But we've gotta give Vanrod a try. Fingers crossed he'll be in a good mood when we meet him.'

Mitchell spoke so cheerfully that Sarah clutched at a glimmer of hope after all.

'I have never heard of Vanrod being in a good mood, unless he was torturing someone,' Fyrddin countered. 'I am quite serious. This wizard is dangerous. I strongly advise you to steer clear of him.'

'All we're gonna do is ask him to help us. If he says no, we're not gonna stop and argue.'

'From my heart, I wish I could force you to stay,' Fyrddin said heavily.

'We'll be very careful,' Mitchell assured him.

Fyrddin sighed. 'Very well. Vanrod is keeping close watch on the dwarves from a cave in Mount Tremor. I can hydrochute you to the Troll River near the foot of the mountain, and from there it's a bit of a climb to Vanrod's cave, which you'll find hidden behind a waterfall.'

'Er – why is the river called Troll River?' Sarah inquired.

'You needn't worry about meeting the troll,' Fyrddin responded with a half-smile. 'The troll's bridge is a long way downstream from where you'll surface.'

'We'll have to change into our own clothes first,' Mitchell put in quickly. 'I'm not going home in tights – no offence, Fyrddin.'

'I'll fetch a couple of waterproof packs,' Fyrddin said. 'You'll need travelling cloaks, for the mountain can get quite cold. And you should be prepared for every eventuality, so I'll pack some healing ointment and unicorn tears as well.'

Chapter 13 – Vanrod's Cave

When Fyrddin promised to hydrochute Mitchell and Sarah to a river near the foot of Mount Tremor, Sarah had envisioned a nice tame river meandering lazily along, much like the Fragrant Forest's Crystal River.

Troll River could not have been more different. Wild and petulant in nature, it originated in the misty heights of Mount Tremor, collecting melting snow on its long descent, before flinging itself over a sheer two-hundred-metre drop onto jagged rocks, where it thundered and foamed and churned before tumbling on in a great hurry.

The icy coldness of the water made Sarah gasp, the raging torrent dragged her under, her mouth and nostrils filled with water, and as soon as she came up spluttering, she found she was being borne along by the current, away from the mountain. Within seconds she knew she was in trouble.

One moment Mitchell was beside her, then she lost sight of him, and now he reappeared, shouting something she couldn't make out over the tremendous rushing roar in her ears.

And then a new worry struck her: she remembered the troll downstream. She began to kick and work her arms, cutting through the water, swimming against the force of the rapids. The river bank was only four metres away, but it seemed an impossible distance to cover. Her pack seemed so heavy. She could feel the heat seeping from her body, feel her extremities going numb.

I can't do this, Sarah thought. *I can't fight the river. It's too hard.*

She felt she had swallowed a bathtub worth of water by the time Mitchell came alongside her again, looking scared. 'Swim!' he yelled.

Sarah kicked as hard as she could, but her muscles were aching, her strength was failing, she was gasping for breath, her heart was pounding. She wanted to tell him she was giving up.

'Not far,' he yelled again.

She lifted her face and saw that it was true. The river bank was nearer now. Not even two metres away. She mustered every bit of energy left in her.

Kick! Kick!

Several stressful minutes later she was floundering up the riverbank hauling her pack behind her, coughing and gagging and spitting out water, grasping at tussocks of grass for handholds.

'I – need – to – rest,' she gasped, and flung herself down on the grass.

Mitchell pulled the travelling cloak from her pack and draped it over her.

And there she lay, body shuddering, teeth chattering, ears ringing, too drained to even think.

It was a good fifteen minutes before Mitchell spoke. 'It's pretty here,' he observed.

Sarah sat up and allowed her eyes to wander over the mountain. The remote peak was crowned with sunlit snow. Lower down, the snow was only a light frosting, and below the mid-way point there was no snow at all, just bare rock.

'D'you see the goats, Mitch? Leaping over the rocks?'

'Yeah. And the bacon.'

'Huh?' Sarah swung round to discover wild boars with long tusks grazing not far away. She wasn't too daunted; she could probably outrun one of those portly creatures if it took the notion to chase her.

The boars didn't seem the least bit curious when Mitchell and Sarah got to their feet and followed the river upstream. The waterfall was throwing up great misty plumes of spray, and the sun had painted a spectacular rainbow right across it. Ordinarily, Sarah would have been captivated by such a sight. But not today. Today she felt like Dorothy about to approach the Wizard of Oz. Every step brought her closer to the dreaded one. Would he send her home, or would he not?

Echoes of Fyrddin's words flashed like neon signs across her mind. Giants turned to stone. Dwarves held as slaves. Elves killed. Now, perhaps too late, she *really* listened. She could almost taste the fear in her mouth as she finally admitted what she hadn't wanted to believe. Fyrddin was right – Vanrod would not help.

She glanced at her brother, wondering if the same thoughts were going through *his* head.

'Mitch?' Sarah said tentatively.

'Yeah?'

If the Cowardly Lion had been by her side Sarah would have caught hold of his paw and fled. But Mitchell looked resolute and fearless.

'Oh … never mind.' She couldn't admit she wanted to turn back. She could never dissuade him from his purpose now they were so close.

***

'This isn't so bad,' Mitchell yelled over the thunder of the waterfall.

He was clinging to the rock face, looking down the thirty or so metres they had climbed so far and puffing from the exertion.

Sarah grunted as she found a foothold and heaved herself up beside him. She glanced around warily. 'Any sign of Vanrod's cave?' she yelled back.

Before Mitchell could answer, a dark shadow rushed over him, and, glancing up, his heart leapt in terror. Monstrous talons reached out and snatched him and Sarah into the air.

Mitchell screamed and screamed and screamed. His screams were almost lost in the roar of the waterfall. He stopped screaming when he ran out of breath. That's when he heard Sarah screaming beside him; she had a strong set of lungs.

Looking out through the talons that held him like the bars of a cage, Mitchell saw the frothing river more than one hundred metres below. If the talons opened, he and Sarah would plummet to their deaths.

Craning around, Mitchell counted four thick scaly legs connected to a massive green underbelly. It was enough to confirm his suspicions. He and Sarah were in the clutches of a dragon.

The dragon was taking them higher still. Mitchell watched the river shrinking. He could hear the whoosh of wings beating the air.

The dragon flew so close to the rushing waterfall that icy spray doused Mitchell's cloak like a shower. Sarah's scream cut out mid-shriek; she had probably copped a mouthful of water.

Where's the dragon taking us?

The answer came soon enough. The waterfall parted in curtains either side of a huge cave entrance; the dragon flew through the opening and landed on its hind legs. Then, from a height of two metres, it dumped Mitchell and Sarah like bags of rubbish onto the hard floor – 'Ow-w-w!' they cried in unison – before bringing its front legs down almost on top of them. And now, several tons of dragon was standing over them.

Mitchell flicked his dripping hair out of his face and tilted his head up at the towering beast, dreading to think what it might do next.

It flexed its claws …

But the dragon appeared to have no further interest in Mitchell or Sarah, for it turned ponderously, spread its serrated wings, and departed the way it had come. The two cascading streams of water united behind it, blocking out much of the bright daylight, and, as if by magic, the mind-numbing roar of the waterfall completely faded until all was still except Mitchell's pounding heart.

'Heh, hem!' A gruff cough sounded behind him.

Swivelling his head around, Mitchell found himself staring at a ridiculously long grey beard. His gaze travelled upwards to a thin slit of a mouth, two hollow cheeks, and a hawk-like nose. Next came two deep eye sockets overhung with heavy eyebrows – the sort that tweak up at the outer ends – and a pair of none-too-friendly eyes – fiery *red* eyes.

Mitchell felt his throat tighten. So, this was Vanrod. An aura of cruelty almost leached from the wizard's pores.

Mitchell hastened to his feet and pulled his sister up. And now that Mitchell was standing, he was surprised at how small he felt, or was it just that Vanrod was exceedingly tall? Sarah drew close to his side.

'HOW – DARE – YOU – DISTURB – ME!!' Vanrod bellowed, almost blasting Mitchell and Sarah off their feet like a water cannon.

It was only with difficulty that Mitchell stopped himself from running. He glanced at Sarah. The blood had drained from her face and he sensed she was quite unable to speak. Mitchell wasn't sure *he* could speak either.

'We're v-v-very sorry to interrupt you, b-b-but we – er – we desperately need your help,' he stammered.

He waited for some sign of encouragement – a nod or the hint of a smile. The wizard's burning eyes didn't even blink; he just *looked*.

'Um.' Mitchell swallowed hard. Now was not the time to crumple in a heap. Maybe the wizard's bark was worse than his bite. Sarah's hand sought his, her grip uncomfortably tight. Mitchell cleared his throat and forced himself to focus. 'We … Sarah and me … were brought here … into *your* world, that is … by witches … and, um, we really want to go back to our *own* world … D'you think … I mean … would you mind …'

Sarah gave his hand a supportive squeeze. It wasn't much, but he found strength to string a coherent sentence together. 'We'd really like you to send us home.'

Vanrod knotted his formidable brows. 'Do I *look* like a fairy godmother?' he demanded, stabbing the floor with his wooden staff.

It seemed that this was not a rhetorical question, for the wizard paused for an answer. Mitchell and Sarah shook their heads.

'No. I do not *look* like a fairy godmother because I am *not* one. I am a mighty wizard. Mighty wizards do not waste time on mundane concerns of no consequence to them.'

There. They had their answer. Exactly as Fyrddin had predicted. Mitchell and Sarah swapped miserable looks.

'And now,' Vanrod continued, 'I shall make the most of this unwelcome interruption – I shall send you into the mine to work.' A cheerless smile curled the corners of his mouth.

It took Mitchell a few moments to digest the wizard's words.

Work? ... In the mine? ... Become Vanrod's slaves?

The idea was preposterous!

Vanrod's long purple cloak swept the floor as he crossed the cave towards a large bronze gong hanging from a metal stand.

Mitchell quickly found his voice again. 'Um ... sorry for bothering you. We'll, um, we'll just climb back down the mount–'

'Silence, fool!' Vanrod struck the gong with a metal striker and a deep boom resonated off the walls.

'Come on, Sarah,' Mitchell whispered as the sound began to die away.

He reached out to seize her hand ... and his head exploded in pain, sharp stabbing pain like he'd never known before, pain like a jackhammer pounding his brain. He dropped to his knees, clasping his head and groaning in agony. The world was nothing but pain, and the pain was building.

Sarah flung her arms around her brother to shield him from the wizard's raised staff. It made no difference. Mitchell collapsed on his side, moaning.

There was nothing for it. Sarah knew she *had* to speak. Her whole body shook as she lifted her face to Vanrod. From the nasty smile on his face he appeared to be savouring the torment he was inflicting.

'Please, oh please don't hurt Mitch,' she entreated in a choked, tiny voice.

'Begging on our knees, are we?' Vanrod took no trouble to conceal his delight at the sight. 'Oh, this is priceless! How touching.'

Sarah could feel her insides sinking. She glanced at her brother, his face poppy red as if his skull must soon burst apart, and she turned back to Vanrod.

'Please!' she cried, her voice shrill with fear. '*Please* stop. He's no use to you dead ...'

Vanrod appeared to consider. 'Fair point,' he conceded, and lowered his staff.

Almost at once Mitchell's moans ceased and his muscles slackened so that he lay quite limp upon the floor of the cave.

Sarah shook his arm gently. 'Mitch? Can you hear me?'

No answer.

An unbidden voice in Sarah's head screamed, *He's dead. It's too late. You're all alone now.*

Sarah shook her brother vigorously. 'Mitch! Talk to me!'

And then, thankfully, Mitchell opened his eyes. 'Neeto ... res ... abit ...'

Sarah hugged him hard in relief.

'Get up,' Vanrod said sharply, and Sarah saw that Vanrod had seated himself at a desk which was off to one side of the cave.

Sarah hauled Mitchell to his feet. He staggered against her.

'Wait there,' Vanrod told them, without bothering to look up from the outspread scroll he was examining in a pool of lantern light.

And now the awfulness of their situation hit her.

Slaves. We're going to be slaves.

Her eyes roved about, seeking some means of escape. A large shadowy archway cut into the back wall looked promising. But where did it lead?

There was nothing much of note in the cave itself, except a squinkle, which gazed back at her from a fish-tank on the sideboard, and four large bookcases whose shelves were graced by hundreds of books, the spines of which bore strange gold symbols.

Sarah's eyes came to rest back upon Vanrod. The insignia embroidered onto his cloak resembled a diving eagle. *Of course!* Each eagle beak formed the point of the letter V. V for Vanrod.

Mitchell pulled away from Sarah, and managed to stand without being propped up.

'You okay?' she mouthed.

He nodded. The vivid colour was starting to fade from his cheeks.

There was the sound of hurried footsteps, and Vanrod turned his face towards the archway. Moments later, a thickset dwarf trotted into sight. Sarah saw him before he saw her – his rough beard, straggly, shoulder-length hair gathered in a pigtail, hobnail boots with iron toe-pieces, hard hat and dusty overalls. It seemed he had been running, for his face was ruddy and his breath came in rasping gasps. He started in surprise at the sight of Mitchell and Sarah, before setting down a covered wicker basket from which appetising smells wafted.

'These feeble creatures have made presents of themselves to me,' Vanrod told the dwarf. 'They wish to join your little mining community. Set them to work and see that they develop blisters and muscles.'

'Yes, master,' the dwarf responded, and signalled for the children to follow.

Sarah shot a beseeching just-do-as-he-says glance to her brother, who replied with a shrug of defeat. After all, what choice did they have?

***

Shortly after the piping of elven music transported Mitchell and Sarah to the Troll River, it also transported someone else. If Mitchell and Sarah had looked hard enough they might have noticed him. He was rather small. Rat-sized in fact.

The swirling current was almost more than he could contend with – it held him down, let him up gasping, and overwhelmed him again – but after a valiant effort his beady eyes and pointy nose re-emerged and he paddled strongly towards the river's edge. By the time he managed to drag himself up the bank he was quite breathless. There, he shook the water from his draggled coat, and settled on his haunches in the rippling grass.

As soon as Mitchell and Sarah roused themselves, so did the water rat, Rodenticus.

He wasn't far behind as they toiled up the mountain.

He saw the dragon swoop down and whisk them up into the air.

He heard their screams.

He watched the dragon enter Vanrod's cave with the children and, subsequently, as he continued to claw his way up the steep rock face, he saw it re-emerge without the children.

He froze the instant the dragon looked in his direction, his grey coat blending beautifully with the background.

The dragon started to turn its gaze away … and the rat took the tiniest of steps.

One tiny movement was all it took to give his position away.

The rat gave an involuntary squeak as a jet of burning flames came gushing towards him. Faster than he'd ever moved in his life, he tumbled nose over tail into a crevice. Just in time. The searing heat would have incinerated him.

He held his nose in the air, sniffing cautiously. There was a horrible odour of burnt fur and flesh.

And then the pain struck, and he gave a squeak of distress. Surely it couldn't be ….

It was.

His tail.

It was gone!

Only a stump remained.

A singed and smoking stump.

Screwing himself right around he fanned the stump with his paw to cool it down, and then puffed out his cheeks and blew on it until the agony subsided.

And there he huddled, whiskers quivering, paws clasped together, facing a rare crisis of confidence. Did he have the nerve to go on? How would he manage without a tail to help him balance? He peeked out at the expanse of rock rearing above.

Then he thought of his five little ratlings at home. What kind of example would he be to them if he gave up now?

More than that, the dignity of all water rats was at stake. Of course he must persist in his mission.

And though his chest felt tight with fear, he stepped back into the open again, and his weary legs began scrabbling up the next rough boulder.

Chapter 14 – Dragon Breath

Mitchell was so furious with Vanrod that he paid no heed to his footing and kept stumbling on the uneven ground. Consumed by fantasies of revenge, he followed the *crunch, crunch, crunch* of the dwarf's footsteps deeper and deeper into the mountain, along a passage hewn out of rock and lit by torches in wall brackets.

Ten minutes passed before Mitchell glanced back at Sarah to see how she was coping. Her head hung low and eyes were cast down.

And now a faint, rhythmic clinking sound pierced his consciousness. They must be getting closer to the mine.

As Mitchell's anger cooled a little, he began to absorb the horrible truth that he and Sarah had no way of returning to their own world. Who would walk Fleabag every day? Who would get his spot on the cricket team? Who would give Grandpa Weaver a hand with the mowing? Who would Grandma make chocolate brownies for? He hastily mopped up a tear that glided down his cheek, fearful that he might start bawling if he let himself go. What wouldn't he have given to be able to crawl onto his mother's knee like when he was little and feel her comforting arms around him?

'Holy guacamole!' Mitchell muttered, halting abruptly just inside a chamber four times the size of his school auditorium.

Sarah blundered into him, and then gasped as if someone had sprayed a glass of cactus juice in her face.

The scene before them was a veritable Aladdin's Cave. Countless rubies and emeralds and opals and sapphires flickered like coloured fire in the torchlight, stacked in great piles that rose up from the ground and towered over their heads.

Mitchell and Sarah drifted spellbound between the mounds of treasure, after their guide, who only paused momentarily to kick five or six sparkling diamonds out of the way. 'Cluttering up the place,' he muttered.

And now they were back in another passageway.

The clinking sound intensified until the passageway brought them at last to a cavern more vast than an aircraft hangar – the throbbing heart of the mountain, where steel clanged against rock and dust hung thick in the air. Sarah clapped her hands over her ears to shut out the intense ringing of hundreds of picks and chisels.

Mitchell ran his eyes around the perimeter of the cavern. There were dwarves on scaffolding and dwarves on the ground, none taller than four feet. They looked filthy and dreary. Their overalls hung off them like rags, their hair and beards were unkempt, and their hard-hats were split and dented. Mitchell watched an old bandy-legged dwarf shovelling dirt into a wheelbarrow and carting it away through one of several dark exits on the opposite side of the cavern.

The scene was dismal, yet its setting was spectacular, for flaming torches brought out the brilliance of glittering amethysts and opals and sapphires speckling the walls.

Their guide stopped beside a disorderly heap of work clothes and work tools on the ground.

'By way of us getting acquainted, my name is Tumblelong,' he said.

Sarah stepped forward to shake the dirty hand he proffered. 'I'm Sarah.'

'I'm Mitch,' Mitchell said unenthusiastically.

'Pleased to make your acquaintance,' returned Tumblelong. 'May I suggest that you rummage through the spare gear to find something that fits?' He bent down and commenced sifting through boots.

'Mr Tumblelong,' said Mitchell, crossing his arms, 'there's *no way* we're gonna work for that wizard.' Tumblelong stood up straight and eyed Mitchell quizzically. 'There's nothing in the world that could make –'

'A cave-in!' Sarah squealed, protecting her head with her hands as the ground shook and loose dirt showered down.

'Not a cave-in. Just a dragon drawing near. It's inspection time,' Tumblelong told her. 'If the dragon doesn't find our work acceptable, it may eat one of us.' He rounded on Mitchell, unable to restrain a grim smile. 'You were saying?'

'Nothing,' Mitchell muttered, unclasping his cloak. As he hurried on a pair of ill-fitting overalls he could scarcely determine whether he was more excited or frightened about seeing another dragon.

'Best not to stand out,' Tumblelong advised. Then, perhaps noticing Sarah's chalk-white face, he added, 'Courage, lass. Courage.'

The ground shook again. Mitchell and Sarah grabbed a pick each from the pile and, tripping on the small rocks that littered the floor, hurried after Tumblelong, ignoring the wondering looks on faces that turned in their direction as they passed.

Closer to the workers, the stench of sweat was strong.

'We're harvesting the gold from these veins running through here, see,' Tumblelong said. 'Gouge out as much as you can. Like this.'

He lifted his pick and struck the wall so hard that a jagged crack ripped through it.

Mitchell gave a low whistle. The dwarves might be small but they evidently had giant strength.

With a heave, Sarah attacked the rock too, but her pick merely bounced off the surface.

'Put some muscle into it,' Mitchell chided. 'Look, I'll show you.'

Mitchell swung his own pick high and smashed at the rock-face with a mighty downward stroke. The impact jarred his neck but made negligible difference to the rock. Surprised and embarrassed, he tried a second time, with no better outcome.

Though he felt Sarah's eyes on him, he would not meet them. 'Not as easy as it looks, is it?' he mumbled.

Sarah had the grace not to say anything.

And now the dragon announced its entrance with a growl.

Mitchell gazed across the cavern at the long poison-green head protruding through an archway. Wisps of steam curled from its nostrils, and its mouth swung ajar, revealing jagged teeth that gleamed in the torchlight. The dragon manoeuvred through the archway with its bat-like wings tucked in close to its body. Keen green eyes skimmed the workers.

'Wow!' Mitchell couldn't help marvelling at the great pointed spikes running along its spine.

'Mitch, the gold's not going to jump out of the rock of its own accord,' Tumblelong said.

'Alright, alright.'

Mitchell threw himself into the pick work – briefly. He could hear the hulking reptile as it made the rounds of the cavern; every step sent loose rocks clattering down the walls.

Mitchell was unable to resist another peek.

'Psst! Keep your eyes down,' whispered Tumblelong.

The dragon continued its slow circle, and Mitchell swung his pick a few more times before stopping to wipe his forehead.

'Is it just me, or has it suddenly got scorching hot in here?' he asked in an undertone.

Neither Tumblelong nor Sarah answered.

There was a very distinctive sniffing sound directly behind him and the smell of rotten meat wafted over him. Dragon breath!

'Keep working,' Tumblelong muttered into his beard.

Mitchell swung his pick at the wall and landed a clumsy blow. Sweat trickled down his face as he tried again. Beside him, Sarah was making a valiant effort, but she may as well have been wielding a plastic toy pick for the results she got.

Mitchell could feel the tickle of sweat behind his knees. He was half-afraid he could smell his hair starting to sizzle.

The dragon emitted a low growl.

Amazingly, bravely, Tumblelong turned to face the dragon. 'Come now, Blaze, these young-uns have only just arrived,' he coaxed.

Mitchell and Sarah also squirmed slowly around, and Mitchell found himself staring into a cavernous mouth crammed with dagger-sharp teeth – three rows. The dragon was salivating, no doubt in anticipation of meat on the bone; long strings of drool swung from its jaws. The heat was so intense it rippled in waves.

Instinct told Mitchell to run, but he was hemmed in. The most he could do was back up, pressing himself against the wall.

The dragon's heavy-lidded eyes seemed to be sizing Mitchell and Sarah up for crunchiness and juiciness as it deliberated over which tempting morsel to devour first.

Mitchell lowered his eyes, hoping not to excite it further, but his grip on the pick handle tightened. He would go down fighting, even if that meant only knocking out a single dragon tooth.

'Think about it, Blaze,' Tumblelong begged, in a rather husky voice. 'Vanrod wouldn't want his new slaves eaten first day on the job, would he now? Give them a week or two to learn the ropes.'

Unwelcome thoughts were flooding Mitchell's mind. *Does the dragon swallow its food whole? Probably not; not with teeth like that. Does the dragon roast its food before eating it? Does it rip it with those terrible talons?*

Mitchell glanced at his sister. Her lips were pressed together and she looked peaky.

The dragon raked its claws along the ground, scoring grooves in the rock. It wasn't happy. But, mercifully, it turned away. And not a moment too soon, for Sarah began to sway, and Mitchell was forced to drop his pick to steady her.

The dragon was clearly irritated as it resumed its circuit. Dwarves were sent scurrying out of reach of its long barbed tail that was now whipping back and forth, sweeping the floor from side to side. Finally, as the dragon brushed through the archway by which it had entered, Mitchell set Sarah down on the ground.

'Thanks,' Sarah said, summoning up a wan smile. 'I'll be okay in a minute. I just got so hot.'

'Dragons take some getting used to,' Tumblelong said sagely.

Chapter 15 – Slaves

The rattle of stones skittering down the walls subsided as the dragon's footsteps died away, and all around Mitchell, workers were downing tools and wiping the sweat from their foreheads.

'Where did *you* come from?' demanded a dwarf with bushy red hair and whiskers, in a tone one might take with a spider on the toilet seat.

'My name's Mitch, and this is Sarah,' Mitchell answered, indicating his sister seated on the ground. 'I know this sounds a bit weird, but we come from a completely different world. A world with only one moon, and really pathetic constellations, but no noxies.' A sea of craggy faces surged closer, some evaluating, some hostile. 'Witches fetched us out of our world by magic because they want our blood for a potion. We only made it out of Wartville because some elves with dragon skins rescued us.'

The cavern swelled with harsh guttural noises as the dwarves conferred in dwarfish. Mitchell caught a few words he understood – not very reassuring words, like 'trick', 'naive', and 'deception.'

Mitchell pressed on loudly. 'We came to Mount Tremor to ask Vanrod to send us back to our world, but he said "No" straight out. He wants us to work for him, here with you –'

'Scrawny and Scrawnier have been sent to *help* us,' a mocking voice rolled across the cavern. 'We can all rest up now.'

The joke was greeted with appreciative chortles and loud guffaws.

'Look at them,' jeered a dwarf whose eyes were half-hidden under bristling black eyebrows. 'Arms frail and useless, flimsy as toothpicks. They can barely *lift* an axe, let alone swing one. No, Vanrod did not send the humans here to *work*.'

Mitchell smarted at the words 'frail and useless'.

'Hear, hear!' a third voice called.

The red-haired dwarf spat contemptuously on the ground. 'If you ask *me*, they've come to spy on us. They're Vanrod's spies.'

Growls and grunts of agreement followed.

'You're kidding, right?' Mitchell said, looking the red-head full in the face.

The red-head's expression hardened. No, it seemed no one was kidding.

'That has to be the dumbest thing I've ever heard!' Mitchell burst out.

The red-head took a menacing step forward.

'In case you didn't notice, one of his dragons almost just *ate* us for a snack,' Mitchell went on, undaunted.

'Dumb, eh?' the red-head said in his gravelly voice. 'Do you take us for fools to be conned by an obvious stunt like that?'

Mitchell was starting to get really annoyed now. 'You *are* fools if you think we'd side with that evil wizard,' he retorted. 'Vanrod almost *killed* me back in his cave.'

'Steady on, Flamebeard,' someone cautioned as the red-head gave every appearance that he would like to cleave Mitchell in two with a swipe of his axe.

Mitchell inched back.

Sarah, meanwhile, had been fumbling in her pack, and now she stood up. 'We are friends of Fyrddin, captain of the elven army,' she declared in a defiant though tremulous voice. 'See what he gave us.'

There was a general shuffling forward to examine the healing herbs and unicorn tears in her hands.

An elderly dwarf with a silver fringe of hair around his bald head cleared his throat. 'These humans speak the truth,' he croaked. 'Such treasures are closely guarded and shared with naught but a trusted few.'

Flamebeard, however, harrumphed and maintained a disgruntled expression. 'They may be friends of *elves*, but are they friends of *dwarves*?' he rumbled.

'Let us give them the benefit of the doubt, Flamebeard,' replied the old dwarf in a placatory tone. 'If their story is true, they are greatly to be pitied.'

'It's a crying shame, in my opinion,' Tumblelong added. 'They're just youngsters.'

This different slant on things seemed to soften the dwarves; suspicion ebbed from many faces and some of the dwarves even managed a sympathetic smile for Mitchell and Sarah.

'We're stopping for a bite to eat now,' Tumblelong said. 'We've food to spare if you're hungry.'

The prospect of a meal lifted Mitchell's anger in an instant.

Crusty bread rolls and hunks of crumbly cheese were extracted from picnic baskets and passed around. The smell made Mitchell's mouth water. 'Does *Vanrod* give you this food?' he enquired.

'Do trolls sing opera?' Flamebeard retorted, ripping his bread roll in two with ferocity.

Tumblelong smiled wryly. 'Our womenfolk climb the mountain every day with food for us. Here – care for some grape juice?'

Mitchell tucked in with good will, and all conversation ceased as the food was devoured. Somehow, everything seemed a little less bleak to Mitchell on an increasingly full belly. And when crumbs had been dusted from beards, the dwarves drew deeply on their weed pipes, issuing a haze of smoke into the dusty air.

Mitchell rather welcomed this opportunity for silent reflection. He drew his fingers through his tangled hair. What on earth were he and Sarah going to do now? One thing he was absolutely sure of: they were not going to moulder away in these caves, they were not going to become resigned to their fate like it seemed the dwarves had.

All too soon, lunch break was over, and the baskets were packed up.

'Humans!' Flamebeard hailed Mitchell and Sarah, who stepped forward cautiously. The red-head's manner was less antagonistic now he had eaten. 'Your muscles are too soft for the pick work, so see if you can find any gemstones buried in the rubble, and give them to Grizzlehead here. He does the polishing.'

'Thanks,' Sarah responded enthusiastically. 'That'll be much easier.'

She was right. It would be much easier, but Mitchell felt a sting of humiliation that he couldn't do the *real* work. 'Whatever,' he said with a shrug.

***

Silvery moonlight was spilling through the waterfall into Vanrod's cave when he finally lifted his head from the book he had been poring over by the light of a lantern. He leaned back in his chair and mashed his fists into his eyes. Then he pushed back his chair and got to his feet with a grunt.

It took him a few muttered words to erect invisible barriers, one at the waterfall entrance, and one at the archway at the rear of the cave, to keep out surprise night-time visitors.

And now the wizard moved from his desk to his bed. He took off his purple cloak and hooked it over the back of a chair. He untied his girdle, to which a leather pouch was attached, and slung it over the iron bed-head.

Finally, Vanrod eased himself onto the bed and tucked the blanket around him. Another muttered word, and the lantern snuffed itself out.

The wizard tossed and turned for a good fifteen minutes until his breathing settled into a regular pattern that betokened sleep.

Only now did the water rat dare to creep out from beneath the sideboard, mindful not to let his tender tail stump touch anything. Whiskers twitching, the scent of bread crumbs drew him towards the meal-table, and he lost no time scampering up onto it.

***

Deep in the mountain, Mitchell, Sarah and the dwarves were still working.

Grizzlehead, by means of cranking a handle, was tumbling gemstones in a rotating barrel not far from where Sarah was sifting through the rubble. The tumbling was a rather noisy operation, but not so noisy that Sarah couldn't hear the voice that rang out.

'Final inspection!'

Immediately Sarah could feel a heightened tension in the atmosphere. Next came the warning tremors, and fear began to twist her stomach. The clatter of small rocks began to build and build, until at last a dragon entered the cavern.

Sarah snatched a peek.

This dragon was a female, a smidgin smaller than the male, but no less threatening. One twitch of her tail and a dwarf found his feet cut from under him; Sarah's hands flew to her mouth to cover a gasp as he toppled backwards with an *ooof!* cracking his helmet against the ground. Rather red-faced, he scrambled to his feet, helmet askew.

The dragon conducted her tour of the cavern with clicking claws and menacing growls, and though Sarah applied herself to her job, her fingers seemed suddenly clumsy, fumbling with the stones she was meant to be picking up.

And then the dragon's hulking form melded into the darkness of the passage that led to Vanrod's cave, her tail slithering noisily after her.

When Grizzlehead paused to blow his nose, Sarah asked him, 'Why's the dragon going to see Vanrod?'

'She's checking the stockpile of treasure,' Grizzlehead answered.

Twenty minutes passed before the dragon returned and halted momentarily in the archway. Her face bore the contented expression of a cat in a dairy.

But no one relaxed yet. The dragon was now nosing through the debris.

Sarah's eyes met Grizzlehead's in an unspoken question.

'Smelling for precious metals or jewels we might have overlooked,' Grizzlehead explained in low tones.

Meanwhile, several dwarves had gathered up the empty picnic baskets. One by one the dragon snuffled them with her big green snout.

'Checking her precious treasure isn't smuggled out when we return the baskets via the eastern exit tunnel,' Grizzlehead whispered.

Now the dwarves bearing the picnic baskets strode into the exit tunnel, and the dragon rustled after them.

'Good riddance,' Sarah muttered, dusting her hands.

'Down tools!' someone called.

'Another day over,' Grizzlehead sighed, leaning wearily against the polishing barrel.

'Can dragons *really* smell jewels?' Mitchell inquired.

'Absolutely,' Grizzlehead replied.

Sarah stepped out of her overalls and folded them neatly. Now that she was still, the bleak atmosphere of the cavern seemed to be exacerbated by the chill that began to seep into her every bone; she located her travelling cloak and snuggled into it. The dwarves were evidently feeling the cold, too, for half a dozen of them had hauled some logs from a recess to build a bonfire. Sarah watched as they lit it and the crackling flames took hold.

'Sarah. Look at this.'

Mitchell had strayed into a dark corner of the cavern. Sarah joined him.

'These must be skins the dragons have shed,' he said, heaving at a great tumble of green, scaly material, raising a great cloud of dust that tickled Sarah's lungs.

'It's nothing – *cough!* – like what – *cough!* – the elves gave us,' she managed to say.

Mitchell examined one of heavy skins more closely. 'Try peeling off the inside layer – I think that's the bit the elves use.'

Painstakingly, Sarah peeled back a strip of dragon skin no thicker than cling wrap. It came away in one piece the size of a bed sheet. She threw it over herself.

'It works. I can't see you at all,' Mitchell said. He twisted his mouth in a pensive expression. 'Fold it up and keep it. It might come in handy.'

Mitchell peeled another thin filmy layer for himself and pocketed it.

The bonfire was blazing now, and its grey smoke was churning up, up, up, losing itself in the deep hollow darkness where the roof of the cavern sprang away above.

Sarah found the glow of the fire cheering. The way it picked out emeralds and rubies sprinkling the walls reminded her of Christmas tree lights.

Dwarves had begun stretching out to sleep inside the bonfire's ring of warmth.

'Good night all,' someone called, and a chorus of answering 'Sleep wells' followed.

Sarah grimaced as she surveyed the rock-strewn floor. *Sleep well? I don't think so!* How she longed to snuggle into her own comfortable bed at home.

Mitchell and Sarah cleared a sleeping spot for themselves a little way removed from the dwarves, and lay down facing each other.

'You know – well – you know there's no way for us to go home now, don't you?' Mitchell said, with a wobble in his voice.

Sarah knew very well, and she suddenly found herself overcome by a suffocating rush of homesickness. Whatever had sustained her all day failed her now, and a steady flow of tears began to trickle noiselessly down her cheeks.

Mitchell reached for her hand and gave it a squeeze. 'Listen, we're not gonna spend the rest of our lives inside this mountain, that's for sure. We're gonna get out of here.' The catch in his throat belied his confidence.

Slumber had stolen quickly over the dwarves and the air was filled with an off-beat symphony of snores that ranged from trombone blasts to piping whistles, punctuated by an occasional chesty cough.

Sarah sniffed. 'D'you reckon we could sneak past the dragons if we wear the dragon skins?'

'I'll ask Tumblelong tomorrow. He –'

'What's that?' Sarah cried, sitting up.

A fluttering firefly?

A strange luminescent moth?

No! It can't be!

Sarah stared through tear-blurred eyes, entranced by the sight of a fair-haired fairy dressed in a business suit.

The fairy alighted on the ground between Mitchell and Sarah, popped open her briefcase, extracted a notepad and quill, set the briefcase upright, sat down upon it, opened her notepad and poised her quill to take notes.

'Well, now. What are the tears for?' the fairy asked crisply, peering up at Sarah through dark-rimmed spectacles.

Sarah rubbed her eyes in disbelief, and looked to Mitchell for confirmation she wasn't dreaming. Mitchell was sitting up now too, wearing a daft, gobsmacked expression, his eyes reflecting a myriad golden fairy dust particles.

Slowly and deliberately, as if she had decided Sarah was a few spots short of a toadstool, Reeks spoke again. 'You – are – crying. – Why?'

'You're ... oh, this is too ... you're a *fairy*!' Sarah gasped.

'Poor dim-witted kid,' Reeks mumbled as she scribbled in her notebook. Then, addressing Sarah once more she said in a coaxing voice, 'I need you to tell me why you are crying so I can help you. Do you think you might be able to do that?'

'Um ... well ... you see ...'

As Sarah began to speak over the rumbled lullaby of snores that echoed around the cavern, Reeks dropped her quill in evident surprise.

115

'Semi-intelligent after all,' the fairy muttered as she recovered the quill, and, applying it to paper, she began to take copious notes.

At length, Sarah finished her explanation, and Reeks blew on her tiny handwriting to dry the ink. By squinting hard, Sarah just managed to read, 'Needs to count her blessings.'

'Well, that explains why you're not on my register,' Reeks said, clapping the notebook shut and standing up. 'You're entirely outside my area of responsibility.' She opened the briefcase and dropped the notebook and quill inside. 'All children from other worlds are, thankfully. The Save-a-Life Division's quite hectic enough as it is. I'm already stretched trying to cover half a dozen countries in *this* world – Wystovia, the Goblin Emirates, Araltica, Treachery Isle, Casparia, the Dark Lands ... Can you imagine?' She snapped the briefcase shut and took it up in her hand, as if set to depart. Then, her face clouded a little. 'You're not planning on applying for an inter-world transfer, are you? The paperwork would be astronomical.'

Sarah was finding it extremely difficult to follow what Reeks was going on about. 'Hang on. Are you saying that you *could* get us out of here, but you're not going to?' Sarah queried.

'That's correct,' Reeks answered composedly. 'It's not my job. Anyway, I can't imagine *why* you were crying. You braved an evil wizard and lived to tell the tale. You fronted a hungry dragon and weren't devoured. This is probably the luckiest day of your life. Anyone else would be celebrating.'

Sarah stared at the fairy in disbelief. Then disbelief turned to indignation. 'Celebrating? We're never going to see our family again. We're stuck in this mountain. We're slaves. Would *you* be celebrating?' she demanded hotly.

Reeks threw Sarah a quelling look. 'Don't take that tone with *me*, young lady. I'm only trying to help. If you go through life fixated on what you *don't* have, rather than being thankful for what you *do* have, you'll never be content.' And with this admonition, Reeks vanished, retracting her golden light with her.

116

Rage roared inside Sarah like an angry beast. She could feel her cheeks burning. 'Can you *believe* that little twerp? I wish I had a fly swatter!' She swished an imaginary fly swatter through the air. 'Whack!'

'What's the problem?' Mitchell repeated in a fine impression of Reek's superior tone. 'Anyone else would be celebrating.'

It took Sarah quite a while to calm down. *Just forget the crazy fairy*, she told herself.

When she finally did put Reek out of her mind, she remembered that the dwarves had been stuck inside the mountain for *years*. Working non-stop. Every day fearing for their lives. And the more she thought about it, the more she found herself stirred by a great sadness for the dwarves and a deep sense of outrage at Vanrod's cruelty.

Then Sarah remembered the dragon skin in her pocket and set to thinking about the possibility of escape.

Chapter 16 – A Good Whipping

'You've done really, really well,' Stella told the broomstick she was flying. 'I honestly didn't think you'd still remember how to get up into the air. But it's time to go back. See, the sun's just popping up now.'

Taking a final breath of fresh air, Stella angled the broomstick downwards towards the olive-green smog that hid Wartville from sight.

Slate tiles and chimneypots only sprang into view when she was almost on top of them, and moments later her shoes touched the slimy cobblestones.

The lane in which Stella landed was sufficiently wide to admit a horse and cart, although the only horse Stella had ever seen in Wartville had been lightly crumbed and fried.

As she dismounted, Stella looked up and down the lane. Apart from a long-haired puss on the prowl, the lane stood deserted.

'Just as I thought,' she said brightly. 'No one's up yet.'

Stella poked her tongue out at the drab grey houses that seemed to crouch like toads waiting to catch a fly, then, clasping her bundled apron in one hand, and shouldering the broomstick with the other, she set off down the lane, humming a little tune.

The moment she entered the town square the tune died on her lips and her stomach gave a lurch of dismay. Why were so many witches up already? The bug-eyed general-store owner was pushing back the shutters on her shopfront, other sisters were trundling out carts, and a voice drifted from Wartville's beauty salon, 'The Uncracked Mirror': 'We have a terrific two-for-the-price-of-one-boil offer, and I can throw in a hairy mole if you like.'

Stella had forgotten that extended trading hours applied during Spellfest.

I hope Horribella's not awake. Stella broke into a fast jog, her heart suddenly thundering in her chest.

'Ow!' She tripped on her overlong hem and nearly went sprawling.

A witch with a face more creased than a dried fig glanced up from the unlucky charms and pixie repellent she was setting out on her street stall.

Stella slowed to a walk. *Act normal,* she told herself, almost stumbling over her feet with nerves.

All was quiet outside *Wartalicious.* The front door to the restaurant was shut. The blinds had not been opened. Chairs were still stacked on outdoor tables.

No sign of Horribella. Everything might be okay after all.

Stella read the menu board. 'Book now for the End of Spellfest Feast, featuring Horribella's famous Baby Bear Stew. Thick chunks of meat and seasonal vegetables simmered slowly over a low heat until tender.'

'Did Horribella write that yesterday or today?' Stella asked the bear cub, whose mournful eyes were looking back at her through the bars of its cage.

And then the front door burst open and a witch with sky-blue dreadlocks charged out. Stella was sprung.

'Where've you been, you lazy loafer?' Horribella demanded, clamping Stella's nose between a pair of tongs and snatching the broomstick.

'Ouch! N-nowhere.'

Horribella rotated the tongs, which left Stella little choice than to twist her head sideways.

'What do you mean, *no*where?'

'I ... um ...'

Even as Stella winced, she couldn't help feeling some pleasure at the sight of the broomstick attempting to whack Horribella. Horribella was compelled to release Stella's nose in order to deal with it. 'Enough, or I'll feed you to the fire,' she promised in a low, dangerous sort of voice.

'No, don't!' Stella implored, straightening her head. 'Don't hurt it!'

The broomstick decided to behave itself, and the witch's critical gaze returned to Stella.

'It's not even *your* broomstick,' Horribella said, sharply. 'It's one of my old ones. What's wrong with *yours*? Lost? Broken?'

'No, Twiggy's fine,' Stella answered. 'It's just ... Don't you think it's sad that the old brooms get left in the cupboard all the time, and never get to fly?'

'Stop talking nonsense and tell me what you've been up to. Come on, out with it!'

Stella looked around wildly for inspiration. The welts on her back were still raw from the last whipping ...

'I was ... um ... I was practising for the flyathon,' she said. 'For that charity, the ... um ... the ...' She faltered under the disbelieving look Horribella gave her.

'The Society for the Torture of Defenceless Creatures?'

Stella nodded.

'Since when did you start supporting *them*? – Eh! What's this? Why are beetles crawling up your sleeve? Explain yourself!'

Stella looked down.

Bother!

Four shiny beetles had escaped from her apron and were marching towards her elbow. The beetles should have been almost invisible – black against black – but Horribella had sharp eyes when it came to spotting anything that would get Stella into trouble.

Clearly there was no point denying the accusation.

'I ... um ... I wanted to try a new recipe,' Stella ventured.

'What recipe?' snapped the witch, furrowing her brow.

'Well ... um ... I was reading the dwarf recipe for vanilla slice with a biscuit crumb base –'

'Eurgh! I'd rather be tossed into a crocodile-infested swamp than eat such muck,' Horribella declared, pulling a disgusted face.

120

'Yes ... yes, of course ... But what if we used crushed *beetles* in place of biscuit crumbs?'

Horribella's expression softened; her dark eyes brightened and her tongue flickered over her lips approvingly. 'Maybe you're not such a dismal failure after all ...'

Stella dared to smile.

'Don't look so pleased,' Horribella barked. 'This is *not* the time to be dabbling with new dishes. There are nightingales to be plucked and worms to marinate and if you *ever* take off without permission again, I'll de-broom you, d'you hear?'

Of course I hear, Stella thought.

'I'll de-broom you *and* I'll lock the broom closet so that you can't steal any of *my* broomsticks.'

'Yes, Horribella,' Stella responded dutifully.

'Now then, get to work.'

Leaping inwardly at her lucky escape, Stella was on the point of entering the restaurant when things took a most unpleasant turn. Not because the unwelcome mat suddenly bellowed 'RACK OFF, LOSER!' (it said that to everyone who entered without gold in their pockets), but because, as if they had been lying in wait to pounce, three particularly nasty, creeping witches spilled out through the doorway.

Stella drew back instantly, her stomach turning over. *Now* she was in for it.

Like a huddle of cunning vultures, the witches eyed Stella. Horribella could be mean when she wanted to, but these three witches were in a cruel league of their own.

The witch with a deep crease in her knobbly chin spoke first. 'You oughtn't let her off so lightly, Horri. She's nothing but trouble, and' – wagging a spiteful finger – 'mark my words, she'll turn out just like her mother.'

Stella dropped her gaze to the ground.

'She's up to no good. Always is,' wheezed the witch with a light moustache on her upper lip.

'If you ask *me*, a good flogging wouldn't go astray,' mused the third witch, stroking the loose skin that wobbled from her neck.

'Nobody *did* ask you,' Stella wanted to retort. If only she dared.

'If you say so, sisters,' Horribella said with a shrug, as if whipping an eight-year-old was neither here nor there.

The bear cub drew his claws across the bars of the cage as if he felt the injustice.

'But I haven't done anything *wrong!*' Stella burst out, bringing her eyes up to meet Horribella's. After all, was it *really* so outrageous to hunt up a few titbits for a bear cub?

'If you haven't yet, you will soon,' Horribella answered, extracting a wand from her gown.

In a flash Stella's shoes felt as heavy as if they were made from lead. She flung her apron on top of the cage, determined that the bear cub should enjoy the honeycomb and beetles it contained. A moment later a crack rang out like a pistol shot and the first magic lash cut into her flesh.

'Aaaargh!' Stella's eyes brimmed with tears.

The gargoyle on the door lintel smiled maliciously, and cockroaches skittered into the gaps between the cobblestones.

Chapter 17 – Fateful Decision

Sarah found herself being shaken awake long before she was ready to open her eyes.

'Back to work,' Tumblelong said apologetically.

Sarah got stiffly to her feet and looked about. The blazing logs of last night had crumpled to ashes, and a handful of dwarves with doleful expressions were already gouging away at the rock walls with a *Clank! Clink! Clank!*

Beside her, Mitchell stumbled to his feet; his scowling face reminded her of the words scrawled across his pyjamas back home: 'I don't do mornings'.

'I dunno how you can stand it, being underground all the time,' Sarah said with a shudder. 'It's horrible.' Even now she could feel the mountain pressing in on her.

Tumblelong nodded as though he understood. 'That's why Vanrod chose *dwarves* for this task. Dwarves make excellent miners.'

'Though we prefer to be our own masters, not pitiful workhorses,' Flamebeard added gruffly, coming up behind. 'Come on, get cracking. Dragons eat shirkers.'

But Sarah wasn't keen to get back to work just yet. She had done some serious thinking last night.

'Can dragons see through dragon-skin cloaks?' she asked.

'No. No they can't,' Flamebeard answered guardedly, as if he suspected this might be a trick question.

'Then, I don't understand,' Sarah said. 'There are heaps of dragon skins lying about. Why don't you make a run for it?'

Flamebeard snorted. 'Fat lot of good being invisible is when dragons can *smell* you.'

'Oh.' Sarah felt stupid. Why hadn't she thought of that?

Tumblelong shook his head glumly. 'That's not the reason we haven't bolted though. Vanrod has threatened to turn our families to stone if we so much as take one step out of the caves or if they so much as take one step in.'

His words carried such sorrow that Sarah almost regretted bringing the subject up at all.

Mitchell, who had been following this exchange with a sleepy expression, stepped forward, looking a little more awake now. 'Last night Sarah and I helped ourselves to a couple of dragon skins. We're going to escape,' he announced.

'Heaven help us,' Flamebeard muttered at the ceiling.

Tumblelong looked serious. 'How do you plan to get past the dragons without them smelling you?' he asked.

Mitchell lifted his shoulders in a shrug. 'Dunno yet.'

Flamebeard gave a loud snort.

'There may be a way around the smell problem,' Tumblelong said, pulling his ear in a thoughtful manner. 'Yes, goat blood should do the trick.'

'Goat blood?' Mitchell echoed, and at the same time Flamebeard grunted, 'Don't encourage them,' with a frown.

'Dragons catch and kill goats on the mountains then deposit them in the tunnels to mature like vintage cheese,' Tumblelong explained. 'I reckon if you smeared rotting goat blood all over you that'd disguise your smell.'

'Sounds like a plan,' Mitchell said, his eyes shining.

'Sounds like complete foolishness,' Flamebeard contradicted.

'Hang on, Mitch.' Sarah didn't want to be a kill-joy but – 'There's one problem. Will Vanrod turn anyone to stone if *we* escape?'

Tumblelong tugged his grizzly beard reflectively. 'I doubt it …'

'Course he won't,' Flamebeard said irritably. 'He knows you're not one of us.'

'Excellent,' Sarah said, brightening.

'What will you do? Where will you go?' Tumblelong inquired.

124

'*If* you make it out past the dragons?' Flamebeard added, putting a whole lot of emphasis on the word 'if'.

'We'll find a country where humans live, and get right away from all this sorcery and stuff,' Mitchell responded at once. 'Try and live normal lives again.'

Sarah looked at him doubtfully. 'You know what happens to kids without parents, don't you? They get stuck in an orphanage.'

Mitchell pursed his lips, considering. 'That mightn't be so bad. Anyway, have you got a better idea?'

'Well ...' Sarah hesitated. '*I* think it'd be cool to live with the elves in the forest. But first, I want to steal the ruby from Vanrod and find the other Banishing Stones.'

Flamebeard threw his hands up in the air. 'Are you *delusional*?'

'No,' Sarah said slowly. 'No, I'm angry. This place is the pits. No one should be stuck in here. All you ever do is work. No holidays. No sunlight. No nice hot baths. And the dragons! No one should be eaten by dragons. I feel sick thinking about it. And some of you've probably got kids?' Tumblelong nodded. 'I thought so. Do they ever get to see you? No. That's really, really sad. Vanrod's a scumbag. He needs to be stopped.'

'Listen, you gumby,' Mitchell said. 'I'd like to stop Vanrod too. I haven't forgotten what he did to me yesterday. But get real. If the Banishing Stones were *that* easy to find, don't you think Vanrod would have found them all by now? We've nothing to go on. No map. No clues. We could search till we're ninety and still not find them.'

Sarah stuck her chin out stubbornly. 'I'd still like to *try*.'

'And how do you plan to steal the ruby?' Mitchell asked. 'Vanrod would kill us if he caught us sneaking around in his cave.'

Sarah shrugged. 'We'll work something out.'

'Nutty as pecan pie,' Flamebeard grunted into his beard.

'No I'm not. I just want to get you out of here. If we could find the Banishing Stones we could send Vanrod back to his own country ... and the witches too. The witches go around turning elves to stone and setting fire to the forest and stealing animals. Someone's got to stop them.'

Mitchell was shaking his head. 'We're just two kids.'

Sarah sighed. She *really* wanted to free the dwarves. Even now the clamour of picks tearing at rock was building as more dwarves took up positions around the walls. Sarah could feel the noise vibrating inside her skull. It was intolerable that anyone should be forced to live like this.

'There may not actually be *three* stones missing,' Tumblelong put in mysteriously.

Sarah drew in a breath.

'What d'you mean?' Mitchell asked.

'Well, our families pass us notes in the food baskets, keeping us in touch with the outside world. There are whispers that the magic sapphire was discovered in the Stormy Sea up north. Vanrod has been torturing sea creatures for information, and day and night his eagles patrol the coast. Apparently merfolk are too scared to surface anymore.'

Sarah could feel a spring of hope fizzing up inside her. 'Then only *two* stones are still lost! Oh, *please* Mitch! Let's hunt for them,' she begged. 'We could meet the merpeople first to check if the rumour about the sapphire's true.'

'For pity's sake!' Flamebeard exclaimed. 'Talk about counting your bearskins before you've trapped your bears! You haven't even escaped from this mountain yet. And even if you *do* get past the dragons, Vanrod's eagles are bound to come after you, you can bet your life on that.'

'Good point,' Tumblelong acknowledged.

Sarah was undeterred. 'We'll have our dragon skins,' she argued.

Flamebeard shook his head, clearly unconvinced, but Tumblelong's clear, frank eyes lit up as an idea struck him. 'Vanrod won't let his eagles hurt you if he thinks you're doing something that might help *him*. So, what if I tell him you've gone in search of the sapphire because you plan to do a trade? I'll tell him that if you find the sapphire, you intend to give it to him in return for him sending you back to your world.'

Everyone mulled over Tumblelong's idea for a moment.

Then Flamebeard clicked his tongue impatiently. 'Make up your minds. The first watch of the day may arrive shortly.'

Tumblelong clapped his hands together, looking at Mitchell and Sarah in turn. 'Righty-o, let's get moving. I'll guide you to the eastern exit. Put on your travel cloaks, it'll be cold outside.' He rushed off and speedily returned with yesterday's leftover bread. 'Here. You'll need this. Ready then? Follow me. Hurry now. That's the way.'

'Totally bonkers,' Flamebeard muttered after them.

Chapter 18 – Tricking a Dragon

Tumblelong hustled Mitchell and Sarah across the vast clanging cavern, through the archway the dragons had emerged from the day before, and along a winding tunnel lit by intermittent torches. The clinking and clanking of picks gradually faded.

'Dragons have sensitive snouts and can pounce like lightning and rip you to shreds, it's true. But just keep your heads and you'll be fine,' Tumblelong began to advise as he strode along the contorted passageway. 'Oh, and dragons can lash out with fire too. But I'm sure you'll be smoking, I mean *sneaking*' – he corrected himself quickly and gave a nervous laugh – 'sneaking past in no time.'

Mitchell's mouth went dry. *Not the most emboldening speech.* He stole a sideways glance at his sister; her face looked pale in the feeble torchlight.

'When you get out of here,' Tumblelong continued, 'just keep following the path down the mountain to the village. Our womenfolk will help you reach wherever you decide to go.'

'How far are we from the exit?' Mitchell inquired after he had been walking for ten minutes.

'It's not far now,' Tumblelong responded.

At last the floor began to angle downwards and oh, what a glorious feeling to round a bend and glimpse a pale prick of daylight, like the light of dawn.

Tumblelong halted and clapped Mitchell on the back. 'This is where I leave you. The tunnel runs straight as a broomstick from here. I wish you the very best of luck.'

'Thanks, Tumblelong,' Mitchell and Sarah chorused.

And then Sarah sprang forward to give the dwarf an impulsive hug. 'I hope you get out of here soon.'

Mitchell set his face towards the exit. 'Right. Let's do it,' he said, trying to inject a note of confidence into his voice.

Together, Mitchell and Sarah marched forward.

The light ahead seemed to be growing with every step.

And suddenly Mitchell found himself fighting down the impulse to gag.

'Oh! That's vile!' Sarah cried, clamping her nose between forefinger and thumb.

Trying to breathe only through his mouth to avoid the dreadful stench in the air, Mitchell almost tripped on something; one of many decomposing goats strewn along the tunnel.

'Got to get lots of this stink on us,' Mitchell reminded Sarah, and stooped to rub his travelling cloak in sticky dark blood. Secretly he wondered if his neat-freak sister would baulk at touching a dead goat. To his surprise, she began smearing goat blood on her wrists as if it were lavender water.

'I'm done,' Mitchell said at last. 'Time to put on our dragon skins.'

'Yep,' Sarah answered, already disappearing into the folds of hers.

Mitchell's dragon skin made a faint whispering sound on the ground as he continued along the tunnel. He hitched it up a little.

Ahead, something was obstructing the exit, something with a saw-edged outline.

'Oh, rats,' Sarah whispered. 'What do we do now?'

Nearer and nearer they crept to the dragon. They had a side-on view of it as it crouched across their path, wings tucked in, big as a bus, taking up the width of the tunnel.

Mitchell debated with himself for a moment. Should he direct his steps left around the dragon's head, or right around its tail?

The dragon's snout was lowered, its teeth busy ripping the flesh from some animal between its forepaws. There was steam rising from its nostrils.

Its tail lashed about randomly, beating the floor and wall with loud smacks.

Best to keep away from that unpredictable tail, Mitchell reasoned. *Better to slip round the front.*

'I'll go first,' Mitchell intoned, just loud enough for Sarah to hear, and proceeded with grim resolve towards the small gap between the dragon's left front foot and the tunnel wall.

There was a rustling noise as the dragon shifted its leathery wings.

Slow and steady, that's the way, Mitchell told himself.

He could have reached out and touched the green scaly paw.

He didn't.

He tiptoed around the curved black spikes that were the dragon's talons.

You're doing good.

The dragon, absorbed in devouring its breakfast, which Mitchell suspected was a couple of wild hogs, had no idea Mitchell was there. Its stinking breath washed warmly over him.

Feeling braver, Mitchell turned for a moment to give Sarah a thumbs-up, after which he edged along the tunnel wall. And now that he was in line with the dragon's muzzle, the heat of its breath was intense. He began to move faster.

Completely unexpectedly the dragon lifted its formidable head.

Mitchell paused and gazed up at the thick milky strands of saliva dangling from its mouth.

Gross!

And then the dragon gave a tremendous belch. Mitchell dodged backwards just in time to avoid a great blast of flames. He shielded his face until the terrible heat subsided.

That was way too close!

Mitchell's heart seemed to be beating in his ears as he watched the dragon return to its meal.

He glanced around at Sarah again. Her eyes looked very large and her lips had formed the shape of an O.

It took Mitchell a full minute to recover his nerve. He could still feel heat radiating off the rock wall. He wiped his clammy palms down his clothes.

Praying that there might be no more burping, he began to cross the distance between the dragon's forepaws once more.

The beast lifted its head a second time, and Mitchell paused, tense as a bowstring, fully prepared to make a run.

The dragon's nostrils flared; it sniffed, and sniffed again.

Had it caught his scent?

Mitchell held himself rigid, scarcely daring to breathe.

The dragon's luminous green eyes darted back and forth. It let out a low, rumbling growl.

Yes, it had definitely caught his scent.

Mitchell clenched his fists, trying to keep his fear under control. *It can't see you,* he tried to reassure himself. He could feel a river of sweat running down his neck.

What seemed like an eternity later, though it was only seconds, the lure of crunchy bones seemed to overcome the dragon's curiosity. It lowered its head and resumed eating with satisfied grunts.

Mitchell allowed himself to breathe more normally again.

Wait ...

Wait ...

NOW!

Ditching the idea of slow and steady, Mitchell sprinted the rest of the way, to freedom.

***

Sarah could have clapped with relief when her brother disappeared safely around the other side of the dragon. But now that it was her turn, a heavy dread settled over her. She felt the insides of her stomach twist and tighten. The glow of the rising sun behind the dragon seemed to be taunting her.

Willing her legs to move, her feet took two timid paces forward, then two hasty paces back.

You big wimp, Sarah chided herself. *Mitch did it, and you can too...*

She counted to three in her head, and began to creep around the dragon.

At every step she feared it would lift its head again.

But things could not have gone more smoothly. The dragon carried on grinding bones to powder, and before Sarah knew it she was standing outside on the mountainside with Mitchell, who gave her a relieved smile.

Sarah gazed about quickly, scanning for other dragons.

There were light scarves of mist suspended in the cool morning air, and further up the mountain snow lay in patches on the ground. Lifting her eyes to the sky, Sarah spotted an eagle circling. But no dragons.

Mitchell beckoned, and together they set off down a well-worn path.

Sarah directed her eyes to the scene far below. A village lay snuggled prettily amongst sloping patchwork pastures, and smoke was drifting from several chimneys. Farmsteads dotted the landscape, set high on hilltops or snugly in glens. Beyond the farmland, rich green vegetation extended for miles.

Every time that Sarah checked over her shoulder to see whether the dragon was on the move or not her spirits lifted a little higher.

No.

Still no.

No again.

It was a good half-hour later before Sarah allowed herself to relax.

'Woohooo!' Mitchell hooted unexpectedly. 'We're freeeeee!'

'Ssh!' Sarah twitched his arm urgently and pointed upwards; the bird of prey was drifting lower, its eyes watchful.

'Don't move,' Sarah whispered, fearful lest a disturbance of dust or a dislodged pebble should give their location away.

Mitchell and Sarah stood stiller than the mountain, heads craned back, watching the eagle descend lower still. The bird was graceful and powerful, black with white wing tips at least three metres apart. Sarah began to make out individual feathers. Its cruelly curved beak reminded her of the master it served.

Abruptly her attention was diverted by a prattle of dwarfish as a band of female dwarves came into view below, journeying up the incline leading donkeys laden with baskets.

The eagle didn't hang around for long after that, and Mitchell and Sarah were able to proceed on their way.

Sarah eyed the dwarves keenly as they passed. Their old-fashioned, ankle-length dresses revealed work-roughened hands and strong forearms. Beneath their sunbonnets their faces looked tired and careworn, but kind.

Sarah lengthened her stride, impatient to reach the village.

Chapter 19 – A Dose of the Truth

Mitchell and Sarah were still descending the mountain when Vanrod shuffled sleepily to his feet. He fastened his girdle with the leather pouch, then splashed water (which magically appeared in his washstand) over his face, and dried himself with his long beard.

A picnic basket had been left for him just through the archway that led into the mountain. In order to retrieve the basket, Vanrod removed the magical barrier he had put up the night before. He licked his lips as he laid out its contents on the table: freshly baked bread, a pot of honey, a slab of butter, and a bottle of cold, creamy milk.

'Not bad,' he grunted.

The wizard ate and drank with obvious enjoyment, noisily licking his fingers. When he was done, he draped his purple cloak over his shoulders and strode into the mountain.

The little grey water rat, Rodenticus, pattered softly behind, keeping to the shadows.

'Hard at work,' muttered the wizard to himself as the clinking of iron on stone became audible.

Brilliant mounds of amethysts, emeralds, diamonds and sapphires burst into sight. Rodenticus could feel his eyes popping as he gazed up at their splendour. But he did not pause.

In no time at all Vanrod was striding towards the centre of a great clanging cavern.

Rodenticus dived into a discarded boot and peeked out the hole in the heel.

'Where are my two new slaves?' Vanrod's deep commanding voice rang out.

The clamour died away as every dwarf turned to face the wizard.

Flamebeard threw an apprehensive glance at Tumblelong, who seemed rather less sure of himself now that the wizard towered before him.

Vanrod's red eyes skimmed the workers, seeking out the children. '*Well?* Lost our tongues, have we?' There was a nasty edge to his voice that hinted if they hadn't yet, they might soon.

Tumblelong took a timid step forward, his axe unsteady in his hand, and looked up at the wizard's face. 'Your g-great wizardship,' he began, 'the two human slaves were w-weedy and worse than useless. Unlike us d-dwarves they were unfit for hard labour. They ate our f-food but did not contribute to the p-piles of treasure. They were incompetent m-miners, hindering your lordship's work in the caves.'

As Tumblelong had been speaking, Flamebeard had been watching the colour mount in the wizard's face.

'Do not trifle with me,' Vanrod said in a low voice. His eyes were glowing like pools of boiling lava.

'Your wizardship?' Tumblelong's voice cracked as he spoke.

'Where are they?' Vanrod said through gritted teeth.

'If it p-please your wizardship,' Tumblelong stuttered, his hands shaking uncontrollably now, 'the p-puny humans realised their mistake – that is to say, they realised that they should n-not have asked a favour of a g-great wizard without offering payment. C-consequently, they have set off in search of the m-magic sapphire. When they return, they will be able to p-pay you properly for sending them b-back to their world ... Do you not find it a p-pleasing plan?'

'A PLEASING PLAN?' Vanrod exploded, his voice filling the cavern.

Tumblelong took several hasty steps backwards, his axe crashing to the ground.

'A PLEASING PLAN? HOW *DARE* YOU DEFY MY WISHES?'

Tumblelong looked about frantically. Nobody seemed keen to step into the fray to assist him. When his eyes met Flamebeard's, he shot a beseeching look.

Curse him! Flamebeard muttered in his head. Then he cleared his throat and spoke up loudly. 'Did you not want the sapphire, my lord?'

Vanrod instantly rounded on Flamebeard. 'OF – COURSE – I – WANT – THE – SAPPHIRE!' he thundered.

'Your mighty wizardness,' said Flamebeard, bowing low in an attempt to appease the wizard's wrath, 'consider the great artfulness, the great deceptiveness of the plan. For months now your eagles have been using … ahem … *harsh* methods to extract secrets from the merpeople, but what have they achieved? Nothing at all. You're no closer to finding the sapphire now than you were before. The seemingly innocent humans, by adopting a more *subtle* approach, by feigning friendship with the merpeople, may actually be more successful.'

Vanrod's nostrils were flaring. Perhaps he sensed he was about to burst a blood vessel, for he took a few deep breaths to regain his composure. 'If *you're* telling the truth,' Vanrod managed to say, 'then I'm a sea slug.' He muttered something under his breath, and what looked like a tiny bottle of perfume appeared in his hand.

Flamebeard swallowed hard; he realised what was coming.

'Open your mouth,' Vanrod commanded. 'Tongue out.'

Flamebeard opened his mouth, and Vanrod squirted a little liquid onto Flamebeard's outstretched tongue.

'Now, tell me again, where have the children gone?'

Flamebeard's brain seemed to have become suddenly sluggish. He could feel his will bending to the potion. 'They talked about going the Stormy Sea,' his mouth answered in a voice that sounded unusually hoarse.

'To search for the magic sapphire?'

'Yes.'

'To bring it back to me?'

Flamebeard wanted to say 'yes'. He tried to say 'yes'.

'No.'

The fire in Vanrod's eyes subsided, and his thin lips spread into a smile of gloating triumph. 'I knew it!' Vanrod crowed. 'Did you really think *dwarves* could outwit the superior intelligence of a wizard?'

Flamebeard stood before Vanrod, head bowed, quaking in his dusty boots. The cavern had grown terribly still. If Rodenticus had sneezed he would have given himself away. Rodenticus decided it was time to be off. He left his hidey-hole and retraced his steps along the mountain tunnel.

When Flamebeard finally dared to look up, he saw that a cunning gleam had taken hold in the wizard's eyes.

'Let the goslings fly the coop,' Vanrod announced in a resounding voice. 'If they *do* manage to find the sapphire, I'll know about it; my eagles won't fail to be watching.'

The entire cavern breathed a sigh of relief.

Vanrod swung round. 'GET – BACK – TO – WORK!!'

The dwarves sprang into action, and the dusty air reverberated once again with hammering and clinking.

The wizard's cloak had barely swished out of the cavern when Flamebeard plumped down on the ground, his legs refusing to support him any longer. He could feel his pulse racing. He massaged his aching temples with his fingertips.

Tumblelong clasped his shoulder. 'Are you okay?'

'Usual side effects,' Flamebeard returned gruffly.

Tumblelong sighed. 'I didn't anticipate truthaliser. But you did well, my friend.'

Flamebeard dropped his head into his hands. 'It was close. Very close,' he muttered. 'We're lucky to be alive, that's what.'

Meanwhile, Rodenticus could hear a set of footsteps growing louder. The rat scooted into the shadows until the wizard had breezed past.

When he was sure it was safe, Rodenticus took himself on a tour of the cavern of glimmering gemstones. There was only one sparkling pyramid that interested him. The crimson one.

Rodenticus clawed his way up it until he came to a stone larger than a chicken's egg. Very gently, half anticipating an avalanche, he levered the stone out of the pile.

Ten minutes later he was pattering along the tunnel towards the wizard's cave with a ruby balanced neatly on his back.

Chapter 20 – Wipple Village

By the time Mitchell and Sarah reached the sun-drenched foothills of Mount Tremor, their legs were jiggling like jelly from tramping down, down, down. The road took them past fields bounded by hedgerows where honey-coloured crops dwarfed the reapers in their midst and straw-stuffed scarecrows welcomed birds onto their outspread arms.

'Hey, Mitch,' Sarah said suddenly, 'don't you think the elves are stupid keeping those dragon eggs? If *I* found a dragon egg, I'd smash it.'

The elves had been far from Mitchell's thoughts. For him, the Fragrant Forest seemed as distant as Australia. He had been agonising in his mind over what to do next. In one respect, it was sheer madness to go after the Banishing Stones; a virtually impossible task, and dangerous, too. In another respect, wouldn't it be brilliant to thwart Vanrod's plans? It might be quite an adventure, too.

Mitchell and Sarah gorged on wild kipberries and washed (as best they could without soap) in a pond, before continuing on, draped in their dragon skins. The stinking travelling cloaks, having served their purpose, were left behind.

'So, have you decided yet?' Sarah appealed to Mitchell. 'Will you help me find the Banishing Stones and rescue the dwarves?'

Mitchell sighed. 'Let's just go to the Stormy Sea and find out if the merpeople have the emerald first,' he said. 'If they do, then I'll help you look for the other two Banishing Stones.'

'Yes!' Sarah twirled on the spot with obvious delight.

'Don't get your hopes up,' Mitchell said quickly.

A rumble sounded behind them, and they turned to watch a donkey-cart advancing towards them at a furious rate, flying over ruts and stirring up a cloud of dust. The cart must have entered the road from one of the farm lanes, Mitchell supposed.

'Feel like a ride?' he asked Sarah.

'Yep!'

The cart hurtled closer, driven by a dwarf boy who was thrashing the reins like Ben Hur in a chariot race.

The two sweat-streaked donkeys were almost upon them.

'Now!' Mitchell whispered.

Mitchell and Sarah raced alongside the cart and jumped onboard. Tucked in between sacks of potatoes, sagging with relief to be off their sore feet, they couldn't have found a less comfortable ride, jolting and swaying like fleas on a hyperactive dwiggle.

The road followed a river for a short distance, past a mill house and a revolving mill-wheel, before veering over a wooden bridge and leaving the gurgle of the river behind.

The driver gave a lusty shout, 'Coming through!' and up ahead, a dwarf herded her straggling cows out of the way.

Mitchell and Sarah presently found themselves rumbling into a charming village. 'Welcome to Wipple', said a banner strung across the road between two poles. The main street was lined with low, thatched cottages set in gardens with nodding flowers.

'Coming through!' their driver yelled again, and a dwarf girl drew back from the road, tugging a toddler out of danger.

Mitchell watched in alarm as ducks pecking for worms refused to give way. The driver tried to navigate around them, the cart tilted on two wheels, and the uninvited passengers leaped off.

'BUNT-YYYYY! SLOW DOWN THIS *INSTANT*!' bawled a buxom dwarf from a porch that fronted one of the cottages.

At the sound of her voice, the donkeys pulled up so sharply that Bunty somersaulted right over their heads, landing face-down in the mud beside the village pond.

'How many times do I have to tell the little imp?' the woman muttered, shuffling into the street to help him.

'Bishle peem womfy,' Bunty spat through a mouthful of mud.

140

By unspoken agreement, Mitchell and Sarah chose to remain cloaked in invisibility – after all, a chance to poke around a dwarf village did not present itself every day.

Mitchell felt like he had stepped back in time as he read the sign-boards swinging gently in the breeze: cobbler, tanner, blacksmith, cooper, draper, wheelwright ...

Just outside the butcher's shop, a hog was rooting for acorns with a ravenous snuffing sound. Mitchell couldn't resist leaning close to its ear to whisper, 'Pork sausages'. The hog bolted, its curly tail bobbing up and down as it fled.

Two dwarf boys traipsed into the toy store, and, on a whim, Mitchell and Sarah nipped inside behind them before the door clicked shut.

'A good morning to you, Miss Jolly,' the taller boy called.

A dwarf straightened up from behind the counter and a sunny smile overspread her face, crinkling the lines around her eyes.

'A very good morning to you, too, Jasper. Hello, young Horace. What can I do for you this fine day?'

'Horace got five silver shuckles for his birthday, and I told him about the new magic carpets –'

'Did one of you boys tread in something?' Miss Jolly interrupted, sniffing the air. 'Check your shoes.'

They checked. Nothing. Mitchell and Sarah exchanged guilty glances.

'Dear me, I don't know what that foul odour could be. Let me just prop the door open. That's better. Now, where were we? Oh yes, flying carpets.' Miss Jolly fetched a miniature Persian-styled rug from the shelf and set it down on the counter.

'Your mouse could fit on that,' Jasper said to Horace, who was bouncing up and down with excited anticipation.

Miss Jolly proceeded to open a pouch of sparking gold powder. 'You only need a *tiny* pinch of fairy dust. Sprinkle it on the carpet, like so, and voila!'

The magic carpet gently lifted up off the counter.

'Take a turn around the store, and return,' she told the carpet.

Horace's rapt eyes followed the carpet as it whizzed around the shop in fancy manoeuvres, tassels fluttering.

'This is the deluxe version – high-performance, anti-gravity, designed according the highest aeronautical safety standards, money-back guaranteed not to cause injury, and comes with two carpet beetles.' Miss Jolly rattled off the words as if reading from a script.

The carpet came zooming towards Sarah and she tried to dodge, accidentally bumping up against a shelf. A deluge of dryad dress-up costumes, novelty genie lamps, and dragon-shaped kites came crashing noisily down on her head.

'Dear oh dear!' Miss Jolly gasped. 'Whatever triggered *that*?'

Mitchell was tempted to take off his dragon skin and confess.

But Sarah didn't move. She seemed afraid of crushing the pretend wizard rings and leprechaun money boxes strewn about her feet.

'Whoa! It flipped right over!' Jasper exclaimed, still watching the magic carpet.

'Do you think my mouse could hold on?' Horace inquired doubtfully.

Miss Jolly returned her attention to the boys. 'Definitely not.' Then, addressing the carpet, she called, 'OK, down you come.'

The carpet hovered near the doorway and shook itself like a naughty child shaking its head.

'Stop that silliness at once! If I have to come and get you …' Miss Jolly threatened.

The distraction allowed Sarah to extricate her feet unnoticed.

The magic carpet deliberated briefly before zooming back to the counter and slapping itself down with obvious annoyance.

'Hey, Horace, try the troll clubs,' Jasper said, seizing a foam club. He landed a whack on his brother's arm, and an evil laugh rang out. Horace burst into shrill giggles.

While the boys duelled, shrieking with laughter every time the evil troll laugh sounded, Miss Jolly busied herself with the window display, sprinkling fairy dust on thumb-sized elf soldiers who began wielding their swords with great ferocity. Miss Jolly tsk-tsked and whisked a couple of swords away. 'Play gently! Who's going buy you with heads and limbs sliced off? Tell me that now!'

Mitchell and Sarah slipped out of the toy store, exchanging grin for grin.

Back on the street a dwarf boy tottered past swinging milk pails from a wooden beam balanced across his shoulders, while a goat trotting along behind was chewing his ankles.

Mitchell slowly circled a signpost, reading the finger signs that pointed in various directions. 'Merpeople. Elves. Witches. Wizard. Giants. Humans.' Rather unnervingly, the 'Humans' finger-sign swivelled around, following him as he moved.

Further on, Mitchell and Sarah came to the schoolhouse.

Mitchell nudged Sarah. 'Look!'

One wall of the schoolhouse was painted with an underwater scene and everything in the painting was moving: the mermaid combing her hair, fish darting this way and that, crabs scuttling along the sea bed, and seaweed swaying in an imaginary current.

A knot of dwarf children stood before the painting jabbering in dwarfish, while a blindfolded dwarf girl was attempting to pin a ribbon on the mermaid's hair. As soon as the girl came close, the mermaid propelled herself out of reach.

'They need a see-through blindfold,' Mitchell whispered.

Sarah tugged his arm. 'Let's sit over there.' She indicated the village well, which had a solid stone wall running around it.

Mitchell settled himself on the well wall with a weary grunt and let his eyes range over the handsome stone buildings that fringed the village centre. Reliefs carved on the eaves gave clues as to their purpose: music hall, gaol, post office. Dozens of pigeons were strutting and fluttering on the post office roof, which was spattered with their droppings.

The delicious aroma of freshly baked bread laced the air, and all at once Mitchell realised he was starving. He consulted the skies. All clear.

'I reckon this place looks safe enough,' he declared. 'D'you wanna let the dwarves know we're here?' *And hopefully they'll give us some food,* he added in his head.

Chapter 21 – New Friends

To the dwarves passing by the well, it must have seemed that Mitchell and Sarah simply materialised out of thin air.

'Gracious goodness!' one exclaimed, oblivious to the lemons spilling from her tilted basket.

'Upon my word!' cried another, tightening her grip upon the chicken in her arms; it let out a half-strangled squawk.

Mitchell found their stunned expressions rather amusing.

Even a goat stared, rattled its head and stared again.

But when a hissing goose came flapping towards Mitchell and Sarah, neck outstretched, Mitchell's smile faltered.

'Ow! It nipped me!' Sarah cried, pulling her legs up so sharply she almost plunged backwards down the well.

'Down, Gerda! Down!' a dwarf girl called, rushing forward.

'Hey!' Mitchell protested, as a beak jabbed his calf.

'Stop it, Gerda!' the dwarf girl said sharply, and the frenzied goose backed off. 'Sorry about our guard goose. I hope she didn't – What a stink!' She gasped, pinching her nostrils together. 'I ... I mean ...' Colour rushed to her chubby cheeks.

'It's okay. We know we stink,' Sarah said, slipping off the well wall with a smile. 'We've just escaped from Mount Tremor. We made ourselves smell like rotting goat to get past the dragons.'

In no time at all Mitchell and Sarah found themselves surrounded by dwarves.

A dwarf whose grey hair was tucked up under a frilled cap asked in shocked tones, 'Where are your *clothes*?'

Sarah glanced down at herself. 'We're wearing them,' she answered uncertainly.

Raised eyebrows showed what the modestly-dressed dwarves thought of t-shirts and shorts.

And now questions flew like elven arrows.

145

'Did you meet my poor Treacletooth?'

'Did you see Strongarm? Was he well?'

'Did Waddlestep send any messages?'

Meanwhile, a dozen dwarf children, having squeezed through the throng, were staring as if Mitchell and Sarah were three-eyed aliens with green skin.

'Everyone was fine, we think,' Mitchell answered as soon as he could get a word in edgewise. 'We weren't in the mine very long.'

Several of the dwarves sighed, and a great sadness crept across their faces.

'It's terribly hard, being apart from our loved ones,' one murmured, dabbing her eyes with a handkerchief.

'Well now,' said a dwarf so overweight she resembled an overstuffed pincushion, 'tell us about yourselves. It's not every day we have *human* visitors.'

Mitchell gave a brief account of their adventures so far, which took a couple of minutes in the telling. 'So,' he concluded, 'first, we're going to check if the magic sapphire really *has* been found. And if it has, we're going to search for the two other missing Banishing Stones.'

Looking around, he expected to see dwarf faces light up with hope, but, inexplicably, many remained downcast. A few dwarves put their heads together and murmured uneasily in dwarfish.

'Is … is something the matter?' Sarah faltered.

'Poppets, there's something you ought to know,' the overweight dwarf said. 'While our menfolk have been captive in the mountain, we womenfolk have not sat idle. Unbeknownst to them – so as not to worry them, you understand – we have done our own scouting around for the lost stones. On three occasions we have sent a delegation to the Stormy Sea to ask the merpeople about the sapphire. On each occasion, the merpeople denied the rumours.'

'Oh.' Sarah's face was an agony of disappointment.

'Come come, Marialda,' said a dwarf with big blue eyes and rosy cheeks, shouldering herself into the conversation. 'You're forgetting one *very* important consideration.'

Marialda bristled, lifting her snub nose. 'Oh *really*? And what might that be?

'Well now, merpeople might not choose to speak openly with *dwarves*, might they? Particularly if they think Vanrod is manipulating us by threatening our loved ones.'

'So you think the merpeople *might* have the sapphire, even though they say they don't?' Sarah clarified.

'I hold out a glimmer of hope, child.'

'Hmmph! You always were an optimist, Daisy,' Marialda said disapprovingly.

'I regard myself more a realist than an optimist, Marialda,' Daisy retorted. 'There's no need to *always* view the world through dismal spectacles.'

A dwarf with crisply curled hair interposed herself between Daisy and Marialda. When she spoke, her voice was even and soothing. 'Marialda, Daisy, you both raise valid points. We have not a shred of evidence that the sapphire has been recovered, not a shred. Nevertheless, there are good reasons why merpeople would not tell dwarves their secrets. Firstly, as Daisy pointed out, there is our unfortunate connection with Vanrod. Secondly, dwarves and merpeople fought bitterly over the stones during the civil war.'

Marialda's mouth was set in a straight firm line, but other heads began nodding, acknowledging the wisdom of the curly-haired dwarf's words.

She ploughed on. 'Two humans with no alliances may be just the recipe to get the merpeople to open up ... Although the children may have to *prove* themselves to gain the merpeople's trust.'

In response to the curly-haired dwarf's little speech, heads came together in a babble of animated dwarfish, and Sarah chewed her fingernails as voices spiralled. Clearly points were being argued and debated.

'What d'you reckon they're saying?' Mitchell whispered to Sarah, who merely shook her head blankly and shrugged.

Mitchell found the suspense hard to take.

147

But finally silence descended, silence that signified agreement.

A dwarf with greying brown hair in a bun stepped up to the children with a warm smile. 'I am Tumblelong's wife,' she announced, 'and there's something I'd like to show you, if you'd care to come with me.'

Mrs Tumblelong conducted them briskly through the village.

A long procession of dwarves straggled behind. 'Like rats following the Pied Piper,' Sarah whispered with a giggle.

The village ended, and Mrs Tumblelong proceeded to march across a field.

'Mind the cowpats!' she called back in warning. She appeared to be making for a sprawling barn with a red roof.

Upon reaching the barn, she grandly swung open the double doors and sang 'Da da-a-ah!' like a conjuror whisking a rabbit out of a hat. Three squealing piglets made a dash for freedom, and dozens of chickens fluttered squawking up to the rafters in a blizzard of feathers.

'Well, what do you think?' Mrs Tumblelong asked eagerly.

Squinting into the shadowy dimness, Mitchell wondered why he was expected to pass comment on a rusty plough. But he had to be honest. 'Looks pretty old. Not much use, if you ask me.'

'Piffle!' said Mrs Tumblelong. 'Swift has *years* ahead of him yet.'

As she spoke, Mitchell made out an oversized ostrich, black with a white tail, squatting grandly on a bed of straw, its round glassy eyes level with his own.

'Yes, of *course* he has,' Sarah said, glaring at her brother.

'There's no finer steed,' Mrs Tumblelong declared, 'and he will fly you all the way to the Stormy Sea.'

Mitchell scratched his head. Surely there had been some sort of misunderstanding. 'Er … isn't that an *ostrich*?'

'He *is* an ostrich, my dear,' Mrs Tumblelong agreed, puffing out her chest proudly.

Seemingly aware that he was being discussed, the ostrich stood up on long gangly legs and unfolded his wings – wings that

148

spanned the entire barn – each twelve feet long. Mitchell took a step back, flabbergasted.

Once it was agreed that Mitchell and Sarah should travel under cover of darkness, the curly-haired dwarf, who introduced herself as Mrs Stockylegs, offered the children a bath and a bite to eat, in that order.

'A bath!' Sarah said rapturously.

Mitchell didn't care a hoot about the bath. His hollow tummy was rumbling.

Unfortunately, Mrs Tumblelong had other ideas. 'In good time, Mildred,' she said. 'The youngsters must bond with Swift before they fly him. That must take highest priority. I'll bring them right over afterwards.'

Mitchell felt like dropping to his knees and *begging* Mrs Tumblelong to reconsider.

'Right you are then,' Mrs Stockylegs said amicably.

Mitchell and Sarah began to pat the mutant ostrich, keeping well away from his broad, flat beak, while Mrs Tumblelong picked strands of straw out of his feathers with obvious fondness.

'Look as his funny feet,' Sarah said.

'All ostriches have feet like that, two toes per foot,' Mrs Tumblelong replied evenly.

Then Mitchell spotted an overflowing barrel of apples and his stomach leapt with joy. 'Nice shiny apples,' he remarked in a would-be-casual voice, nodding towards the barrel.

'Aren't they?' Mrs Tumblelong agreed. 'We picked a decent crop this year. I'll be busy bottling shortly.'

'Probably really tasty,' Mitchell hinted.

'The nicest we've had for years, no question. The weather's been in our favour.'

Mitchell sighed as he tore his gaze from the fruit.

Sarah shot him a you're-such-an-idiot look, and asked directly, 'Mrs Tumblelong, Mitch and I are starving. Can we have two apples to eat?'

'Laws, child, by all means. Help yourself.'

Gradually the audience lost interest and drifted away, except Mrs Tumblelong's own two children who had overcome their shyness and were now bouncing from one bale of straw to another, each holding an elf action figure sporting a glowing fingertip.

'Noddie, Tilly. Are your chores done?' Mrs Tumblelong wanted to know.

They shook their heads.

'Righto, scram,' Mrs Tumblelong said briskly. 'And when you've finished, get washed up for dinner.'

It was only once Noddie and Tilly had skipped away that Mrs Tumblelong made her *real* purpose for detaining Mitchell and Sarah clear. Glancing about to check they were quite alone, she murmured, 'I have something *else* to show you.'

She guided them out of the barn and back across the field past chirruping grasshoppers until they came to a low stone wall. 'Cheesyface! Over here!'

One of several Jersey cows trotted obediently closer, with a blade of grass poking from her mouth. Mrs Tumblelong checked the skies, then reached up and unfastened the large bell about the cow's neck. Upending the bell, she fiddled briefly before presenting –

'The magic diamond!' Sarah burst out.

Mitchell almost choked on the apple he was chewing. And once he stopped coughing, he just stood there, mouth agape. He did not doubt that this was the magic diamond. Not because it was large as a chicken's egg, nor because it sparkled tremendously, but because it seemed to pulsate with an inner light that was startling even in the bright sunshine.

'My husband found it. In the mine,' Mrs Tumblelong told them. It was impossible not to notice her smug expression.

'And ... and didn't you tell your friends?' Sarah asked incredulously.

Mrs Tumblelong shook her head. 'My lips are sealed.'

'But why? Wouldn't it make them happy?'

By now, five other cows had crowded up to the wall to peer at the diamond.

'Oh, it may well cheer them up, dearie, but then again, they might want their menfolk home so badly that they'd hand the diamond over to Vanrod. I can't risk it. That beastly wizard must *not* get the stone. Besides, the fewer who know, the better, because he's pretty liberal with his truthaliser and we all know what *that* means.'

Actually, Mitchell and Sarah didn't know, but they nodded as if they did.

'How did Tumblelong get the diamond to you? Not in a picnic basket – the dragons would have smelled it,' Mitchell said, feeling rather knowledgeable on the subject.

Mrs Tumblelong assumed a conspiratorial tone. 'You know how the dragons stockpile dead goats for eating? Well, my Mr T wedged the diamond inside one of the carcasses. The dragons couldn't detect it then, could they, over the stench of decay? Then he scrawled me a message on a serviette: "A dragon broke a tooth today eating his dinner. Dragon dung makes excellent fertiliser".'

'We constantly send notes back and forth, mostly in code in case Vanrod sticks his great big nose in. Of course, I couldn't make head nor tail of what my Mr T was getting at when I first read his words. It worried me no end. Then it struck me – wham! – like a giant's foot, and over the next week you should've seen me charging around the base of the mountain digging through every fresh pile of dragon dung I could find.'

She screwed up her nose and shuddered at the memory. 'Foul, totally foul. But well worth it. The diamond had passed straight through the dragon. It got a *very* good wash – *that* you may be sure of – and it's been safely hidden ever since. I sent Mr T a note in return saying, "Dragon dung is a brilliant idea." Anyway, I would like you to take it,' Mrs Tumblelong said, offering the diamond to Sarah.

'But … but … *why?*' Sarah spluttered, looking completely overwhelmed.

151

'Isn't it safer here with you?' Mitchell put in.

'I have a feeling that you will need to convince the merpeople to trust you,' Mrs Stockylegs replied, 'and I don't like your chances without it, because, goodness knows, merpeople are not the most trusting of races … Well, go on, take it.'

Sarah extended her hand to take the diamond, and retracted it smartly as if she had touched an electric fence. 'Oooh!'

The dwarf chuckled. 'It won't bite. All four Banishing Stones vibrate like that when Wystovia's in danger. When you bring the stones together and banish the evildoers, they'll settle down.'

The way she spoke, as if their success was a foregone conclusion, troubled Mitchell. He fitted a smile to his face, but it felt artificial. Quite suddenly he felt burdened by the weight of hope this good dwarf was resting on him and his sister. And what a huge responsibility this precious diamond would be.

'Well now, let's not keep Mildred waiting,' Mrs Tumblelong said. 'She's probably cooked you up a storm.'

***

Mrs Stockylegs lived in a whitewashed circular cottage with round windows, much like all the other cottages.

Mitchell and Sarah entered via the back entrance, which took them past pumpkin vines that straggled along the ground and onion shoots bursting through the soil and trellises tilting under the weight of passionfruit.

The first thing Mrs Stockylegs did when she welcomed Mitchell and Sarah into her home was to insist they take turns in a rather short bath tub. When they were smelling fresh, and when their faces were rosy from scrubbing, and when they were wrapped in quilted dressing gowns, she led them into a kitchen filled with a rich tantalising aroma.

'Take a seat, take a seat. You must be half famished,' she fussed, setting two large bowls of piping hot stew on the table. 'Careful you don't scald your tongues.'

152

The stew set Sarah's tastebuds tingling, it was so delicious. As she alternately blew on each spoonful and swallowed, her eyes lingered on gleaming copper pots, polished silver utensils, and orderly shelves stocked with colourful pickles and jams.

Mrs Stockylegs dished out more stew before Mitchell could scrape the pattern off his bowl.

'Your house is a bit neater than the witches' houses,' Mitchell put in mischievously.

'Well, *really!* What a comparison!' Mrs Stockylegs sniffed.

'Mitch just likes to tease,' Sarah scrambled to explain. 'Your kitchen is the cleanest I've ever seen.' Honestly, she could have tipped her glass of cold, creamy milk right over Mitchell's head; she shot him a reproachful glare instead.

'Oh, stirring the brew, is it? Well then,' Mrs Stockylegs clucked, returning to good humour. 'Eat up now.'

As Mitchell and Sarah downed their second helpings, Sarah pointed out a smiling family portrait to her brother. 'Do you see anyone you know?'

Mitchell chuckled.

The artist had perfectly captured a three-year-old Brodin poking his tongue out. No mistaking *that* naughty face.

'Did Brodin used to live here, Mrs Stockylegs?' Sarah asked.

'Brodin? Yes, I brought him up from a baby. Here, petal, have a tad more,' Mrs Stockylegs pressed, scooping up another ladle full of stew.

'Oh, I couldn't fit in another drop,' Sarah objected, covering her bowl with her hand. Neither could Mitchell.

'I suppose dwarf food isn't quite to your liking,' Mrs Stockylegs said, returning the ladle to the pot with a disappointed sigh.

'No, no, it was great,' Sarah insisted. 'We're just full.'

'*Really* full,' Mitchell added, patting his bloated belly

'Well, if you're sure,' Mrs Stockylegs said doubtfully. 'Now then, I 'spect you could do with forty winks. Up you get and I'll show you to a bedroom.'

'We don't need a rest, Mrs Stockylegs,' Mitchell argued.

Mrs Stockylegs only shook her head knowingly. 'I daresay you think so now, but if you're going to fly all night you'll need your wits about you. We don't want you toppling through the clouds, do we?'

Mitchell protested all the way through the cottage. 'We're not – *ow!* – tired. We couldn't possibly sleep in the middle – *ow!* – of the day.' He kept cracking his head on the low door lintels.

'Careful, child!' Mrs Stockylegs cautioned. 'You'll knock the sawdust out if you keep that up.'

Sarah's eyes roved over the bluebells on the mantelpiece, the rocking-chair by the hearth, the grandfather clock in the hallway.

'This way now,' Mrs Stockylegs said firmly, marshalling them along.

They entered a children's bedroom with twin beds and a rocking unicorn.

'Just you nap awhile,' ordered Mrs Stockylegs pulling back a patchwork bedspread on one of the beds to reveal crisp lemony sheets.

Sarah flopped down on top of the sheets. It was the softest feather bed imaginable. 'Mmmm, nice,' she murmured.

Mitchell dropped onto the other bed, yawning. His toes peeped over the end.

At this juncture a rooster with a scarlet comb and green tail feathers fluttered onto the windowsill and crowed, 'Cock-a-doodle-doo!'

'Wake-up!' Mrs Stockylegs cried in frustration. 'You'll ruin my nice lace curtains. Shoo!'

Wake-up retreated the way he had come, and Mrs Stockylegs called, 'I should think so,' after him.

'Have a good rest,' she said to Mitchell and Sarah, and rustled away.

'I'm not tired,' Mitchell remonstrated one last time.

Wind chimes tinkled like fairy music through the open window, and Sarah's hand closed over the diamond tied around her waist under her nightdress. What luck! To have found one of the Banishing Stones so quickly. Only three more to go.

Within minutes, her eyes began to close …

***

Half an hour later, when two sets of t-shirts and shorts were flapping merrily in the sun where they had been pegged out to dry, Mrs Stockylegs stole back softly into the bedroom.

'Bless their little freckled faces,' she said tenderly and pottered back to the living room to write a note to the captain of the elven army.

'Dear Fyrddin,

Vanrod did not send Mitch and Sarah back to their world. Swift is flying them to the Stormy Sea to search for the magic sapphire, which they hope to present to Vanrod so he will send them home.

Mildred Stockylegs.'

She chuckled as she set off for the post office. If eagles intercepted the post pigeon, Vanrod would learn nothing new. But Fyrddin was smart – he would read between the lines.

Chapter 22 – Horribella is Horrified

'Watch where you're poking that broomstick, you klutz.'

'Believe me, I *am* watching. Now shove over or I'll poke harder.'

'GET – OFF – MY – TOES!'

'Your feet are so big, it's impossible *not* to tread on them.'

'You want this wand jammed up your nose?'

'You want this *broom* jammed up yours, you smelly dung beetle?'

'Hey! Who knocked my hat over my eyes? Who did it?'

With hundreds of witches jostling for space in the town square, Wartville was simmering like one of Horribella's sturdy iron cauldrons. It could signify only one thing: the Spellfest witch hunt was about to get underway.

'Raffle tickets!' someone called as she wormed through the throng. 'Buy your raffle tickets! Win a chin extension at The Uncracked Mirror, Wartville's prestigious beauty salon.'

'Wartville's *only* beauty salon,' Grotchetta sniggered.

'How much?' Sleazilla demanded.

'One gold glotz buys five chances in the draw,' answered the ticket-seller.

Sleazilla handed over the money just as a toad-like witch stepped out of the bakery, holding a basket of rock-chip fortune cookies. 'Good fortune! Bad fortune! Take a gamble!' the bakewitch hollered.

Within seconds all the cookies had been snatched up and gobbled down.

Meanwhile, the hunt mistress was climbing onto one of Horribella's outdoor tables in order to see over the forest of pointed black hats. She almost slipped on the layer of grease that coated the table.

'LISTEN UP!' she screeched. 'LISTEN UP!'

The crowd quietened down and riveted their eyes on the hunt mistress, an impressive-looking character with curved fingernails fully two inches long and abundant mauve hair that cascaded down her back all the way to her feet.

'This year, sisters, our quarry will be –' she paused, and the audience rubbed their veined and bony hands, shivering in anticipation, '– *FAUNS!*'

Howls of delight erupted.

'We're going to catch baby deer?' Sleazilla questioned, disappointed.

'No, Sleazy. We're going to catch two-legged goat-men with pointed beards and little horns,' Grotchetta corrected her.

The hunt mistress raised her hands for quiet before proceeding. 'Perhaps a silly young faun who strays too far from his friends, or, even better, a whole ring of them in a hidden glade skipping about to the music of a lute.'

There was a great deal of cackling.

'Morbidia will pay handsomely for each set of hoofs you collect. But *great* will be the reward for anyone who can actually catch a faun *alive*. Thanks to our generous sponsors, Hags-in-a-Hurry Broomsticks, you'll enjoy one week, all expenses paid, at Hag Island Resort.'

The town square seemed to explode with shrieks of glee, and again the hunt mistress signalled for the crowd to settle down.

'Sisters, hush! It is time. Mount your broomsticks.'

The competitors obeyed.

'And awaaaaaaay!' cried the hunt mistress.

A blur of broomsticks leapt into the air to the cheers of a handful of onlookers too old for such recreation. In moments the competitors had disappeared through the dense, churning smog, and the town square fell blankly silent.

'Drinks, sisters?' suggested a squat little witch with ankles like sausages that bulged over her shoes. 'There's a tavern just across the way.'

157

And so the wizened, the stooped, the hard-of-hearing, took themselves off to 'The Witching Well' to while away the afternoon. For them, Spellfest was all about rest and recreation, and in no time at all they were downing fiery millipede liqueurs and creamy slug cocktails.

***

Stella's day, by contrast, had been neither restful nor recreational, right from the moment she had entered the steaming *Wartalicious* kitchen.

'Get to work, you little wretch,' had been Horribella's morning greeting.

Uh oh! Someone's in a bad mood, Stella thought.

'Morning, Horribella,' Stella said quietly. Her calloused hands set to work preparing cabbage jelly while her brain whirred like a spinning wheel. What had upset Horribella, who was now banging oven doors and slamming lids on pots with ferocity? Surely she hadn't found out …

For the past two nights, while Horribella had been tucked up in bed, Stella had been training two broomsticks and two mops to fly around the restaurant in unison, side by side. At first, they were so excited that at least one of them would keep racing ahead of the others. Stella had to threaten to lock them back up in the broom closet before they settled down.

After what seemed like hours, they mastered parallel flying, four abreast. Stella was delighted, but it still wasn't good enough. They needed to narrow the gaps between them. With a little effort and encouragement, the brooms and mops managed to fly so close to one another that their heads were touching. Stella showered them with praise.

The progress made on the first night had given Stella reason to persevere with the training. On the second night, she taught the brooms and mops to carry heavy iron pots balanced across their handles – first one pot, then two, then more and more.

'Don't let any of the pots smash to the ground, or you'll wake Horribella,' Stella had warned them.

The brooms and mops were painstakingly careful. None of them wanted Horribella to put an end to their fun. Of course, to Stella, it was more than just a midnight prank; it was part of her rescue plan ...

Horribella continued to storm about, muttering imprecations, until Stella could bear the suspense no longer. 'Horribella, what's wrong?' she inquired timidly.

Horribella set a pie tin on the bench with a vicious thud and rounded on Stella, chest heaving. 'What's *wrong*? What's *wrong*? As if you didn't know!' she almost yelled. She jabbed an accusing finger in Stella's direction. 'You *know* what you did.'

Stella could feel her insides starting to quiver. *How had Horribella found out?*

'I woke up trembling all over,' Horribella went on furiously. 'Sweating too. It was dreadful, heart-breaking, watching my restaurant burn to the ground like that.'

Restaurant burn to the ground?

'After everything I've done for you, to think you could deliberately set fire to it.'

Set fire to it?

Stella continued to stare at Horribella's flushed face for a few seconds before the truth dawned on her.

Horribella's had a nightmare. She's angry at me because of something she dreamed.

Stella let the spoon she was holding clatter to the ground, and then crouched down to retrieve it, venting her relief in a fleeting grin that she was wise not to let Horribella see.

As Stella straightened up, her empty tummy gave a loud rumble.

'Don't think you're getting breakfast, you little vixen,' Horribella snarled.

The rage in Horribella's eyes convinced Stella that it would be foolish to point out that *clearly*, since they were standing in it, the

159

restaurant had *not* been burned to the ground. Stella set to scrubbing a blackened pot instead.

As the morning wore on Horribella's anger dissipated by degrees. Gradually the cockroaches dared to crawl out from hiding, the crickets in the jar stopped trembling, and finally the cat crept back into the kitchen.

Horribella opened an oven door and peeped inside. One tap of her wand and the dozing wood fire leapt awake. She straightened up and glanced around at the self-stirring pots. 'You're not doing too badly, Horri. Things are coming along nicely.'

Stella sniffed. 'Er ... something's burning ...'

'Thefishgutstrudel!' Horribella wailed, throwing open a second oven door and dragging out a cremated mess. 'Look lively, Stella! You'll have to make another one.'

'Yes, Horribella.'

'And put the thing on the thingamajig.'

'I beg your pardon?'

'Put the thing on the thingamajig,' Horribella said irritably.

Stella scanned the kitchen for some clue ... *What* thing on *what* thingamajig?'

Horribella twisted her head to give Stella a frustrated look. 'Are you *completely* stupid? Put the lid on the jar before the cockroaches eat all the sugar.'

'Yes, Horribella.' Stella did as she was bidden.

'There's so much to do,' Horribella muttered. 'That bear needs butchering, for one thing. Mmmmm. Fresh baby bear stew. I can almost taste it.' Dribble leaked from the corners of her mouth as she leaned over a congealed green concoction on the stove. 'Did you taste the risotto?'

Without waiting for an answer, Horribella extended her wand and began to chant the flavour-enhancing *Delishify* spell with an effort of concentration that contorted her face. A jug of insect stock soared gracefully through the air and tipped its contents into the pan. Next, an assortment of herbs and a claw grinder glided over.

160

With Horribella completely engrossed in her spell, and with the town unusually silent, Stella decided it was time to put her rescue plan into action. Stealthily, she moved to the broom closet and beckoned the two brooms and two mops. Silently, they followed her out of the kitchen.

In due course, Horribella transferred her attention to another pot, from which she fished out a mouldy old sock. She dipped a finger into the mixture and sucked it clean. 'Bucking broomsticks!' Horribella exclaimed. 'This needs *far* more toadstools. *Far* more. Run down to the basement and fetch another basket.'

There was no reply.

Spinning round, Horribella realised that Stella was no longer peeling scorpions. Horribella checked underneath the centre work bench in case Stella had fallen asleep and tumbled off the stool. No, not this time. Only toenail clippings, a nest of cockroaches, and a very strong scent of rat pee under there. Oh, and a small cube of diced carrot. Waste not, want not – Horribella picked it up and dropped it into the stew.

'Stel–laaa!'

Horribella dabbed her forehead with her apron as she waited.

Stella did not come running.

Horribella raised her nasal voice to a yell: 'STELLL-LAAAAA!' – and stood fanning herself.

Still no response.

Horribella heaved a martyred sigh. 'By all the whiskers in Wartville, where *is* that useless child when I'm so busy?' she asked the pots. 'Must I do *everything* myself?'

When the pots failed to reply, Horribella sought sympathy from the cat.

'I just can't work the girl out. Here she is, employed by the finest restaurant in Wartville, and yet where's the gratitude? I ask you!'

The cat paused from chewing on a scorpion and blinked serenely.

'Getting that little jade to help around here is like trying to drown a mermaid. Impossible.'

The cat still said nothing.

'I'll teach her to sneak off without so much as a by-your-leave,' Horribella muttered, snatching up a spatula and waving it about vigorously. 'A good clout over the ear is what she'll get, that's what. Keep an eye on things for me.'

Horribella stalked out of the kitchen, through the empty restaurant, over the unwelcome mat, and into the town square.

The place was quite deserted, apart from Stella who stood facing her, shifting from foot to foot.

'Hanging about like a giant waiting for a thought,' Horribella said sternly. 'Haven't you any *work* to do?'

Then she noticed Stella's guilty expression, and registered that Stella was nervously knotting and unknotting her fingers ... and saw Stella's eyes slide towards the cage.

If ever Horribella was to come close to having a heart attack, this was the moment. The moment she beheld the cage door standing open. The moment she realised that the key ingredient for her renowned Baby Bear Stew had vanished.

The spatula fell to the cobblestones, and her face steadily turned the colour of beetroot.

'AAAAEEEEEEOOOOOOOOWWWW!!'

There was the sound of shattering glass as racks of not-so-clean glassware in The Witching Well tavern exploded into sharp, flying shards.

Horribella turned on Stella, looking almost apoplectic. With one bound, she caught hold of Stella's arm so tightly that Stella yelped.

'I'll have you boiled ... boiled alive in a vat of wax,' Horribella shrieked, spraying flecks of spit over Stella's face. 'And then I'll have you beheaded,' – she drew her finger across her neck to make the point – 'and then I'll have you beaten ... beaten until the flesh is stripped, yes *stripped*, from your bones!'

Chapter 23 – Witches' Prey

Evening was falling softly over Wipple village when Mrs Stockyleg's sunny, 'Rise and shine,' woke Sarah from a restful sleep. 'I've filled your rucksacks,' she said. 'There's food and drink for your journey, and I've popped your dragon skins in too, plus your elven gifts. Wake up, Mitch. Just strap this money belt around your waist. It's got five shuckles in it.'

Sarah checked the rucksacks. Yes, Mrs Stockylegs had been thorough.

Dressed in their shorts and t-shirts once more, and shrouded in fresh woollen cloaks, Mitchell and Sarah made their way through the village, past cheerily lit cottage windows, towards Mrs Tumblelong's barn. Sarah felt a pang of sadness to be leaving Wipple.

A crowd of well-wishers was waiting for them outside the barn.

Inside the barn, Mrs Tumblelong was holding a torch that flickered light and shadows over her face. 'Swift's ready and waiting,' she announced brightly, indicating the seated ostrich.

'Hello, Swift,' Sarah said, running her hand along the thin layer of down on his neck.

Mitchell clambered onto the ostrich first. 'Nice,' he remarked. 'Heated seating.'

'Just as well, cookie,' Mrs Tumblelong said, 'for you've a long journey ahead of you.'

Sarah got up behind Mitchell and settled into Swift's fluffy feathers.

'That's the ticket,' encouraged Mrs Tumblelong.

A shrivelled, snowy-haired dwarf hobbled closer with the aid of her walking stick, and shook Sarah's leg.

'You might need this,' she croaked, squinting up through thick glasses and poking something at Sarah.

Sarah found herself accepting a floral-patterned night-cap that smelled of mothballs. 'Oh!' She forced a smile. 'Great. Thanks.'

'Outa the way, Granny Dreamaday. You don't want to get knocked over,' Mrs Tumblelong said loudly.

Granny Dreamaday shuffled away, and not knowing what else to do with it, Sarah stuffed the night-cap into her pocket.

'Lost her marbles, but wouldn't hurt a pixie,' Mrs Tumblelong whispered, tapping the side of her head. 'Now, have you got the you-know-what?'

Sarah patted her belly. 'Uh-huh.' Strapped to her waist under her t-shirt, the diamond kept up a continuous throb, like a heartbeat.

'Right then. Up you get, Swift,' Mrs Tumblelong instructed, and Swift stumbled to his feet.

'Whoa!' Mitchell cried, clutching a handful of feathers as he almost slipped off sideways taking Sarah, who was gripping his waist, with him.

'Hold tight,' Mrs Tumblelong cautioned, somewhat belatedly. 'Atta boy! And now, Swift my friend, you've a very important job ahead of you. Take the humans to the Stormy Sea, fast as you can.'

The bird answered with a deep booming noise and strutted through the open doorway into the dusky field. When the ostrich unfurled his expansive wings, Sarah was forced to tuck her legs up like a jockey to allow Swift's wings to extend straight out either side of her. Mitchell looked to have the more comfortable position, with his legs dangling down in front of the wing joints.

'Clear a path!' Mrs Tumblelong instructed the crowd. 'Make way!'

Shuffling to the left, shuffling to the right, the dwarves formed a runway straight through the middle of the assembly.

'Stormy Sea, here we come,' Mitchell said, sounding a little nervous.

Sarah tried to grip with her knees as Swift broke into a clumsy jog. 'Bye, everyone,' she called.

Faster and faster, Swift's wings rose and fell, swishing the air.

'Cheerio.'

'Take good care of yourselves.'

'Stay vigilant.'

'Could've – done – with – a bit – of – suspension,' Mitchell muttered as they bounced giddily up and down.

And all the while, Swift was pumping his wings with mighty beats. He seemed to be straining harder and harder.

Suddenly something came whizzing up on Sarah's right – a terrified-looking mouse, with its whiskers blown back against its face, on a mouse-sized flying carpet. The carpet kept pace with Swift for a moment before it swerved away, with the mouse clinging on for dear life. Sarah only had time to wonder briefly at the sight before she poked her head around Mitchell's shoulder in order to see ahead. They were already coming to the end of the field. She clutched Mitchell tighter. It seemed that Swift was about to slam into a tall hedge.

'Lift off!' Mitchell cried, and Swift staggered awkwardly into the sky.

In her relief, Sarah let out a whoop. Looking down, the ground appeared to be falling smoothly away. She cricked her neck to look back at the winking village lights, and gave a hearty wave.

It wasn't long before Swift levelled off his climb and set his wings in a fast, steady rhythm.

'This is better,' Sarah said, adjusting her cloak so that it stopped flapping. She ruffled Swift's feathers and began enjoy the feel of the night air that streaked against her face and plucked at her hair.

When she cast a look back one last time she saw stars twinkling over the snowy peak of Mount Tremor.

* * *

Mitchell was deeply impressed by the ostrich. The bird truly could fly at remarkable speed.

Sarah prattled cheerfully about the cosy dwarf cottages, Mrs Stockyleg's delicious cooking, Tumblelong's secret discovery …

165

Mitchell took in only about one in every five words. He hated to spoil Sarah's mood, so he kept his thoughts to himself, but he couldn't help feeling a little tense. Would the magic diamond *really* be enough to gain the merpeople's trust?

Suddenly, Swift was winging through a dense clot of cloud, which obscured absolutely everything from sight.

'Yuck! I'm all wet!' Sarah grizzled, hitching her cloak tighter.

Hardly had the words left her mouth when, out of nowhere, without the slightest warning, four dark shapes plunged through the whiteness on a collision course with Swift, who promptly let out a hiss. Mitchell almost tumbled off Swift in shock, and Sarah erupted in an ear-splitting scream.

Witches! Mitchell felt the blood drain from his cheeks.

Swift put on an instant kick of speed, beating his wings more strongly, and Mitchell wound his fingers more tightly into the bird's feathers.

Just as suddenly as they had entered the cloud, they were out of it.

'They'll come after us for sure,' Mitchell muttered, throwing a look over his shoulder.

He was right. Four broomsticks had slewed around to give chase.

As he faced forwards again, he felt Sarah twisting around to look too. 'Far out!' she cried. Mitchell felt her grip tighten around his waist. 'They'll petrify us any second now.'

'No. They want our blood, remember? They won't kill us – *yet.* Go, go!' Mitchell urged the ostrich, which seemed to be gathering still more speed. Mitchell squinted his eyes against the rushing air. 'We've gotta shake them.'

Shrieks of diabolical merriment sounded, and Mitchell checked back over his shoulder again. The witches were keeping up, four menacing figures in black, blending with the inky darkness of the night.

'Faster, Swift! You can do it!' Mitchell yelled, trying to inject confidence into his voice.

'D'you think Swift can beat them?' Sarah asked anxiously. Mitchell bit his lip and did not answer. Time would tell.

Again and again, Mitchell craned his neck to check what the witches were up to. Not once was a wand raised, which seemed to support Mitchell's 'capture first, kill later' theory. It wasn't very cheering.

If the broomsticks had been the pointed battle variety, Swift would have been overtaken in seconds. Fortunately, the broomsticks were the lightweight long-distance sort, and Swift managed to keep the length of a cricket pitch ahead of them for hour upon nerve-wracking hour. All the while, Mitchell alternated between hope and despair. His hands grew numb from gripping Swift so tightly.

'Swift's exhausted,' Sarah wailed. 'I can hear him panting.'

He wasn't just panting, he was gasping, as his wings thrashed the air.

Of course he's exhausted, Mitchell thought. No bird could maintain that superfast pace indefinitely. Mitchell was exhausted just sitting there holding on and worrying.

And then snatches of conversation reached his ears – the witches talking amongst themselves. They began cackling. Evidently they were feeling sure of success.

He glanced over his shoulder for the hundredth time. It had been almost imperceptible at first, but now he was sure of it – the witches were gaining on Swift. Mitchell could feel his chest constricting. He clenched his jaws tightly. *Don't let them catch us. Don't let them catch us.*

Sarah had noticed too. 'This is ba-a-ad. They're getting closer,' she moaned.

'Faster, Swift,' Mitchell yelled in desperation. He wished he could *do* something, wished he had some kind of weapon, something to throw at the witches.

'Either we're getting slower or they're getting faster,' Sarah said just minutes later, her voice rising in pitch.

Mitchell checked. Yes, the witches were closing in. They were now only four metres behind. He could make out their hideous faces in the moonlight.

'Swift, you mustn't slow down!' Mitchell shouted. Swift gave no sign of hearing or understanding. He just continued flapping his wings and gasping for breath. Flapping, gasping, flapping, gasping. Mitchell's fear was increasing with every passing moment. It seemed inevitable that the witches would catch up.

'Swift, can't you go any faster?' Sarah wailed despairingly just minutes later.

Mitchell snatched another look behind him. The gap had closed further. The leading witch, who had a face wrinkled like cabbage, flashed him a gap-toothed grin. The hump-backed, pinch-faced witch trailing her had a greedy gleam in her eyes.

'Come *on*, Swift! You've gotta go faster!' Mitchell yelled, almost beside himself in panic. He waited, hoping Swift might still have some inner reserves of energy to call upon. But no, it seemed that Swift had given his all already.

The witches were talking again now.

'The girl's mine.'

'No, *I* want the girl.'

'I'll have the boy.'

'I'll take the bird.'

Mitchell clung tighter than ever to Swift, steeling himself for what he knew must come.

Two tense minutes passed before Swift gave an agonised squawk.

'YES!' cried a witch. 'We've got them!'

Snapping his head around, Mitchell saw cabbage-face clasping a fistful of Swift's tail feathers. 'Tell your bird to stop, sonny!' she ordered.

'The girl's mine, I say,' insisted the hump-backed witch riding alongside her.

'Not if I get her first,' retorted cabbage-face, groping for Sarah's plaits.

'Get away!' Sarah shrieked. Mitchell was terrified she would fall off Swift as she twisted this way and that. 'Don't touch me!'

'Tell the bird to stop!' cabbage-face repeated.

Sarah yelped with pain, and Mitchell saw that cabbage-face had seized Sarah's arm. He wriggled around and prised the awful claw-like fingers off his sister. Then he whipped around to face the front again and bellowed, 'GO, SWIFT! GO!'

Cabbage face and hump-back began squabbling in earnest.

'Shove over. *I'll* make the little wretches stop!'

'No, *you* shove over!'

Then – 'Yeeaaaoooow!' There was a furious howl.

Mitchell looked to see what was going on. The witches appeared to be wrestling one another.

'Oh no!' Sarah cried.

The witches' wands were out, and almost instantly the air exploded with deafening cracks and bangs like fireworks.

'Duck!' screamed Mitchell as green sparks shot past, perilously close.

Mitchell faced the front once more, and leaned flat against the ostrich's outstretched neck, wrapping his arms tightly around it. A blaze of green light flashed past his cheek. Then another. His mind was a whirl of terror, his heart was pumping like mad. Intentional or not, it seemed only a matter of time before one of the hexes would hit him or Sarah or Swift.

And sure enough, Sarah suddenly shrieked, 'Swift! ... He's ... We're gonna ...' The rushing air snatched her words away. Swift's enormous wings had retracted and the bird was falling, taking Mitchell and Sarah with him. They were dropping like a boulder, gathering momentum.

Mitchell's stomach left him.

Faster and faster, dizzily plummeting down, down, down.

'We're gonna die!' Sarah screamed; Mitchell was beyond screaming.

Time seemed to slow as he felt himself being sucked earthwards. The ground was surging upwards ... this was it then.

Mitchell screwed his eyes shut, bracing for impact ... Sarah had buried her head into his back ... Would it hurt or would they die instantly, snuffed out like a candle?

Mitchell was expecting to smack into the ground. Instead, he felt a jolt, much like a freefalling skydiver experiences when the parachute opens.

His eyes shot open.

Just metres above the ground, Swift's wings had fanned out, catching the air and slowing their fall. And as Mitchell goggled, Swift began flapping his wings evenly, regularly, as if nothing untoward had occurred.

'Far out! Swift's okay!' Sarah whispered, detaching herself from Mitchell's back. 'I thought he'd been hit!'

Mitchell remained in a sort of marvelling stupor, his mouth slightly open. *We didn't crash,* he told himself slowly, *we didn't die.*

'The witches are still fighting,' Sarah observed, and Mitchell looked up at the sinister green flashes that continued to slash the sky. He tried to speak, but his voice failed him.

Very gradually, as Swift continued on course just skimming a plain of dense low shrubs, Mitchell's terror leaked away and he began to relax his white-knuckled grip on Swift's feathers. The light show was receding with every passing minute.

Mitchell cleared his throat and made another attempt to speak. 'Swift, you're a star!' He leaned forward and hugged the ostrich about the neck. 'You saved our lives.'

Swift gave a jerk of the head in agreement.

Chapter 24 – Bold and Brave

While Swift was winging purposefully through the night, only the wizard Vanrod's even breathing disturbed the dark stillness of his cave.

It was time for Rodenticus to be a hero, and his little heart fluttered wildly.

Precariously balancing the ruby on his head, Rodenticus proceeded to scale Vanrod's wooden bed-leg. The ascent was particularly challenging without a tail. Halfway up, he could sense the ruby teetering. For a moment he hoped it might right itself, but no, it was tumbling, and as he lunged for it, he found himself falling too.

'Ummmph!' The air was punched from his lungs as he slammed into the hard ground.

He forced himself to wait for his thudding pulse to slow a little before attempting the climb again.

The second attempt was a success.

Rodenticus paused beside Vanrod's pillow and cocked his head sideways. The wizard was grinding his teeth. Was he *really* asleep?

Jumpy with nerves, but treading with utmost care, Rodenticus tiptoed across the pillow and gently lifted one of Vanrod's eyelids. An evil red eye stared at him, but the wizard did not stir.

This was very pleasing.

Rodenticus released the eyelid, which slid back into a closed position.

And now ... the moment he had been waiting for ... Rodenticus felt a thrill of anticipation.

Reaching up towards the pouch slung over the bed-head, he loosened the drawstring.

A reddish glow of light sprang from the pouch.

Rodenticus could have leapt for joy. His hunch was correct.

He dipped a paw into the pouch, and then lurched back in surprise. The magic locked up in the stone had rattled his whole frame.

Rodenticus collected himself with haste, and advanced to complete the task. Out with the magic ruby. In with the ordinary ruby. Tighten the drawstring once more. The Banishing Stone in his forepaws radiated light like a beacon, almost shouting to be noticed.

Rodenticus retraced his steps stealthily across the pillow.

Suddenly the wizard began to cough.

The rat threw himself on top of the gem in an attempt to hide its light.

Cough! Cough! Cough! Bed covers lashed up and down like mighty surfing waves ... and then settled.

The water rat clambered down off the bed in all haste, clutching his booty.

He positioned the ruby under the sideboard, executed a little dance, then fetched a crisp linen napkin from the table, stopping briefly to savour a few crumbs. The napkin concealed the ruby nicely.

And now Rodenticus was forced to be patient, for Vanrod's magical barriers prevented any immediate departure. He dusted his fur coat, smoothed out his whiskers and bided his time.

It wasn't until Vanrod was pouring his morning cup of coffee that the little grey water rat brazenly exited the cave. No dragons saw him descend the cliff-face – or if they did, they ignored him. Really, why should a great important dragon be bothered with a pesky rodent stealing a napkin when there was mountain goat to terrorise?

After following the rushing river for a good distance, Rodenticus bunkered down in the grass with a singing heart. What did it matter that he had a frizzled ugly stump for a tail?

Chapter 25 – The Stormy Sea

Sarah caught her breath as the sun peeked over the horizon, staining the sky a glorious magenta colour, and a great glistening ocean came into view ahead.

'Must be the Stormy Sea,' Mitchell said.

Sarah inhaled deeply. She could almost taste the salt in the air.

'It's not very stormy,' she commented as Swift drew closer and she could see how gently the waves caressed the shore.

A broad ribbon of sand followed the water's edge for miles, and a vast wilderness of windblown scrub backed onto the beach.

'Hold tight. We're going down,' Mitchell cautioned.

There was nothing graceful about Swift's landing; seabirds left off sunning their wings to watch the ostrich hit the beach at a run, slowing to a jog, slowing to a jerky walk, until he plonked down on the sand. His passengers rather more fell off than climbed off.

Mitchell picked himself up and strutted around, stiff-legged like a rooster. 'My bum's completely numb.'

'Mine's got pins and needles,' Sarah moaned, rubbing her backside.

Swift gave an indignant grunt.

'Oh, we're not complaining,' Sarah said hastily.

'Not at all! You're a champion, Swift. That ride was unbelievable,' Mitchell said, mussing the bird's feathers.

Swift guzzled the entire contents of Sarah's water flask ('Crikey!' she exclaimed), polished off a loaf of bread in three enormous pecks, and then gave a huge yawn. Sarah smiled at his gaping beak. If any bird deserved a nap, this one did.

'Have a long, long rest,' she told him.

The ostrich stretched his neck across the golden sand and closed his eyes – a picture of perfect contentment with the sun kissing his face and a breeze stirring his feathers.

'D'you think we should wear our dragon skins?' Mitchell asked.

Sarah looked up. Neither eagle nor witch marred the cloudless sky. 'No, we're right for now. But keep it handy. Let's eat.'

It felt splendid, sprawling bare-foot in the sunshine, tucking into sandwiches and fruit. Seabirds converged noisily to quarrel over the scraps Sarah cast them.

'You know, this is what our holiday *should've* been like,' Mitchell remarked wistfully. He scooped up a handful of crumbly sand. 'Hey, don't drink all the water!'

Sarah replaced the lid on Mitchell's flask. 'So. Where d'you reckon the merpeople are?' she asked.

Mitchell mused for a moment before answering. 'Probably in the deepest part of the ocean, where Vanrod can't spy on them. We should build a raft and go look for them.'

Sarah gazed out over the turquoise water. Conditions couldn't have been more perfect. 'Okay. But can we have a little sleep first?'

'We might miss the merpeople if we don't look straight away. It's probably a bit like fishing – you have to catch them at the right time,' Mitchell said. 'You know, early morning or late at night.'

Accordingly, Mitchell and Sarah went in search of driftwood to build the raft with. That's when they stumbled across a dead sea-turtle half-buried in seaweed.

Mitchell strode around the massive carcass examining it from every angle. He tapped the dome-shaped shell on the turtle's back. It appeared strong and undamaged and had a lovely tile pattern on it. What could be seen of the lower shell that encased the turtle's belly appeared to be broken, and it had come away from the upper shell. 'This top shell would make a good boat. It'd hold us easy.'

'*I'm* not touching that disgusting thing,' Sarah said, backing away with her nose screwed up.

'You're such a princess,' Mitchell scoffed.

'I am not,' Sarah shot back. 'I'd just rather build a *raft*.'

'This is *better*.'

'No, it's not.'

'Yes, it is.'

'No, it's not.'

Mitchell lifted his eyes skyward and sighed with exasperation. 'Fine, *I'll* clean it by myself.'

'Fine.'

Sarah pattered further along the beach hoping to discover a freshwater stream. Every so often, her eyes drifted longingly towards the rows of gentle waves coming in, one after the other – ideal for a dip.

When Sarah eventually gave up on finding drinking water and retraced her steps, the turtle shell was floating like a little round dinghy fairly low in the water.

Sarah crossed her arms and regarded it apprehensively. 'As soon as we hop in, it'll sink.'

Mitchell's expression was scornful. 'Don't be ridiculous.'

'What about oars?'

'Here.' Mitchell held up two pieces of driftwood. 'And I've got our dragons skins too, in case any eagles show up.'

Sarah shrugged her shoulders in a gesture of resignation. 'OK.'

Mitchell held the boat steady while she clambered in and seated herself. Then he scrambled in too and plopped down, cross-legged, facing her. The little vessel was still buoyant and Mitchell looked very smug.

'I'll row,' he said, taking up the oars.

'Don't go too far out,' urged Sarah. 'We need to test this thing first.'

Mitchell rowed clumsily, while Sarah leaned over the side, trailing her hand in the tepid water. She felt particularly vulnerable in the little boat, though the dragon skins provided some measure of comfort.

The air was warm, the breeze was pleasant, and the water was so clear that sunlight penetrated all the way to the submarine forest. A sailing ship just visible in the distance provided the only sign of civilisation.

'Any merpeople?' Mitchell queried at length. As he spoke, a magnificent flying fish leapt out of the water and glided through the air for several metres, before making its re-entry.

'Nope, only sardines nibbling on seaweed, a stingray with two tails, and a three-eyed squid,' Sarah answered.

By and by, Sarah twisted her head to see how far they had come. 'Mitch, stop! This is far enough. Look. Swift's only a tiny dot now.'

Mitchell stowed the oars. 'My arms are about to drop off anyway,' he admitted, and joined his sister gazing into the watery depths. 'Hey, that lobster's blue!'

Sarah watched it sweep past on the current, and then spotted a ripple of something long and slim. 'Down there! See that shadow?'

'It's an eel, I think.'

Sarah felt her face fall. She could see now that it *was* an eel, and not a mermaid as she had hoped.

An hour passed pleasantly as the little boat drifted. In fact, Mitchell and Sarah were so engrossed studying the underwater world that they missed what was taking place overhead; missed the fact that clouds heavy with rain were galloping across the sky, obscuring the sun and transforming the sea to the colour of lead. It wasn't until a sudden swoop of wind cut right through Sarah, startling her out of her serenity, that she noticed the angry sky.

'Er ... Mitch ...' She tapped him on the arm.

Mitchell looked up too. 'Awesome. A really big storm's on the way.'

Enormous plopping raindrops and the menacing rumble of thunder galvanised Sarah into action. 'Quick. Back to shore.' She grabbed one of the driftwood planks and Mitchell wriggled himself round until he was facing the same way as Sarah.

Rowing was not as easy as Sarah had imagined.

The sea began to roll in large, scary swells. Rising. Falling. Rising. Falling.

Mitchell and Sarah found themselves battling against white-capped waves that reared higher and higher; water slurped into the boat with every wave they encountered. Sarah tucked the dragon skins underneath her, lest they wash away. She wished she had a life jacket strapped on.

'I don't feel so –' Mitchell began, but salt spray smacked Sarah's face and she didn't hear the rest.

The situation grew more perilous as the wind continued to whip up the sea. A fork of lightning split the sky, followed by a cannon blast of thunder – Sarah nearly leapt overboard with shock – and then the storm swooped down with sweeping gusts of rain that filled Sarah's eyes and left her freezing and drenched.

Now the waves had grown as tall as trees, and the sea seemed like a raging creature bent on devouring them. Sarah was calmly desperate as she tried to row and hang on at the same time. It was a miracle neither she nor Mitchell had fallen out or lost their oars.

The turtle-shell teetered on the ridge of a monstrous wave, and Sarah's breath caught in her throat as she looked down; it was like being at the highest point on a roller coaster, but without a safety harness. At that very moment, a mermaid shot high out of the water, turned a somersault in the air, and plunged back down. It was only a fleeting distraction. Sarah's stomach left her as the little boat pitched forward and careened to the base of the wave.

'Keep paddling,' Sarah screamed, for Mitchell was twisting around to look for the mermaid as the little boat was shunted up to the rim of the next wave. Down they hurtled, spinning towards another trough. Just ahead the mermaid launched out of the water to execute two somersaults, her gurgling peals of laughter muffled by the roar of wind and waves and ear-shattering thunderclaps like a thousand heavenly cars backfiring at once.

Massive heaving mountains and valleys tossed the tiny boat carelessly up and down, up and down. Sarah strained at her oar with aching muscles, slitting her eyes against wind and rain. The shore hardly seemed to be getting any closer, and Sarah felt sick with apprehension.

The mermaid appeared again, giggling, spinning like a top.

177

Then, almost too fast to follow, an eagle dived out of the clouds, and with a shrill scream of agony the mermaid was plucked high into the sky.

Rain pelted Sarah's face as she watched in helpless horror. The mermaid's tail was thrashing as she tried to extricate herself from the eagle's talons. She must have been strong for, with a frustrated screech, the eagle relinquished her and she plummeted a hundred metres into the booming waves. The swirling water enfolded her, and the eagle retreated beyond the clouds.

'Keep rowing. That eagle might come after us next,' Mitchell yelled.

It was a horrible thought.

Looking back later, Sarah couldn't say how long they had been tossed about on the sea with the storm howling and shrieking around them. She remembered thinking that the foaming breakers along the shoreline seemed dismally beyond reach. She remembered doggedly plugging at her oar, muscles screaming, holding out little hope of surviving. And then, wonderfully, a huge wave lifted up the turtle shell and carried it all the way to the beach.

'I'm wrecked,' Sarah moaned, stumbling out of the boat. A violent wave tried to knock her over.

Mitchell stumbled beside her and Sarah grabbed his arm. 'You okay?' she shouted over the crashing surf. He had turned rather green.

'Feeling crook,' he mumbled. He staggered out of the water and slumped on the sand letting the downpour pummel his body.

Sarah wrestled the little boat out of the waves and onto the sand. She retrieved the dragon skins from it, folded them neatly and set them down beside the food packs.

Astoundingly, the storm had not disturbed Swift's sleep. Sarah could see him further down the beach where they had left him.

With sudden inspiration, Sarah remembered the empty water flasks and unscrewed the lids so the rain could collect inside.

Her eyes kept returning to the skies and then to the wild breakers driving sand and seaweed onto the shore.

How long's this storm going to last? she wondered. *And will that eagle return?*

Chapter 26 – Aquatica

Five minutes later, the rain began to ease and the thunder dropped to a distant murmur.

Ten minutes later, the wind dragged the clouds away to cause havoc elsewhere, and sunlight dazzled down upon a placid sea of cobalt blue.

Mitchell didn't care about any of this as he lolled in the sand gripping his stomach; his breakfast was threatening to make a re-appearance.

'Come and eat something,' Sarah suggested sympathetically. 'It might help.'

Kipberry pie with a latticed crust turned out to be just the thing to settle his tummy. As the sun dried his clothes, he could feel the colour creep back into his face.

Sarah packed up the remains of the pie, and slipped a dragon skin into each rucksack. 'Now what?' she asked.

'No more rowing, that's for –' Mitchell stopped abruptly. Something further down the beach had snagged his gaze; something that glinted as the surf washed in and out around it. 'What's *that*?'

Sarah shaded her eyes to see. 'Dunno. Let's check it out.'

As they drew closer, Sarah darted forward with a cry.

The sea had vomited up the mermaid.

'Is she dead?' The mermaid lay so still and pale that Mitchell felt quite sure she must be. And she was only young too.

Sarah, who was feeling for a pulse, her face intent, did not reply.

Mitchell winced at the gashes in the mermaid's sloping shoulders. Her bare arms and dainty shell top were spattered with blood. Mitchell shifted from foot to foot until he couldn't bear the suspense. 'Anything?'

'She's alive,' Sarah declared at last. 'Get the unicorn tears.'

Mitchell sprinted to his rucksack and returned in a trice.

'Just one drop,' Sarah told him.

He slid a single drop between the mermaid's slightly-parted lips.

The effect was immediate.

The mermaid's flukes began to twitch. Pink flooded her cheeks. Her eyelids fluttered open to reveal lovely sea-green eyes – eyes clouded with fear.

'Don't be frightened,' urged Sarah. 'We saw what happened with the eagle. We want to help you. '

The mermaid's fear didn't seem to lessen. She flexed her tail, endeavouring to sit up.

'Your shoulders look pretty bad,' Mitchell told her. 'Let me put some medicine on them.'

The mermaid sank back helplessly.

Sarah picked up the jar that contained the elves' healing herbs, and took off the lid. 'I'll hold this, so we don't get sand in it,' she said.

And so, Sarah held the jar, while Mitchell applied its contents to the mermaid's injuries.

As Mitchell anticipated, the mermaid's wounds closed over almost instantly, leaving only needle-thin scars. 'All better now,' he announced. 'See for yourself.'

The mermaid tried to sit up again, and this time managed it. She pushed back her long clinging hair to examine her shoulders, and traced and retraced the scars with her fingers.

Then her flukes began to thump against the wet sand, and she turned to Mitchell with a look of deep admiration. 'You are a wondrous healer. I am sorry I doubted you. I am called Aquatica.' Her voice was clear and musical. 'I had been warned about the eagles and forbidden to play in the storms, but today I couldn't help it. The waves were just perfect.'

Mitchell checked the sky and Sarah grimaced. 'Perfect for *you* maybe. I thought Mitch and I were goners,' she said.

'She's not your girlfriend, is she?' Aquatica asked Mitchell, nodding towards Sarah.

'What – Sarah? No way,' Mitchell said, with a laugh. 'She just my sis–'

'Assistant,' Aquatica finished for him. 'Yes, I thought so.' She continued to gaze upon Mitchell as if he were her knight in shining armour. 'Now that you've saved my life, I must repay you. Tell me what you wish for – eels for your dinner perhaps or pirate gold from forgotten places of the sea? Or would you like to kiss me?' She batted her eyelashes.

Aquatica was very pretty. Mitchell felt it would be a reward indeed to kiss those lovely lips …

'Ahem!' Sarah coughed in an obvious manner. Mitchell looked at her. 'The *stones*,' she said, giving him a meaningful look.

'Oh yes … er, Aquatica, there *is* one thing we want,' he said.

Mitchell told Aquatica their story, and the mermaid listened with an adoring expression.

'So you see,' Mitchell ended, 'what we *really* want is to know if you have the magic sapphire? Are the rumours true that –?'

His voice trailed away as Aquatica shook her head. 'I've heard of the Banishing Stones of course, but I've never seen one,' she said. 'I wish I could have given you the answer you wanted. Are you sure you wouldn't like to kiss me instead?'

The green of her lovely eyes had deepened. Once more Mitchell was tempted to accept the kiss she offered …

Sarah's insistent voice cut into his thoughts, and Mitchell turned to her. 'What did you say?'

Sarah gave him an indignant look. 'I *said*, help me get Aquatica back into the sea.'

'I *do* feel a bit like a beached whale,' Aquatica admitted.

She was not an easy burden to lift. Not that she was heavy; on the contrary, her frame was slender and light. The problem lay exclusively with her silvery tail.

Sarah gently hooked her arms under Aquatica's armpits but Mitchell, who attempted to seize her flukes, found they kept wriggling, so that again and again her tail slipped from his grasp and flopped on the wet sand with a *smack!* Not only were her scales abrasive as sandpaper, the sharp edges of her flukes kept catching his fingers.

'What's wrong with you, Mitch? Just get a good grip,' Sarah told him crossly, while Aquatica launched into giggles as he stood there examining his fingers which were covered in what looked like fine paper cuts.

Mitchell was feeling distinctly rattled by the time he mastered the technique of carrying a mermaid tail and together he and Sarah floundered waist-deep into the water.

Aquatica let go a whoop and took off, racing through the waves like a dolphin; seconds later she sprang out of the water fifty metres away to sashay across its surface on her flukes like a ballerina on tippy toes, before dropping into the surf.

Mitchell was still watching the spot where she had disappeared when her head popped up close beside him. He tried not to appear startled.

'Don't you think I'm clever?' she inquired.

'Yes, very clever,' Mitchell answered earnestly.

'I like your legs,' Aquatica said, blinking coyly at him.

Darting a glance in Sarah's direction, Mitchell saw her rolling her eyes.

'It's the calf muscles that make them look good,' Mitchell responded with a perfectly straight face. 'I play lots of sports – cricket mostly, and soccer.'

'Pur*lease!*' Sarah exclaimed, and Mitchell could not suppress a grin.

'Oh …' Aquatica seemed at a loss what to say; Mitchell guessed she had never heard of cricket and soccer. 'Don't go anywhere. I'll see what I can find out about the Banishing Stones,' she promised.

'Okay then, see you soon,' Mitchell replied.

'Promise?'

'Promise.'

Aquatica's lips parted in a mischievous grin, and with a flick of her tail she sent a spray of water directly into Mitchell's face.

'Hey!' he objected, as her gurgling laugh dived under the waves.

Sarah clucked disapprovingly.

'What?' Mitchell asked. 'I can't help it if girls like me.'

Sarah snorted. 'It's only because she thinks you're a great healer.'

Mitchell sloshed back to the beach, found a warm spot of sand to sink down onto, and lay back with his head pillowed on his arm. He couldn't help feeling flattered by the mermaid's admiration.

Sarah planted herself beside him and waggled her toes. 'D'you think Aquatica was telling the truth? About not having seen the sapphire?' she asked.

'Dunno,' Mitchell answered, through a great yawn. All he knew was that he was immensely tired. 'Wake me when she gets here.'

Even the sea seemed worn out from its earlier exuberance, and the waves washed sleepily backwards and forwards. Lulled by their soothing rhythm, Mitchell drifted into a peaceful slumber.

Chapter 27 – The Picnic

A considerable way south of the Stormy Sea, in the Fragrant Forest, something was about to happen which would have unfortunate consequences for Mitchell and Sarah.

It all started with a quiet picnic by the Crystal River.

Fyrddin (captain of the elven army), Jevelle (his wife) and Tristor (their son), made up one half of the party. Elteace (who had punched Mitchell), her mother and her younger brother made up the other half. The picnic had been Jevelle's idea, to help cheer up the dead elf's family.

Elteace didn't feel the slightest bit cheered. She sat apart from the others on the grassy riverbank, hugging a book in her arms and staring mistily at the water as it caught up leaves and twigs and whirled them around before letting them go. Her heart ached so badly she could have screamed with the pain. She wanted to smash her fist into something, kick something …

A dwiggle crept up and draped a hairy arm around her shoulder.

'Get lost,' she said fiercely, shrugging the arm off.

The dwiggle regarded her with a wounded expression, then moped away.

'Why didn't Brodin join us, Mum?' Tristor asked wistfully.

'I caught him cutting the whiskers off a dwiggle-bub when he should have been in class. He's grounded until he catches up his bookwork,' Jevelle answered.

A white tiger came padding sleekly along and butted Elteace with its nose. She turned her face from it.

And now Tristor was coming over. He squatted on his haunches and trailed his fingers through the thick coat on the tiger's back.

'What are you reading, Elteace?'

Elteace didn't bother looking at him. She wasn't going to make conversation and pretend to be happy. 'Nothing.'

185

'So what's the book you're holding?'

'It was Dad's ...'

'Oh.'

Elteace could sense Tristor's discomfort. He nudged his glasses up his nose, then plucked a caterpillar from the grass and appeared to be examining it intently, before he tried again.

'Did you hear that a bear cub escaped from Wartville? Dad said the witches were keeping it in a cage outside a restaurant.'

Elteace didn't care about stupid bears. She wished Tristor would just go away. She didn't bother answering.

'It flew into the forest balancing on two very worn broomsticks and two dirty old mops flying together side by side,' Tristor pressed on. 'Can you believe that?'

A laugh sounded, and Elteace turned indignant eyes upon her brother who was constructing a headdress of tiver-feathers under Fyrddin's direction. She was sure *she* would never laugh again.

Tristor finally left Elteace alone, and she watched him set a little leaf boat sailing along the river before he turned back to join the others.

Elteace pricked up her ears when the discussion turned to Mitchell and Sarah.

So they set off to see Vanrod, did they? That's pretty stupid.

Shortly after this, a post pigeon arrived. Fyrddin detached the note from the bird's leg, scanned the message, frowned faintly, and then passed the note to his wife. Jevelle had a quick read, traded concerned looks with her husband, and tucked the note into her pocket – partially. The slip of paper hung half-in half-out of Jevelle's pocket, and minutes later wafted lazily to the ground before, as chance would have it, a rogue breeze whipped it up into the air and slapped it against Elteace's leg where it stuck.

Elteace took hold of the note, fully intending to hand it back to Jevelle, when a burst of curiosity got the better of her. She skimmed Mrs Stockylegs' curling handwriting, and was appalled.

How dare the humans even think *about giving Vanrod a Banishing Stone!*

A quick glance told Elteace no one had seen her: Jevelle was biting into a slice of merrin-fruit tart, Tristor and her brother were racing their elf-lights around an obstacle course of plates and cups, Fyrddin was watching the race, and her mother was knitting a snufflelump-wool blanket.

How can Fyrddin take the news so calmly? Maybe he thinks the merpeople won't trust the humans. But what if they do?

Elteace slipped the message into her own pocket. Something had to be done, and she, Elteace, would do it.

'Mum,' she said.

Her mother lifted her face enquiringly and swiped a pale gold strand of hair away from her puffy red eyes.

'I need some time alone,' Elteace said, taking care that nothing in her expression betrayed her sudden excitement.

'Sure, my sweet,' her mother replied, with an attempt at a smile.

Elteace took herself off along the riverbank, and, once out of earshot, she extracted her pipe from her pocket, lifted it to her lips, and struck up a haunting melody that began to stir the river water.

Chapter 28 – Squatters' Wreck

'Please get down,' Sarah implored. 'Before you fall.'

Grandpa responded with a wink, and commenced another loop of the garden.

He was cruising five feet off the ground on a broomstick, dressed in blue-striped pyjamas and tartan slippers, and didn't seem at all concerned what the neighbours might think.

'Better than a bicycle, isn't it?' he called, looking at Sarah rather than where he was going. Next second he was brushing up against the big gum tree; Rainbow Lorikeets that had been hiding in the foliage scattered in panic.

Sarah could feel herself getting annoyed. 'Grandpa, *please*! If Grandma sees you she'll have a heart attack.'

Grandpa pretended he hadn't heard. 'How fast can these things go?' he inquired.

'Grandpa, come down!'

Grandpa chuckled. 'Not on your Nellie!'

The broomstick was coming around again, getting nearer. Hoping to catch hold of Grandpa's ankle, Sarah leapt into the air … and promptly woke up.

She closed her eyes directly, willing the dream to continue, but it had slipped beyond her grasp, leaving a hollow, desolate ache inside her. The painful reality was that dreams were probably the closest she would ever get to seeing Grandpa again.

'Aquatica didn't come back?' Mitchell mumbled, sitting up all tousled and sleepy-eyed beside her.

Sarah yawned as she sat up too. 'I don't think so, but I accidentally fell asleep.'

The sun had dipped low in the western sky, elongating Swift's shadow as he stood stooped over the tortoise-shell boat drinking rainwater. Thankfully there was no sign of eagles.

188

Sarah began sifting through her rucksack, looking for a snack to eat. 'Hey, where's my dragon skin?' She looked up. 'Mitch, did you take my dragon skin?'

'Course not.'

A horrible thought struck her and she bent over her rucksack again, rummaging furiously. 'No ... it can't be ... the unicorn tears are gone.' She ran her eyes over the beach, suddenly wary. 'Someone must've been here.'

Mitchell rifled through his own pack. 'My dragon skin's missing too.' He studied the scuffed sand. 'I can't see any strange footprints ...'

'*Elves* don't leave footprints,' Sarah said slowly.

'Yeah, but the elves are our friends. Why would they take what they've given us?' Mitchell challenged. He looked up and down the beach.

Sarah shivered. It was most disturbing. 'We're stuffed now,' she said. 'There's nowhere to hide from eagles.'

Mitchell stared across the flat sea for a moment, then jumped up. 'I'll get some driftwood. To defend ourselves with,' he said.

All too soon, twilight fell.

'Doesn't look like Aquatica's coming back,' Sarah said despondently.

Swift ambled closer in his ungainly manner, and prodded and poked their rucksacks until Sarah said, without enthusiasm, 'Dinner time, is it?'

The bird watched keenly as she shared out the chocolate muffins. Only the ostrich had any appetite. Mitchell and Sarah just nibbled and waited restlessly.

And then, almost imperceptibly, came a faint stirring of what might have been called music; a humming kind of noise with the merest suggestion of a melody.

Sarah strained her ears. 'D'you hear that?'

Mitchell stood up and gazed searchingly out to sea.

It was like the sea itself was singing, calling, beckoning with an invisible hand.

'It makes me want to charge into the water,' Mitchell said.

'Me too.'

Sarah's urge to dive in only increased as the wild song persisted. The music seemed to have possessed her.

'I can't stand this much longer,' Mitchell confessed, digging his toes into the sand in an effort to hold himself back. 'Do you suppose it's bad magic or good magic?'

Sarah considered briefly. 'It doesn't *feel* bad …'

Mitchell nodded. 'I agree. Let's go swimming.'

Without bothering to strip down to their swimming costumes, Mitchell and Sarah raced down the sand and dived under the cool waves.

They hadn't swum far when Sarah felt the sea tugging gently at her legs. At first she thought she was imagining it. Then she became quite sure. And suddenly it was dragging her down, pulling her under. She reacted at once by kicking out strongly and stroking hard with her arms. She struggled for all she was worth, but to no avail. The sea seemed intent on swallowing her up. Shouting Mitchell's name, her head slipped beneath the waves.

Sarah held her breath. How long could she keep holding for? Two minutes? Three? Panicky thoughts were overtaking her …

And then the most startling thing happened. The water in which she was suspended was sucked away and she fell with a thud onto the sea bed.

'Holy guacamole!' Mitchell spluttered beside her. He scrambled to his feet and brushed his sopping hair from his face.

Sarah stood up too, her mouth wide open.

They were standing in an air tunnel that reminded Sarah of the underwater viewing tunnel at Sydney Aquarium. Sarah could see a parrotfish grinding its teeth on coral, a cone snail sneaking up on a small sleeping fish, and a turtle flapping past. Tentatively, she poked a finger at the invisible barrier holding back the water on either side and above her head, and found herself touching water. There was no glass, no plastic, nothing.

'This is amazing,' Mitchell breathed.

Something latched onto Sarah's ankle. 'Ouch!' She shook off a crab, and it waved an angry claw at her.

The air tunnel followed a sandy road that inclined downwards, running through a rich and varied landscape of luminous coral, and extended far into the distance.

'We've gotta see where this goes,' Mitchell said, and set off in a state of great excitement.

'Waitaminute!' Sarah called after him. 'Is this even *safe*?'

Mitchell did not wait.

Tempting as it was to follow him, Sarah held back, full of misgivings. What if the tunnel collapsed? What if some danger lay ahead?

A spectacular shoal of fluorescent fat-lipped fish drew her eyes. A mammoth stingray glided overhead. Then a dugong and its calf paddled closer, cropping the sea grasses.

The temptation was too strong, and Sarah yielded.

'I hope you know what you're doing,' she called, jogging down the slope after Mitchell.

Strange crustaceans with three eyes and serrated pincers scuttled across the sandy floor. A school of pin-striped fish swirled this way and that, as if they were performing an underwater ballet, and then were lost from sight.

The colours of the coral were a visual feast, the sea creatures were enthralling, but Sarah could not shake off her worries, especially as the tunnel began to enter a tall forest of kelp whose waving spires cast a green glow over everything. Anything at all might be hiding in the lush foliage.

Sarah caught sight of a small epaulette shark chewing on something it had just eaten.

She could feel a nasty prickling along her skin. 'Don't you think we should turn back now?' she asked.

'Just a bit further,' Mitchell replied without pausing.

Sarah tried humming a tune, to bolster her courage.

By the time she ran out of tune, dark craggy rocks were rearing up on either side of the air tunnel instead of kelp. A nasty-looking octopus emerged from a crevice in the rocks and stared at her.

'I want to go back,' Sarah announced.

'Stop stressing,' Mitchell responded with a touch of annoyance. Sarah dragged her feet after him.

Minutes seemed like hours before the landscape flattened out in another impressive display of coral. A pulsing jellyfish drifted closer, and a school of rainbow-flecked fish darted away.

The tunnel continued on and on ahead.

Sarah decided she had to be firm. She stopped and spoke in her most authoritative voice. 'Mitch, this is far enough.'

'Look at that!' he exclaimed, pointing to something ahead outside of the air tunnel.

'What? … Oh!' Sarah's eye's encountered a sunken galleon in the distance, resting on the ocean floor.

'Hold it right there.'

Sarah stepped backwards in astonishment and Mitchell spun around.

A merboy had pushed his torso into the air tunnel, and proceeded to scrutinise first Mitchell, then Sarah, as he picked at something, possibly seaweed, caught between his front teeth.

Sarah stared right back at him – his short black curls that exposed the gills behind his ears, the satchel slung over one shoulder, and the swordfish tattooed on his left arm.

'Who invited you here?' he inquired at last.

'No one invited us. We just kind of … dropped in,' Sarah answered.

The merboy gave her a shrewd look. '*Some*body must have invited you. Otherwise the dryway wouldn't have opened up, would it?'

'We know Aquatica … if that helps,' Mitchell said.

Surprise flickered briefly in the merboy's eyes. 'Friend of yours, is she? Wouldn't have thought she'd associate with *you*.' From his satchel he extracted two scrolls of paper which he presented, one each, to Mitchell and Sarah. 'Anyway, you can't go no further unless you sign an indemnity.'

Each time the merboy moved, he gave off an unpleasant fishy odour. Sarah did not recall Aquatica smelling at all fishy; perhaps this merboy's hygiene was poor.

Sarah unfurled the scroll she had been handed, which seemed remarkably intact considering it was soaking wet, and proceeded to read the tiny handwriting. 'The undersigned hereby promises to remain strictly within the confines of the dryway, and takes full responsibility for any damage or injury that may be incurred by entering, either partially or fully, the water. Damage and/or injury may include, but is not limited to, one or more of the following: loss of life or limb, electrocution, bites, stings, pinches, cuts ...' *Blah blah blah.* Sarah couldn't be bothered reading the dozens of lines that followed.

'Here,' the merboy said, thrusting a quill into Sarah's hand.

She signed her name awkwardly (never having used a quill before) and passed the quill to Mitchell, who did likewise.

'That's the way,' said the merboy, accepting the signed scrolls. 'That'll be two shuckles.' He held out his palm, as if for payment.

'Shuckles?' Mitchell repeated.

'Yes, two shuckles, as agreed, for the guided tour.'

'Er, what guided tour?'

'The guided tour of Squatters' Wreck that you just signed up for,' the merboy answered.

'We didn't sign up for any tour,' Mitchell countered.

'You must learn to read the fine print when you sign fishall documents,' the merboy chided. 'It's all there in the contract. So, if you'll kindly hand over the money, we can get on with the tour. Unless you'd rather be sued for beach of contract?'

'Might be interesting...' Mitchell muttered to Sarah with a hopeful countenance.

Sarah shrugged. 'Can't hurt.'

Mitchell unzipped his money belt and pulled out two silver coins. 'These okay?'

The merboy snatched the coins, tested his teeth on each in turn, and seemed satisfied. 'Welcome to Squelch Tours,' he announced, assuming a brisk, professional manner. 'My name's Squelch, and I shall be your guide. Swim ... I mean *step* this way.' He withdrew from the air tunnel and proceeded to propel himself slowly alongside the tunnel by undulating his tail. Mitchell and Sarah hurried along the sandy road to keep up.

'*The Adventurer* embarked on a voyage of trade and exploration eighty-two years ago,' Squelch informed them, his voice sounding faintly muffled now that he was speaking in water, 'but sank in a storm, like all the wrecks in these waters. A dreadful clamity. Twenty-four human souls were lost. If you look closely, you'll spot porkfish, trumpetfish, butterflyfish, and angelfish flapping about – descendants of the fish that ate the bodies.'

'How do you know they're the descendants?' Sarah queried. 'Do you tag and track the fish or something?

With a lightning fast whisk of the tail, Squelch spun about to peer at Sarah. 'You some kind of oceanogrouper?'

'Er ... don't you mean oceano*graph*er?'

Squelch gave Sarah a hard look. 'Are you porpoisely trying to annoy me?'

'I think you mean pur–' Sarah began.

'The wreck looks *totally* amazing,' Mitchell interrupted hastily. 'I can't wait to see it.'

Within three minutes they had drawn as close to the fat-bellied galleon as the tunnel permitted.

Squelch floated to a stop. 'Got any questions? Ask away. I ain't been floundered yet.'

The clear water afforded Mitchell and Sarah an unimpaired view of the wreck and its surrounds, which were lit by torches whose underwater flames transfixed Sarah; surely there was magic at work here? With rusty cannons poking through the gun ports, the hull frowned down on them like a crumbling fortress. Most of the portholes flickered with light, suggesting there were torches *in*side the wreck as well. Graffiti had been scrawled across the

194

barnacle-encrusted sides ('Lobsters Rock!' and 'What do you call a pet carp? A carpet. Ha ha.') and there was a jagged hole in the hull through which bare-chested mermen and bikini-topped mermaids came and went at leisure.

The sandy patch of reef into which the galleon's keel had lodged itself was littered with sea chests, barrels, crates, blotchy mirrors, ruined paintings and rotting furniture, all of which had presumably come from the ship. A patched-up wooden hut, doing a reasonable trade selling take-away through a serving window, reminded Sarah of a fast-food drive-through, except that customers swam past rather than drove past. More than a dozen merpeople lolled on armchairs and lounges eating and chatting, while a curvaceous mermaid crooned a love ballad in the background. Sea grasses planted in old boots scattered here and there added a homely, cared-for touch to the scene.

'Tentacles of love have entangled my heart,

Electric eels couldn't keep us apart,' the mermaid sang soulfully.

Sarah would have liked to swim right up to the wreck and inspect the flaming torches. 'How d'you get fire underwater?' she asked.

'Are you *seal*ious?' Squelch replied, in the most emphatic tone of amazement.

Sarah nodded.

'It's dragon fire. What else could it be?'

Squelch was giving her such an odd look that Sarah felt compelled to explain her ignorance.

'Mitch and I come from another world. A world with no dragons and no merpeople and no –'

'A world with no *merpeople*?' Squelch scoffed. 'What a lot of abalone! Think I was spawned yesterday?'

'Pizza! And burgers!' Mitchell exclaimed, reading a crudely painted sign over the hut.

Squelch addressed his attention to Mitchell. 'Not had dinner yet? Floe's famous for her anchovy pizzas and whiting burgers.'

'Don't they go soggy?'

'Blimey! You're dolphinately behind the times. Water-resistant additives was invented *decades* ago. Want to try the pizza?'

Mitchell shook his head.

'What about the mackareli cheese?'

'No thanks.'

''Fraid of packing on the pounds? Floe's got healthy options too,' Squelch said. 'There's fishcakes cooked in krill oil?'

'No thanks.'

'How about sashimi?'

'No, really, I'm not hungry.'

'Crab cakes?'

'No thanks.'

'A low-joule oyster juice?'

'No! Stop pestering me!'

'Okay, okay, no need to get snappery! I'm just trying to make a little honest commission.'

The mermaid was still warbling her heart out:

'Your love ebbs and flows like the waves on the shore,

Is it draining away with the tide?'

Meanwhile, Sarah had been running her eyes over tablecloths and blankets pegged to washing lines strung between broken masts sunk into the sea-bed. An octopus had its arms fully occupied washing tea-towels in a soapy tub, wringing them out and draping them over the washing line. It looked neither content nor happy in its work.

'What's the point of hanging out washing under the sea?' Sarah asked.

Squelch tilted his head to one side and studied Sarah as if it were a curiosity to see a being so stupid. 'D'you think only *humans* like the feel of a nice dry blanket or towel?'

Sarah was perplexed. 'How can they be dry? They're soaking in water.'

'Well, duh! They're made from waterproof sea sponge,' Squelch replied rather rudely.

'Why's the octopus got chains on its legs?' Mitchell asked.

Sarah hadn't noticed the chains.

'Convicted felon. Gets locked in the brig at night,' Squelch answered.

'Do merpeople *live* inside the ship?' Mitchell asked.

'Certainly do. Not everyone can afford their own sea cave, y'know. Reef Safety Inspectors move us on, though, when they come round … reckon it's a fire hazard, what with everyone squished together like sardines.'

'What do merpeople *do* all day?' Sarah asked. 'Just swim around?' Immediately, she wished she had phrased the question differently.

'What do *humans* do all day?' Squelch returned tetchily. 'Manicure their toenails?'

'Human kids go to school and adults go to work,' Sarah said weakly.

'Same for us. We mine sea-salt, farm kelp, breed oysters, dig for oil, harvest moonshine to keep our tails glistening …' Squelch indicated a merman with fleshy cheeks and a receding chin who was eating at a table. 'That there's Briny. He's a bookie. You probably want to place a bet on tomorrow's water-hockey match, yeah? Which team d'you follow? Planktonites or Kelpmunchers?'

'Neither.'

'Then which d'you want to put money on?'

'Neither.'

'What other jobs do merpeople do?' Sarah asked.

'Oh … well, see the merman sitting on the anchor under a beach umbrella?' Sarah's eyes picked out a rough-looking merman. Little stirrings of current kept lifting his sweep-over hairstyle to reveal a balding head. 'Nauticus does fintastic tail piercings. Very tasteful. He did mine.' Squelch drew his flukes around to show off a line of silver studs.

'I like that,' Sarah said sincerely.

Squelch appeared pleased as he tucked his tail back. 'A friend of mine, Salina, got her tail pierced by a dodgy merman who

197

didn't sterilise his needles. Her flukes got finrot and a fungal infection.'

'Oh, that's horrible!' Sarah cried, wrinkling her face at the thought.

'Yeah, she can't swim at all now, and her family's disowned her 'cause finrot's contagious. It's turtally tragic.' Squelch heaved a heavy sigh. 'She had to prawn her only necklace to buy medicine and a morsel of food. I'm collecting donations to help her. Not that I'd expect *you* to make a donation of course. You've never met her and got to know how shy and sweet she is. You've never heard her weeping her little heart out.' Squelch wiped an invisible tear from his eye. 'It makes me want to start howling in shrimpathy when I hear her. *Don't cry*, I says to her. *You're making the sea level rise.* But she can't help it. All that awaits her is a life of misery and poverty.' Suddenly overcome, Squelch's features crinkled with emotion, and he turned his face away.

Sarah looked at Mitchell. He was staring awkwardly at his feet. Sarah nudged him and gave him a meaningful look.

'Salina would n-never' – Squelch let out a sob – 'never d-dream of asking a *human* for help' – he let out another sob – 'though she spent her life rescuing d-drowning sailors.' He broke down and sobbed piteously.

'Here you go,' Mitchell said. He gingerly pushed his forearm into the water and handed another coin to Squelch.

'Oh!' Squelch stopped sobbing at once, and gave a loud sniff. 'You don't know what this means. You're very kind, very unshellfish.'

Sarah was pleased to be able to help.

'Hey, what's swishing?'

A merboy with matching red hair and red pimples had swum up, holding a basket filled with little bottles. 'Why, you'll never make a splash with a complexion like that, miss!' the merboy said, making a careful study of Sarah's face. 'What *you* need is sea cucumber eye gel and a seaweed face mask.' He extracted a couple

198

of bottles from his basket. 'Pop these on before bed each night, and wake up to skin that's clear and bright. Only two shuckles.'

Sarah planted her hands on her hips. 'I'm quite okay with my face as it is,' she declared. *If the face mask works so well, why are you all pimply?* she thought. *And maybe you should clean the algae off your tail.*

'Prickly as a pufferfish, ain't she?' Pimple-face remarked to Squelch.

By now a third merboy had swum closer, clasping a colourful bunch of coral blooms. He wore a fish hook through one ear and sported a limp sea-snake – presumably dead – like a scarf around his neck. 'Care to buy a bouquet for the young lady?' he inquired of Mitchell. 'It's a steal at one shuckle.'

'No thanks,' Mitchell answered.

'How about a pet sea snake? She's very friendly.'

The sea snake lifted its head towards Mitchell, who promptly started back, with a half-suppressed gasp. The look the snake was giving him might have been friendly for a sea snake, but it looked remarkably *un*friendly to Mitchell. 'No, that's okay.'

Hook-ear dropped his voice and cupped his mouth with his hand in a secretive manner. 'Don't have a reptile-keeping licence? I can get you a forged one.'

Mitchell shook his head. 'No, *really*, I *don't* want a sea snake. I don't want to buy *anything*'.

'Then what did you come here for?' Hook-ear demanded, his voice tinged with disappointment.

'We're looking for Aquatica,' Mitchell answered. 'Does she live in the ship too?'

'Aquatica? No-ho. The likes of *her* don't associate with *us,*' Hook-ear replied.

'She's from an *up*reef family,' Pimple-face chipped in. 'They've got money up to their gills, that lot.'

His words rang true; Sarah recalled that Aquatica's top had been made from hundreds of tiny pearlescent shells stitched together, a far superior garment to the simple clam-shell bikini tops worn by the mermaids around the wreck.

'Think they're the catfish's whiskers, they do,' Hook-ear sneered.

'Upreefers like Aquatica attend caviar appreciation classes and go on whale spotting tours,' Squelch said in a posh voice.

'Can you tell us how to find her?' Mitchell asked.

'Directions ain't included in the price of the tour,' Squelch said, and thrust his hand into the air tunnel for more money.

Sarah detected that fishy scent again.

Mitchell produced a fourth coin from his money belt and dropped it into Squelch's palm.

'Just keep following the dryway,' Squelch said as he retracted his hand.

Mitchell and Sarah continued to look at him, expecting more instructions.

The singing mermaid had retired by now, and a mergirl was rapping out the words:

'This leaking tub, this sunken wreck,

with peeling paint and tilted deck,

is such a hole. I will not stay.

I'll seek my fortune far away.'

'You'll stay right here where I can keep an eye on you!' called the shrill voice of a mermaid, presumably her mother, through one of the portholes, evoking some laughter from the audience.

'That's *it*?' Mitchell checked. 'Just keep going?'

'Sure. The dryway don't branch out nowhere. Either you go forward, or you go back.'

Mitchell and Sarah exchanged annoyed glances for parting with that last coin too easily.

'Well, I'm sorry you have to split,' Squelch added, sounding not at all sorry. 'Don't let us keep you then.'

Mitchell and Sarah farewelled their tour guide rather coolly and proceeded on their way.

Hook-ear's voice drifted after them. 'Bit strange, ain't they?'

'I've never met such flatheads in my life,' Squelch returned. 'It's like they've been living on one of the moons or something. They bought the whole tour guide thing, and they even believed the Salina story.'

'Noooo!' Hook-ear exclaimed.

'Hook, line and sinker,' Squelch assured him. 'Soooo gillable.'

Sarah whipped back around.

Hook-ear was chuckling. 'How much d'you make?' he asked.

'*Four* shuckles all up,' Squelch answered.

'Way to go.' The merboys slapped their flukes together.

Indignation blazed up inside Sarah; Squelch was a con artist, and she had been conned. 'You stink, you know that, Squelch?' Sarah began in a loud voice, striding back towards the merboys. Squelch looked at her, entirely unabashed, smug even. 'You stink like a dirty fishmarket. And you should read the dictionary, because half the words you say are wrong.'

Squelch's smug expression wavered.

'Stop it,' Mitchell said, clamping a hand on her arm, and feeling mildly satisfied, Sarah allowed her brother to drag her away.

Chapter 29 – Marinarvius

A five-minute uphill walk from the wreck brought Mitchell and Sarah to an expanse of reef dominated by hillocks of rock that bulged out of the sea bed like giant beehives. Around these rocky mounds, sea grasses and fluorescent coral had been set out in orderly plots, like garden beds, bordered with scallop shells. Milling about these gardens Mitchell spotted half a dozen merpeople whose gently swishing tails gleamed with moonshine. A manacled octopus appeared to be raking sea urchins off the coral.

Four mermen, in deep discussion, emerged through a curtain of seaweed from one of the rocky mounds, and the seaweed fell back in place behind them, concealing the entrance once more.

'Those must be the sea caves,' Mitchell whispered to Sarah.

The tranquillity of the scene was abruptly disturbed by a silvery stream of tuna racing past and a dozen merpeople tearing after them, brandishing spears. The tuna and their pursuers swept away, and as the water settled behind them, two dumpy mergirls erupted from another sea cave, squabbling over a baby turtle. An irate mermaid hastened after them, ordering them to 'Come back inside. *NOW!*'

All at once, the merpeople became aware of Mitchell and Sarah. They glided closer.

'Hello,' Mitchell ventured with a grin.

There were no answering smiles. Rather, there was an air of contempt about the merpeople's refined faces as they subjected Mitchell and Sarah to careful appraisal from outside the tunnel.

'I hope they haven't brought sea-lice with them,' a merman said, without troubling to lower his voice.

In response to his statement, several merpeople edged back a little from the air tunnel.

'Humans can't be very clean, living out of water,' another remarked, equally loudly.

'Certainly not,' answered a third. 'Some humans go for days at a stretch without even taking a bath.'

A chorus of appalled oooh's followed.

Snobs, Mitchell thought.

More and more merpeople approached, until quite a crowd had congregated. There wasn't a friendly face among them.

Was Aquatica here somewhere? Mitchell's eyes darted from one merperson to another. A burly merman with bulging muscles and a threatening bearing. A fragile white-bearded merman with a scornful expression. A mermaid with red-gold hair that fanned out around her head, who knew she was beautiful. An older mermaid with a proud bearing and dripping with pearls.

There was something almost accusatory in the merpeople's expressions that struck coldly at Mitchell's heart.

He felt a prod between his shoulder blades. 'Over there,' Sarah said, and pointed.

Mitchell relaxed a little as his eyes picked out Aquatica – one small, reassuring figure amongst many flanking the tunnel – waving madly.

No sooner had Mitchell reached her than Aquatica's head and shoulders pushed into the air tunnel, and her cheeks dimpled. 'I'm soooo glad you came, Mitch,' she said in her sweet, melodious voice. 'I told my relations that you're a mighty healer and that you saved my life.'

Glancing around, Mitchell observed that the relations did not appear at all impressed or grateful.

'You're my *hero*,' she said ardently. 'My gallant rescuer.' Then she cast her eyes coquettishly downward, which showed her lovely long lashes to best advantage.

A grave-faced merman with a receding hairline and a well-developed paunch poked his torso through the air-water divide to join the conversation. 'I am called Marinarvius,' he announced in a deep voice.

A beautifully crafted silver trident in the merman's hand caught Mitchell's eye for the briefest moment. Then he met the merman's piercing gaze. 'I'm Mitch and this is Sarah,' he said.

'Aquatica has told us your story,' Marinarvius said. 'Quite a story it is, too. But whereas she is young and naive, *I* am not. To me, your lies are transparent as jellyfish.' The iciness of his tone sent a chill right through Mitchell.

Aquatica gave a muffled exclamation. 'What do you mean, Grandfather?'

Marinarvius looked into Aquatica's troubled face and stroked her hair. 'These drownable ones are in league with Vanrod,' he explained gently, evidently sensitive of upsetting her. 'The eagle attacked you in order that these humans might stage your rescue to earn our trust.' This explanation only served to increase the confusion on her face. Marinarvius switched his focus back to Mitchell and Sarah, and his tone hardened as he concluded. 'The deed was despicable, and you shall be punished.'

Sarah was the first to respond, and Mitchell was surprised by how cheery she sounded. 'The dwarves said you probably wouldn't trust us,' she said. 'Sooo …' She started fiddling with something around her waist.

Marinarvius made an impatient huffing noise.

By the time Mitchell realised what Sarah was doing, and tried to signal her not to, she was holding up the magic diamond.

'There. How's that?' she asked, smiling. 'The dwarves gave it to us, to prove you can trust us.'

A merboy whistled, and a trail of bubbles issued from his mouth.

Other onlookers uttered exclamations of astonishment. A buzz of comment passed through the crowd. They pressed closer.

'*See.* We're *not* on Vanrod's side.' Sarah put the statement to them all, clearly confident she had presented a convincing argument.

Mitchell was not nearly so confident.

Marinarvius's baritone voice broke the stillness, superbly scornful. 'Even if we *did* believe your story, your ignorance astonishes me. The earth-dwellers never chose to share with merfolk the great honour of safe-keeping the Banishing Stones, yet you assume we would overlook this insult?'

The smile slid from Sarah's face, and an anxious, knotted feeling took hold in Mitchell's stomach.

Quick as snapping shark jaws, Marinarvius reached out and plucked the diamond from Sarah's hand. 'No indeed. Now that you have, quite unexpectedly, brought this treasure to us,' – he fingered it greedily – 'we shall keep it. One day *we* shall be masters of all *four* stones.'

Sarah looked like she'd been cuffed across the ears. Mitchell knew how she felt. How could they return to Wipple without the diamond?

'Oh, ho!' Marinarvius went on disdainfully. 'Look at their shocked faces.'

Then his eyes swept the assembly, and a tacit understanding must have passed between the merpeople, for with a swishing of silvery tails they disbanded, leaving Mitchell and Sarah alone with Marinarvius who smiled an irritatingly superior smile and said, 'I know *all* about your little scheme.'

'And what's *that* supposed to mean?' Mitchell demanded.

'It means that an elf paid us a visit earlier today,' Marinarvius answered, suddenly brandishing a piece of paper.

Mitchell tore the paper from the merman's hand and read Mrs Stockyleg's missive.

'Dear Fyrddin,

Vanrod did not send Mitch and Sarah back to their world. Swift is flying them to the Stormy Sea to search for the magic sapphire, which they hope to present to Vanrod so he will send them home.

Mildred Stockylegs. '

'Well?' Marinarvius said impatiently, moving his lined face closer to Mitchell's.

Mitchell took a step back.

'We weren't *really* going to give the sapphire to Vanrod,' Sarah said in a voice that wobbled. 'That's just what Tumblelong was going to tell Vanrod … so he wouldn't send his eagles after us.'

'Oh sure. Anything you say.' Marinarvius' tone was mocking now.

'You've got it all wrong, really you have! We were *never* going to give Vanrod *any* of the stones,' Mitchell pleaded.

The merman's face clouded. His eyes flashed dangerously. 'I grow weary of lies and I have a good mind to send in the sting rays.'

Sarah's eyes widened in trepidation. 'But –'

'But torture is, lamentably, illegal,' Marinarvius steamrolled on. 'So you shall be imprisoned instead.'

'Imprisoned?' Sarah repeated hoarsely.

With a tap of his trident on the seabed, the long air-filled passageway shrank to a bubble as big as a minibus, with Mitchell and Sarah inside it.

'You can't keep us here!' Mitchell exclaimed indignantly.

'Try me,' Marinarvius returned, in a voice now distorted by the water.

The injustice made Mitchell's blood boil. He could feel his cheeks flushing. He could feel his hands shaking. 'You think you've got it all figured out but you can't even see the obvious!' he said angrily. Marinarvius glared back. 'Everyone needs to work *together* to beat Vanrod. You, the dwarves, the elves. It's your only chance. And do you honestly think you're gonna find the missing stones when you can't even walk on land? Maybe the salt water's rusted your brains, if you've actually got any.'

A muscle in Marinarvius's clean-shaven jaw was twitching with fury. Mitchell waited for the explosion. But the merman merely looked down his nose at Mitchell and said, 'Think upon this riddle.'

'*What?*'

'I love to stretch and shrink, I love to leap and play, but when the darkness swallows light I have to hide away. What am I?'

'*Huh?*'

Marinarvius did not bother to expand. His powerful tail muscles rippled as he swept away with the diamond, muttering something that sounded very much like 'a pain in the gills.'

Mitchell's voice rose furiously. 'YOU'RE – MAKING – A – BIG – MISTAKE – AND – YOU'LL – REGRET – IT! – YOU – OLD – TROUT!'

'Shush! You'll make him more angry,' Sarah urged.

Mitchell turned on his sister. 'Why d'you have to go and give him the diamond? You're such a twit!' Even as the words left his mouth he knew he was being unfair, but it was easier to be angry than admit he was frightened.

Sarah recoiled, her face reproachful. 'I was trying to prove we were telling the truth.'

'Well, it didn't work, did it?'

Hitting out at the edge of the air bubble, Mitchell's fist came into contact with, not water this time, but a solid barrier. He kicked it hard, but it only flexed slightly. Up until this moment he had nurtured the possibility that he and Sarah would be able to break out and swim to the surface. Now he wasn't so sure.

'Check your pockets for something sharp,' he ordered.

Sarah turned out Mrs Stockylegs' white handkerchief and Granny Dreamaday's bright night-cap and wrung water from them both.

'Real useful,' Mitchell said sarcastically, though his own pockets only produced a couple of shells and a handful of sand.

Mitchell could see Sarah was close to tears. Nevertheless, he continued his rant. 'If we had the diamond we could've cut our way outta here. It's *your* fault we're stuck.'

'It was *you* who kept going along the tunnel when I wanted to turn back!' Sarah burst out in a flood of tears. She sank down onto a clump of mottled seaweed and covered her face with her hands.

'Oh, that's right. Cry like a baby. That'll do a lot of good.' Mitchell turned his back on Sarah's heaving shoulders.

A school of exotic-looking fish came to goggle. Mitchell scowled so dreadfully at them that they zigzagged away in fright.

Mitchell struggled with his conscience for a full minute before he dropped down beside Sarah with a sigh of surrender. 'I'm sorry,' he admitted in a small voice.

Sarah lifted her miserable face to his. 'What – *sniff!* – are we – *sniff!* – going to do?'

'Dunno. But I hope Marin-stupid-arvius ends up in the belly of a whale.'

While Sarah blew her nose on the wet hanky, Mitchell picked up Granny Dreamaday's nightcap and turned it around in his fingers. The monogram *G.E.* embroidered on the frill seemed wrong. Shouldn't it say *G.D.*? He tossed it aside.

Merpeople appeared to be retiring into their sea caves for the night.

'Oooh!' Sarah cried, raising one foot to reveal a partially-buried sea cucumber.

The sight triggered an idea in Mitchell's head. Maybe he and Sarah could tunnel their way out of the bubble, and then swim to shore.

He waited until all the merpeople had gone, and then, without a word, started gouging a hole in the sea bed, scooping out sand with his hands.

'What're you doing?' Sarah queried.

'Getting us out of here,' Mitchell answered, digging energetically.

The hole was getting bigger. Mitchell was feeling hopeful.

Then a blast of sea-water struck his face and he lurched backwards, momentarily blinded. He heard Sarah gasp, and when he wiped his eyes he saw that where he had dug, he had released a five foot fountain of water. And as water continued to gush up into the air and rain down over him, it wasn't draining away. It was pooling ankle-deep.

'We'll drown!' Sarah squealed, throwing herself on top of the powerful jet. 'Quick! Plug it up!'

Mitchell was back on his knees in a heartbeat, scrabbling feverishly with handfuls of sand, patting it down. He could feel the water creeping up his legs.

It took five stressful minutes to stem the flow, another two minutes to stop it completely, and a quarter of an hour for the water to drain away.

Now Mitchell knew, without a doubt, that they were trapped. He dropped his head in his hands, and gave himself up to hopelessness.

Chapter 30 – Wartville Dungeon

Stella huddled on the stone floor with her legs tucked up under her, hugging herself against the chilling cold. She had not been boiled or beheaded or beaten for engineering the bear cub's escape. Rather, the Witches' Council had sentenced her to death by starvation in Wartville's underground dungeon. Horribella cursed and ranted and jumped up and down, railing against the soft justice system, to no avail.

The dungeon was an eerie place, dimly lit by torches and infused with a brutal stench of sewerage and decay. Stella imagined herself mutating into a bee and flying out through the floor-to-ceiling iron bars. In reality, however, she was trapped, for long ago a *Bind* spell had been woven over the dungeon to prevent prisoners from using their magic.

'Neck of phoenix,

brain of bat,

eye of beetle,

wing of gnat.

Melt and stir to make this potion

turn into an itching lotion,' muttered a dry, crackly voice that belonged to Hazar, the old prune-like prisoner two cells away. Perhaps she was mad. Or maybe she just rattled off spells to pass the time.

The tread of approaching shoes and a soft brushing noise brought Stella to her feet.

The iron bars provided ample view of the passageway between the cells and of the cat that sat there like an ebony carving, its eyes reflecting the torch light. For a second, a shadow slid along the floor of the passageway, and then Cruella the gaoler strode into view dragging a young faun by his horns that weren't yet fully grown.

Cruella, whose most prominent feature was a long chin that curled upwards, did not spare Stella a passing glance.

It was clear, from the way the faun offered no resistance, that he had been stunned; his hairy brown legs and black cloven hoofs trailed uselessly along the ground, and only his terrified eyes moved of his own accord. He had every reason to be terrified, as Stella knew, for Wartville's Illness Research Institute liked to test their latest viruses and diseases upon fauns when they could be caught.

The faun was shoved into a cell; Stella heard the door clang shut and the key turn in the lock.

Footsteps again – the gaoler retracing her steps.

Cruella's chin preceded her.

'Cruella? Can I please have a glass of water?' Stella entreated.

Cruella paused and flicked an eye over Stella. 'Hmmm, let me see ... NO!'

No! ... No! ... No! chorused the echoes as Cruella marched away.

Stella's shoulders sagged. Though she was entirely unrepentant about freeing the bear cub, she certainly didn't want to die in the dungeon, like so many prisoners before her. Like the shrivelled leprechaun with unblinking eyes across the passageway. Like the canary-sized giant slumped in the hanging birdcage. Like the trolls whose ugly heads graced the walls.

'Your granny Mortadora was left to rot here too, you know,' Hazar piped up. 'Funny how things turn out, isn't it?'

'Hysterical,' Stella muttered.

'Eh? What's that? Speak up.'

'Er ... D-did you know my granny?' Stella inquired loudly.

''Course I knew her,' rasped Hazar. 'Real strange, she was, just like your ma.'

Stella had been told as much a million times.

'Why were they different from everyone else?' Stella asked. 'Horribella wouldn't talk about them much. All she would say is that they had bad blood.'

'Bad blood?' Hazar repeated slowly, as if she were thinking. 'Maybe. Maybe. But my guess is that one of your ancestors drank from the Cup of Kindness, and it's infected each successive generation. Never mind, the disgrace will die here with you.'

Stella's shoulders sagged even more, and Hazar ploughed on. 'You know that your ma was caught stealing a dozen griffin eggs, don't you?'

'Yes,' Stella answered dully. Sleazilla and Grotchetta never stopped harping on about how her mother had been a thief.

'Those were the good old days,' Hazar reminisced. 'Well I remember your ma's face when she found herself caught out. She looked terrified. She knew she was in big trouble. I mean, we'd gone to so much trouble to get those griffin eggs – flown to the remotest lands, to the highest mountain peaks, and fought the wild griffins protecting their nests. We were hoping to raise an army of vicious griffins. Can you imagine if we'd succeeded? We could have had such sport terrorising the dwarves and the elves. But your ma had other plans. Like I said, she was terrified when we caught her stealing the griffin eggs – you could see it in her eyes – but she kept her nerve, she didn't drop the eggs. She leapt onto her broomstick and took off. Several of us gave chase, as you might imagine, but your ma was a fine flyer and gave us the slip. Before we could track her down, her broomstick returned to Wartville on its own, a sure sign she was dead. We had no way of knowing what happened to the eggs. Maybe she found a purchaser who double-crossed her and killed her. Those eggs were worth a fortune. Anyway, *someone* had to be punished for what she did, didn't they? But *you* were just a tot, so we imprisoned your granny instead.' Hazar sighed, as if reliving happy memories.

It was painful enough that her mother had been a thief. But what hurt Stella *most* of all was that her mother had abandoned her. Surely if a mother loved her baby she wouldn't just fly off and leave it behind? Tears insisted on falling, despite Stella's resolve to be brave.

The cat arched its back and waved its tail as it strolled away.

Upon receiving Stella's tear alert, Reeks the fairy consulted her notebook, read 'a whinging and whining sort of child', and took her time responding. In consequence, Stella, who had been thirsty earlier in the evening, was well and truly parched by the time Reeks made an appearance, bathing the stone walls and iron bars in a golden glow.

The fairy's first words were, 'Pooh! Not exactly a fairy bower, is it?'

'You again!' Stella gasped, blinking up at the hovering fairy whose wings were a glimmering blur. Reeks had no briefcase with her on this occasion; she was holding a notebook and a quill in her hands.

'Yes, me again,' Reeks returned a little frostily, 'and I don't mean to be rude, but I'd like to make this zippy.' Then, flashing wary looks around, she added, 'The last fairy who visited this stinky dump left it sprouting a tail. Some witch's idea of a joke, I gather.'

'Lots of witches think fairy tails are funny,' Stella admitted in a voice that sounded husky because her throat was so dry.

'Hmmm. I'm sure. Anyway, what did *you* do to wind up here?'

Daring to hope that Reeks might help this time, Stella began to explain about rescuing the bear cub. Reeks flitted around Stella's head, scribbling notes.

'Keep it brief. I don't think my nose can take much more of this place,' Reeks interrupted. 'It stinks worse than a troll's bathroom.'

Stella kept it brief. 'Can you get me out of here?' she wound up in pleading tones.

Reeks paused an arm's length in front of Stella's face.

'So the bear cub did not belong to you?' Reeks clarified with a disapproving edge to her voice.

'No-o-o, but –'

Reeks raised a tiny finger to cut Stella off. 'And you knew the cub was meant to be kept in the cage?'

'Ye-e-e-es, but –'

Another finger. 'Then what do you expect, Stella?' Reeks emitted a frustrated sigh. 'At your age, surely you know it's wrong to steal. I can't release you when you're being justly punished, can I?'

'*Justly* punished? It's not –'

'However,' Reeks said loudly, holding up her delicate hand to silence Stella's objections. 'I can't have you starve to death either. That's against rule one thousand and forty-one.'

Stella looked at Reeks beseechingly as the fairy seemed to deliberate, then –

'Behold!' Reeks said grandly. 'Your once-in-a-lifetime intervention.'

A glass of water and a slice of bread on a plate appeared on the ground by Stella's knees.

Stella grabbed the glass and began gulping down its contents.

'Well, that's that then,' said Reeks, tucking her notepad into her jacket pocket. 'I'd best be off now.'

'W*hat?!*' Stella spluttered, slopping water all down her front. 'That's all I get? Bread and water? When Cinderella got a coach *and* a dress *and* slippers!'

The fairy drew herself up, apparently deeply affronted. 'Can you *eat* slippers, tell me that now?' she said snappishly. 'Can you *drink* a dress? I don't think so! And why ever would you need a coach? You're not *going* anywhere, *clearly.*'

And with that, the fairy vanished.

Tears gathered afresh in Stella's eyes, tears of bitter, bitter disappointment.

Eight hours later she discovered that her gift was a little bit special after all – both the glass and the plate magically replenished their contents. When another eight hours had passed the same thing happened again. Thanks to the Save-a-Life Division of the International Association of Fairy Godmothers, Stella could look forward to an extended stay in prison.

Chapter 31 – Password

It was a worrying sight: Aunt Alison standing in the Fragrant Forest holding a chain-saw and running her eyes over the trunk of a majestic merrin tree.

'Aunt Al, what are you doing?' Mitchell asked nervously.

'I'm going to build a cubby house for Rufus,' Aunt Alison answered, with a ready smile. 'Don't worry, munchkin. I've read *Tree-lopping for Dummies*, and I intend to keep all my limbs.'

But that wasn't what Mitchell was worrying about.

Aunt Alison ripped the chain-saw to life.

'No! You mustn't!' Mitchell yelled. 'You'll kill the dryad!'

Aunt Alison wasn't listening. 'Stand further back, Mitch,' she shouted, lifting the chain-saw purposefully.

'No!' Mitchell made to run towards the gap between his aunt and the merrin tree, arms outspread …

'Wake up!' came an urgent whisper. 'Oh, *do* wake up!'

Mitchell's eyes popped open.

Just a dream. It was just a …

Mitchell leapt up like a jack-in-the-box.

A pair of bluish-grey shadows with pointed snouts, grinning white teeth and gleaming eyes was circling the air bubble. Never had Mitchell seen such villainous-looking sharks, even in the movies. He kicked his sister hard.

'Ouch! What was that for?' Sarah complained, her voice thick with sleep.

He kicked her again.

'*Ouch!* Stop –'

The protest died on her lips and she stood up quick smart beside him. 'They can't get in, right?'

''*Course* they can get in,' Mitchell almost yelled. 'Look at their teeth!'

'Shhh! You'll wake everyone,' said a low voice behind them. Mitchell and Sarah swung around.

If Mitchell hadn't been so petrified, he would have felt heartened, for Aquatica had returned.

'Oh Mitch,' Aquatica said sorrowfully, 'it's *tragic* to see you locked up like this, like a common criminal. And after you saved my life and healed my shoulders and everything.'

Mitchell's gaze followed the sharks' light tail movements. 'Er … yeah …'

'Don't worry. Rip and Tear won't hurt you.'

Mitchell dragged his eyes back to the mermaid. The fact that she was looking distinctly ill at ease, fidgeting with her necklace and swishing her tail like a windscreen wiper did not inspire confidence.

'Trust me, Mitch. Rip and Tear are quite harmless,' Aquatica repeated. 'You must hurry. You must flee before my people awake. You *did* figure out the password, didn't you?'

Mitchell was fighting to control his shaking hands. 'What password?' he asked.

'*What password?*' Aquatica repeated. 'I hope you're pulling my tail? … Oh, this isn't good.'

'What? Tell us,' Sarah prompted.

'You need to solve Grandfather's riddle to undo your enbubblement. The answer to the riddle is the password. It's never hard.'

Mitchell rubbed his temples, utterly confused. 'What kind of air-head would lock someone up and give them a password to break out?'

Aquatica pouted a little and lifted her head with a touch of pride. 'It's mer tradition. For centuries, ever since a sailor was found to have been wrongfully imprisoned, my people have provided a password. We believe that the innocent will figure it out, and the guilty will not, so justice will always be served.'

Mitchell threw up his hands. 'Fabulous! I suppose that makes us guilty.'

'No, no. You just need to remember the riddle and think about it.'

Sarah shook her head hopelessly. 'I dunno. I can't think at *all* with those sharks watching.'

'Come on, you have to try!' Aquatica scolded.

Easier said than done. Mitchell had been so angry at the time, he hadn't really been listening to Marinarvius. 'I *think* the old tr–, I mean Marinarvius, said something about light … and dark.'

'What else?'

'Leaping and playing, maybe?' Sarah put in.

'It must be fire,' Aquatica said quickly. 'Just say *fire*.'

'Fire,' said Mitchell.

Aquatica's tail brushed back and forth at an increased tempo and Mitchell cast his eyes around expectantly, but nothing happened.

'You mustn't have remembered properly,' Aquatica said with a touch of exasperation. 'Try to recall *exactly* what grandfather said.'

Mitchell groaned.

Aquatica gnawed her bottom lip, the sharks circled, and Sarah twiddled one of her plaits. What *had* the merman said? Whatever it was had been sucked into the quicksand of Mitchell's mind.

Quite unexpectedly Aquatica let out a squeal. 'You've got a thinking-cap! Why ever don't you put it on?' She was gazing with sparkling eyes at Granny Dreamaday's night-cap which was partially concealed under Mitchell's foot.

'That's just a plain old night-cap like people used to wear in the olden days,' Sarah said as Mitchell stooped to pick it up.

'No, silly! It's a *thinking*-cap! A genuine, *goblin-made* thinking-cap!' Aquatica's voice was rising with each word. 'How did you get it? They're scarce as turtle teeth. Never mind, we don't have time. Put it on. Put it on.' Aquatica executed a tumble-turn out of sheer excitement.

Mitchell looked at Sarah, who looked back at him, unconvinced.

217

'Just try,' he mumbled, forcing the crumpled night-cap into Sarah's hands. He figured they might as well humour the mermaid.

'*You* try,' Sarah said, shoving the night-cap back at him.

'It's for *girls*,' he said disdainfully, and dropped it on her head.

'Now think back to what grandfather said,' Aquatica pressed.

Sarah rolled her eyes. Mitchell guessed she was feeling pretty stupid standing there with a floral nightcap on her head.

Quite abruptly, Sarah's expression completely changed. Her face lit up, her eyes sparkled, her lips parted in a smile.

'What's up?' Mitchell queried. 'Don't tell me it actually *worked?*'

Sarah nodded. I can remember everything Marinarvius said, word for word.

'Well? … Tell us then …'

'I love to stretch and shrink, I love to leap and play, but when the darkness swallows light I have to hide away. What am I?' Sarah quoted. 'That's *exactly* what he said. And' – she spun on one foot – 'I know the answer –'

'Stop! You can say it aloud in two shakes of a lobster tail.' Aquatica was speaking rapidly now. 'But first, I'll tell you the plan. Eagles are watching your ostrich, so Rip and Tear are going take you south down the coast to the Crystal River.'

'The *sharks?*' Sarah yelped.

'Oh, no,' objected Mitchell hastily. 'I'd rather stay right where I am.'

'It's the only way, Mitch,' Aquatica urged. 'Our sea horses are bred for racing and would buck you off quick smart. And dolphins are always playing; they just won't be serious. No, sharks are much more reliable, *and* they can fight back if eagles attack.'

Mitchell and Sarah just looked at her.

'Well? What else are you going to do?' Aquatica said impatiently.

'What's the rush?' Sarah implored. 'We can wait till the eagles are gone. Anyway, we've left our sneakers on the beach.'

'No. You must leave at once.' Aquatica turned her head this way and that, before dropping her voice to a dramatic whisper. 'The kraken is drawing nearer.'

Mitchell and Sarah gazed back at her blankly.

'Oh, don't tell me you haven't heard of the kraken!' Aquatica exclaimed.

Mitchell and Sarah shook their heads.

'It's a giant octopus that chomps ships in half and eats all the humans that fall into the sea. You're in great danger here. At least my family and I can swim away and hide, but you stand *no* chance.'

Mitchell and Sarah shared uneasy glances. It seemed like they didn't have a lot of alternatives.

'Looks like we're going for a shark ride,' Mitchell said.

'I suppose we have to now,' Sarah conceded.

Aquatica's face relaxed into a half-smile. 'Good. Then say the answer to the riddle.'

'I'm ready when you are,' Mitchell told Sarah.

Sarah spoke the password. 'A shadow.'

It happened in a split second. The bubble burst, a weight of water rushed in, and Mitchell found himself being boosted upwards by one of the sharks, propelled against a sweep of water. Seconds later he broke the surface, spitting out salty water. As he shook the hair out of his eyes the heads of Sarah and Aquatica popped up close by.

'Good old Granny Dreamaday!' Mitchell exclaimed. 'She's not so loopy after all.'

'I hope she didn't want her cap back,' Sarah said. 'It got washed away.'

Mitchell glanced about, keeping a jittery eye on the two pointy shark fins. The tranquil sea sparkled in reflected moonshine and in the distance Mitchell could just make out the shore.

'Don't think badly of Grandfather for enbubbling you,' Aquatica said, looking at Mitchell out of big, pleading eyes. 'It's just he's got his tail in a knot over that letter.'

'Er, I'm sure he's really nice,' Mitchell said, privately hoping Marinarvius might get tangled up in the nets of a fishing trawler.

Aquatica beamed at Mitchell. 'Up you get then. You can ride on Rip.'

Mitchell didn't know quite what to do once he found himself astride a shark.

'Get a grip on the dorsal fin,' Aquatica instructed.

'Am I holding too tight?' Sarah asked.

Mitchell was amazed by his sister's question. 'You're worried about hurting a – *aagh!'*

Without any warning, the sharks were off, waggling their tails back and forth to pick up velocity.

'Bye,' Sarah called softly over her shoulder. 'Thank you.'

'Good luck, Mitch,' Aquatica called. 'Keep your eyes on the skies.'

Chapter 32 – Bent to Breaking Point

If racing through the sky on an ostrich had been thrilling, cutting through gentle waves on a shark was more so. A long beach slipped past, then a small harbour came into view, and then the coastline changed again to wide rock platforms over which the sea spilled placidly.

The kraken did not show itself. The eagles kept away.

If only Sarah still had the diamond Mrs Tumblelong had entrusted to her, she might have enjoyed the ride. Even so, her tension gradually drained away.

Sarah glanced at her brother. Only his head and shoulders showed above the water. He grinned as he caught her eye and said, 'How good is this?'

The miles sped by at a furious pace, a big moon and a little moon climbed higher and higher in the charcoal sky, smiling to one another in greeting, and all the while the constellations held Mitchell and Sarah enthralled.

'See that flower, like a tulip?'

'See that hammer?'

'Oh, look! There's a minotaur.'

Mitchell was just a little way ahead of Sarah when she first became uneasy. She squinted hard into the darkness above. There was something there, she was sure. By the time she worked out it was an eagle, the bird was already swooping.

'WATCHOUT!' she shrilled, yanking hard on Tear's dorsal fin to make him stop.

In a horrible confusion of feathers, claws and waving arms she saw Mitchell fall off Rip with a splash and the eagle dive after him.

'NO-O-O!'

There was a flash of movement as Rip made a sharp U-turn and – *SNAP!* – before Sarah could even blink the huge bird was trapped between powerful jaws. Shark food.

Scanning the water feverishly, Sarah spotted Mitchell's head bobbing above the surface.

'Are you okay?' she asked.

'Its claws snagged me,' Mitchell answered shakily, holding up an arm.

'Mitch! There's blood gushing all down you!' Sarah cried.

'I'll need to bandage it. Have you still got that hanky?'

As he swam closer, Sarah fumbled in her pocket and pulled out the handkerchief. She gave it a quick wash in the sea since she had used it to blow her nose. 'Here.' She secured it around Mitchell's arm to stem the bleeding.

Three minutes later Mitchell was straddling Rip once more.

'I didn't see the eagle coming,' he said. 'I was watching that spouting whale.'

Sarah's heart was still thumping as the sharks took off again. Her plaits streamed out behind her as the sharks built up speed. On and on they rushed, past long stretches of rugged cliffs rising steeply from the sea. Tired but wakeful, Sarah kept a vigilant eye on the heavens.

'What's that?' Mitchell asked suddenly.

In the distance a small light was flashing at regular intervals.

'Lighthouse, maybe?' Sarah suggested.

As they drew nearer, they saw her guess was correct. Within minutes the sharks had rounded the promontory upon which the flashing beacon stood, and left it behind.

Though Sarah was beginning to feel enormously sleepy she forced herself to stay watchful, and as it turned out she was glad she did, for, although there was nothing out of the ordinary for ages, she began to make out a deeper blackness against the night sky, and as she followed it with her eyes, familiar shapes suddenly showed up in silhouette crossing the face of the large moon.

'Witches,' Sarah whispered. She gave Tear's fin another yank before slipping off his back into the water. Mitchell dismounted Rip in a shot.

Their luck held out – the witches flew past, and after a few tense minutes Mitchell and Sarah hoisted themselves onto the sharks again and continued their journey.

Not long afterwards, a ship with coal-black sails loomed out of the darkness ahead. The flag attached to the masthead unfurled briefly to reveal –

'Skull and crossbones,' gasped Mitchell.

'Just what we need,' Sarah moaned. 'Try and steer around it.'

Sarah leaned hard on Tear's dorsal fin and nudged him with her knees in an attempt to make him change direction, but the shark did not respond. Mitchell had no success with Rip either. Both sharks kept right on towards the pirate ship.

There was a lookout in the crow's nest and lusty singing from the poop deck. Every third word sounded like 'rum'.

The sloop was almost on top of them when the lookout called, 'Merpeople. Portside,' and a shadowy figure leaned over the bulwark waving a tumbler about.

'Blood 'n bones!' he exclaimed.

'Hold your breath!' Mitchell called to Sarah, just before the sharks dived underneath the keel. They surfaced on the other side of the ship, and kept going.

The rest of the voyage was uneventful. The stars faded, the sky lightened, a splendid fiery sun rose across the water, and by mid-morning, when the sharks entered a serene bay lapping at a curve of golden sand, every fibre of Sarah's body was yearning for sleep.

Quite suddenly the perfume of merrin flowers reached Sarah's nostrils. The bay turned out to be the mouth of the Crystal River, which led directly into the Fragrant Forest.

After travelling along the river for a couple for minutes, Sarah tasted the water. It was only a tiny bit brackish. A pair of tivers on the bank twisted their long necks in alarm, an otter paddled energetically away, and frogs croaked warnings amongst the reeds. No one, it seemed, was pleased to see sharks.

'We've made it,' Sarah said, with a feeling of comingled gratitude and exhaustion.

The sharks came to a stop in a pretty spot where merrin trees overhung one bank of the river and a little wind was playing among the treetops. A dryad in a soft, fluttering green dress swept out of a solid merrin trunk, blushed shyly, and morphed right back into the rough bark like a momentary trick of the eye.

'This way?' Mitchell said, thumbing towards the opposite bank where a grassy area like a small meadow swept down to the river. 'We can dry in the sun.'

Sarah was undecided for a moment. It *would* be nice to feel warm and dry once more, but shouldn't they hide in case of spying eagles?

A nightingale in the branches had tilted his head back to trill with all his heart. The sound had a soothing effect on Sarah. The forest seemed to enfold her in a sense of well being. 'Okay.'

Rip and Tear waited until their charges had swum to shore before shooting into the air in a parting salute, their wet skins glistening in the sunlight.

'Bye, Rip!' Mitchell called, raising a hand in farewell.

'Bye, Tear!' Sarah called. 'Thank you!'

And their unlikely rescuers departed.

Sarah threw herself on the grass in the drowsy warmth of the sun, quite prepared to fall into a doze. Mitchell flopped onto his stomach beside her.

Sarah's sense of well-being shattered in an instant.

Time almost slowed to a standstill as an eagle hurtled straight down from the sky, with its wings folded, to land on the grass not two metres away. The eagle's outline shivered, twisting and stretching as atoms shifted and rearranged, and resolved into a tall human-like figure; a figure draped in a purple cloak and with a beard that fell to his knees.

Noooooooo! Sarah wasn't prepared for this at all.

It felt like a cloud had come between her and the sun.

The nightingale fell silent.

Both Mitchell and Sarah scrambled back on their feet.

'Well, well. Look what *I've* just found,' Vanrod said in a silky-smooth voice, sweeping his hand to take in Mitchell and Sarah. 'My two absconded slaves. You don't look at *all* pleased to see me.' He bestowed upon them an indulgent smile that sent a crawling sensation down Sarah's back. 'Had a disappointing visit with the fish people, did you? I see you've returned empty handed. I must admit I'm mildly curious to know how you stole the ruby that I carried on my person …'

Stole the ruby? Had someone stolen the ruby?

Though Vanrod paused for an answer, he didn't get one.

Dispensing with the smile, he roared, 'HOW DID YOU STEAL IT?' so unexpectedly that Sarah jumped like a scalded dwiggle. She could feel her heart pounding in her ears.

'We *didn't* steal it,' Mitchell said boldly.

'No. Of *course* you didn't.' The smile was back on again. Vanrod's cooing voice chilled Sarah to her core. 'In hindsight, I should have killed you outright. Clearly, you are cleverer than I suspected; but not so clever that you can hide from *me.* '

In the dreadful pause that followed, Vanrod's eyes lingered piercingly on Sarah. Never had she felt so utterly smothered by dread. She shuffled closer to her brother, and he caught her trembling hand in his.

'You!' He indicated Sarah, and she felt a tightening in her chest. 'Tell me where you've hidden the ruby. Unless of course you would prefer to see the boy turned into an earthworm?'

'We don't have the ruby. We never took it,' Sarah pleaded.

'But we're glad if someone did,' Mitchell declared, flashing defiance from his eyes.

Sarah's fear swelled to a crescendo. *Shut up, Mitch! Don't be stupid!*

It was too late. Mitchell's hand was ripped from her own and he disappeared.

Sarah gasped. Had he been turned into an earthworm? Not daring to move her feet, Sarah examined the leaf-strewn ground.

This cannot be happening!

A few heart-stopping seconds passed before Sarah realised that Vanrod's gaze was directed upwards, and she too craned her neck. She drew in a sharp breath. Several metres above the ground Mitchell's body was spreadeagled face-downwards, rotating like a helicopter propeller, twirling faster and faster, whipping around and around. Sarah tried to follow with her eyes as her brother morphed into a spinning blur.

'Please stop!' Sarah appealed to Vanrod in a strangled voice. *'Please!'*

'Why would I stop?' Vanrod asked in genuine bewilderment. 'I'm having too much fun.'

Sarah stared at him, and, as he looked back at her, a hateful grin stole over his face.

It was too much to bear. This same wizard who was oppressing dwarves and terrorising merpeople was now killing her brother. None of it was fair! All of it was wrong!

And before Sarah was even aware of what she was doing she was swinging her fist at the wizard. 'BRING – MITCH – DOWN!'

'Aaargh!' she doubled up in pain. For all the good it did, she might as well have punched concrete. Vanrod's protective ring shielded him, as she had been told it would.

The malice of his ever-widening grin only incensed Sarah further. 'Boxing isn't really your forte, is it?' he said, clearly amused to see her wringing her hand.

A moment later she lashed out again. This time Vanrod caught her wrist and shoved her away so that she fell hard onto her back, hitting her head. Senses reeling, she lay there until the stars cleared from her eyes, then she pushed herself slowly into a sitting position.

It was hopeless. She could not hurt Vanrod.

As she looked up at her blur of a brother, her mouth went totally dry. She could hardly swallow. Her heart seemed to die within her. She wanted to crumple in despair.

'Tell me what you've done with the ruby,' Vanrod said in a calm, deadly voice.

Sarah gained her feet again, choking on tears, and laced her fingers together to steady her hands.

In the awful silence that waited for her response, Sarah's mind groped for a way out of this nightmare. Perhaps she could tell him that the merpeople had the diamond ...

Never!

Yet Vanrod could play this torture game indefinitely, and Sarah knew she could not hold out against him. She couldn't watch her brother suffer. She couldn't let him die. Like a plastic ruler that had been bent too far, she was about to break.

Chapter 33 – Monster

'Raaarrrgh!'

Sarah looked past Vanrod, and felt an immediate upswing of hope. Completely unnoticed, two white tigers had crept up behind Vanrod. The only creatures that sorcery held no power over. The only creatures that could make a mockery of Vanrod's ring.

Vanrod wheeled around to face the rippling-muscled male tiger and the supple female tiger.

The tigers coiled, ready to pounce.

In an instant, Vanrod vanished. A split second later an immense column had arisen in his place; a column that looked very much like it was covered in leathery elephant skin.

Astonished, Sarah took three steps back, following the column upwards with her eyes. Then her heart crashed with despair.

This was no column. This was a huge foreleg. Vanrod had shape-shifted into some kind of monster. He intended to overcome the tigers with brute strength.

Quick smart, Sarah got out from beneath the monster and skirted around it, towards its rear. As she did so, a muscular tail swung overhead and smacked into the trees on her left. *Crack!* A thick branch snapped like candy-cane and came crashing down, and Sarah ducked under the shower of twigs, leaves and flowers.

Her foot caught on something, and she found herself looking down at a body.

For a moment, Sarah's limbs seemed to freeze, and a terrible fear clutched at her chest.

'Mitch!'

He must have fallen when Vanrod's attention was diverted. His face was pale, his eyes vacant.

Then the thud of a monstrous foot behind her impelled her into action. Grabbing hold of Mitchell's arms, she managed to half-drag, half-carry his limp body a good ten metres off to the side, and lay him under a tree where sunshine shafted down through the spreading branches. She knew she should take his pulse, but she couldn't do it. She didn't want to know if ...

And then Mitchell groaned.

Sarah plumped down heavily beside him, relief surging through her. He was alive. She could have sobbed with thankfulness.

As she took a deep breath, her eyes strayed back to the monster. She had a side-on view of its two snaking necks and two dragonish heads that reached as high as the forest's leafy canopy. The monster's saliva hissed and steamed like acid when it dripped onto the ground, leaving brown patches in place of green grass.

The tigers looked like tiny kittens by comparison. They were keeping their distance, shoulder to shoulder, craning up at their new enemy.

Vanrod let out such a shattering roar that Sarah was forced to clap her hands over her ears. The male tiger opened his mouth to respond, but only a scared little mew trickled out.

'Run! Get away!' Sarah urged under her breath. It seemed senseless to stay and fight.

With ferocious speed the monster's crushing jaws snapped at the tigers; Sarah stifled a scream and the tigers recoiled just in time. Then a shrill whistle sounded, and the monster wheeled around, its eyes drawn to a human boy beside the river. Brodin produced another piercing leaf-whistle, but the monster didn't seem interested in him, and promptly returned its attention to the tigers.

Sarah jumped up and waved, and Brodin made his way towards her.

Vanrod struck again, this time with a swipe of hooked talons, and Sarah caught her breath as the tigress sprang out of reach. Was Vanrod just playing with the tigers before he *really* did some damage?

'You okay?' Brodin asked Mitchell, who, Sarah realised, was sitting up now, gaping at the monster.

'Tell me I'm dreaming,' Mitchell murmured.

Sarah saw pain flit across his face, and he clutched his shoulder. 'What's wrong?' she asked.

'Nothing. I'll be right,' Mitchell answered. 'Where did that monster come from?'

'It's Vanrod. He shape-shifted. No, don't get up.' Mitchell had pushed himself onto his hands and knees with a groan. 'Take it easy –' Clasping onto Sarah for support, Mitchell pulled himself up into a standing position.

'STO-O-O-P!' Brodin hollered.

A snufflelump calf had come charging out of nowhere, horn-first, straight for the monster. The calf was as tall as Sarah and easily ten times her weight, but – *thwack!* – with a casual kick, the monster sent it flying. Sarah cringed as the calf slammed into the ground. It trumpeted in pain, briefly struggled to heave itself up, and crumpled.

Seizing upon the diversion, the tigers had separated, and were now circling the monster in opposite directions. The monster turned slowly on the spot, stretching its two necks to keep them in view. Surely it was only a matter of time before Vanrod would be parading two tiger heads on his wall.

Sarah stole a sidelong peek at Brodin; he was clenching and unclenching his fists as he watched.

A deep rumble sounded from the monster's belly – Vanrod was laughing. Yes, this was all a game to him. Then his scalpel-sharp talons whipped through the air again, and what Sarah had been dreading actually came to pass. She forgot to breathe as a trail of vivid red welled along the male tiger's flank; he faltered.

The monster exploited his advantage. A huge foot pressed down upon the tiger, crushing him, forcing the air from his lungs, until there was a snapping sound.

'Noooo!' The cry sprang from Mitchell's lips.

It was too cruel. The beautiful white body lay motionless in the grass, pooled in blood. The sight was so horrible, it would forever remain imprinted on Sarah's memory. She looked away, sickened.

'Soldiers will arrive soon,' Brodin said bracingly.

Mitchell spread his hands in a hopeless gesture. 'So what? Vanrod's got that ring, remember. Soldiers can't hurt him.'

Brodin shook his head in disagreement. 'They can if the tiger manages to rip through the ring's shield.'

Mitchell snorted to show what he thought of the tiger's chances. Yet he didn't suggest escaping while they had the chance, Sarah noticed. Like her, he couldn't tear himself away; perhaps he too was praying for a miracle. His face twisted with pain for a moment and he looked ready to throw up.

'Is your shoulder hurting?'

'I'll be fine,' Mitchell grunted.

Distractedly, Sarah scanned the trees for the smallest movement that would indicate the arrival of swords and arrows. But the forest was perfectly still, perfectly quiet, as if it had turned its back on a horror it didn't want to see.

'Come quickly, please come quickly,' Sarah muttered under her breath.

'More tigers!' Mitchell exclaimed, as three fresh tigers advanced with great bounding strides along the riverbank.

The monster roared a fearless challenge. 'Bring it on!' it seemed to say.

But four tigers were harder to keep track of than two. In a twinkling the newcomers had leaped onto Vanrod's back, and Sarah dared to feel a smidgeon of hope, watching them clawing with all their might. She soon slumped in disappointment. It seemed that the monster's tough wrinkled hide could not be slit by tiger claws.

Monstrous teeth suddenly locked around the original tigress and wrenched her into the air. An agonised cry tore from Brodin. Sarah watched hopelessly as the tigress dangled from Vanrod's jaws, as good as dead. Vanrod thrashed his head from side to side like a pit-bull shaking its prey, before releasing the body.

Sarah felt like she was viewing a horror movie she couldn't turn off. Vanrod would dispense with each of the tigers, one by one.

Her eyes moved to the tree-line again, willing the elves to arrive. She waited … and waited … and meanwhile, the three remaining tigers had scaled the monster's wrinkled back as far as its neck, working their claws and teeth furiously.

A drizzle of purple blood began to show.

'Yes!' Mitchell burst out. 'The skin on the monster's necks must be thinner.'

But the monster was having none of that. With one slick movement, its tail swung like a wrecking ball, and a tiger was knocked to the ground, either dead or unconscious.

Sarah cringed; she heard Mitchell's heavy indrawn breath. The monster issued a triumphant ear-splitting bellow, and then Brodin was diving across the intervening space towards the motionless tiger.

'What's he doing?' Sarah cried fearfully.

Stupidly, valiantly, Brodin began trying to haul the tiger to safety, just as the monster's huge front feet began stomping purposefully.

In a heartbeat Mitchell and Sarah were beside Brodin, lending their muscles.

'He's alive,' Brodin told them.

Sarah kept her head down as she dragged the heavy tiger away from the monster's clumsy thumping feet; if the monster was going to stomp on her she'd rather not see it.

Completely unexpectedly the monster screamed with pain.

'Look!' Mitchell was pointing up at the purple blood cascading down one of the monster's long necks.

'A bit further,' Brodin urged, still tugging at the tiger. 'We're too close.'

Only when the tiger had been concealed among a mass of ferns did Mitchell, Sarah and Brodin hurry back to the tree-line to watch the fight.

The monster was by now throwing its weight against a merrin trunk, obviously hoping to crush its last two tormentors. It was a smart move. Before a minute had passed a loud *snap!* sounded and one of the tigers dropped to the ground on three legs, holding the fourth leg up. Sarah let out a cry of dismay, and the injured tiger limped away into the trees.

'Four down, one to go,' Mitchell groaned.

One tiger that must be starting to tire, one tiger that would not withstand being rammed against a merrin trunk for much longer.

Sarah was on the verge of despair.

'Finally!' Brodin burst out, punching the air, while Mitchell yelled, 'Alright!'

And then Sarah saw that five elven soldiers had sprung onto the scene; the Special Recovery Team she had first met just outside the Dead Wood.

The monster suddenly looked a little less sure of itself.

Skirting around it to get a clear shot at its wounds, the elves lost no time. A volley of arrows thudded into its neck, some piercing the wounded skin, others deflecting off the wizard's protective shield.

To Sarah's bewilderment, the monster broke into howls of horrible anguish.

Another flight of arrows. More howls.

'GO ELVES!' Brodin bawled, bouncing on the balls of his feet. 'GOOD SHOT, RHENYD!'

'Why's it making so much fuss?' Sarah wondered out loud. 'The arrows must be like tiny pinpricks.'

'Poison,' Brodin said.

'Poison?' Sarah repeated.

'On the arrow tips. GO RORTHAN!' Brodin hollered. He couldn't keep still, shifting from one foot to the other.

After that, things developed swiftly.

Arrow after arrow bit into the monster's wounds. With crazed eyes and harsh bellows, it made a run at first one elf, then another, scoring deep grooves in the ground with its claws as the light-footed elves eluded it.

'CELEDUR, LOOK OUT!' Brodin warned.

Sarah was convinced Vanrod's reflexes were slowing, that his movements were becoming sluggish, yet, propelled by rage, he kept charging at the elves even though he stood no chance of catching them. He was breaking into a sweat.

'He'll shape-shift back any second now,' Mitchell said darkly, 'and then he'll petrify the elves.'

'He wouldn't dare. Not with that white tiger so close,' Brodin replied with certainty.

Sarah watched with a mixture of glee and horror as purple blood began squirting from the monster's neck in rapid pulses. The monster wavered on its feet and made a choking gurgling sound.

'Yes!' Sarah crowed. 'He's dying!' She could have exploded with joyful relief.

But she spoke too soon.

In a flick of a frog's tongue, the monster vanished.

The purple-splattered tiger that had been raking at the monster's neck dropped to the ground, breathing hard.

Silence.

Elves, humans and the tiger checked this way and that, tense, wary. But all that remained of Vanrod was purple blood pooling in the deep furrows churned in the dirt.

'The villain has eluded us,' Celedur growled. 'He probably shape-shifted into a fly.'

Sarah looked at him dismally. She couldn't believe it. She had felt so certain that Vanrod's time was up.

The tiger, with its head and tail hanging low, appeared even more wretched than Sarah felt.

Suddenly Sarah became aware of someone calling her brother. 'Mitch! Mitch!'

Following the sound, all eyes turned towards the river.

'Mitch!' It was a female voice.

Mitchell set off across the grass, still clutching his shoulder.

Curious, and a little apprehensive, Sarah strode after him.

'Aquatica!' Mitchell gasped just moments later, and Sarah blinked in surprise.

The mermaid was in the river, gazing adoringly up at Mitchell from beneath her long lashes.

'Oh, Mitch, I thought you were going to *die* when I saw you spinning in the air,' Aquatica said tragically.

'So did I,' said Sarah, coming to a halt alongside her brother at the water's edge. 'My insides are still shaking.'

Aquatica's eyes slid over Sarah for the briefest second then returned to Mitchell. 'Was it really *dreadful?*'

'It was pretty bad,' Mitchell answered.

'You were *enormously* brave.'

'Yeah, well,' Mitchell said with a little swagger, 'I tried to be.'

'The way you spoke back to Vanrod, it's something I'll *never* forget.'

Mitchell stood a little taller.

'If he'd kept his mouth shut, he mightn't have been tossed in the air,' Sarah rumbled.

'I did something bad, Mitch,' Aquatica confessed.

Mitchell's eyes widened in surprise.

'You know I told you there was a kraken coming? It wasn't true. I just told you that to make you leave.'

'Oh.' Mitchell didn't seem sure how to respond to this news.

'Did you come all this way just to say sorry?' Sarah asked, her mouth tweaking with amusement.

'What's *she* doing here?' Brodin called out, bounding across the grass towards them.

Sarah flicked a look around. Rhenyd was also drawing closer, eyeing the mermaid with interest.

But the besotted mermaid only had eyes for Mitchell. 'I know you'll forgive me, Mitch, because I'm going to make you *so* happy,' Aquatica declared. 'There's something I wanted to tell you before, but I didn't know if I should trust you. So I followed you here. And I saw what happened with Vanrod. Now I trust you *completely*. I'd trust you with my *life*. It's obvious Vanrod hates you.'

Sarah shuddered all over. It wasn't a comfortable feeling to be hated by a powerful wizard.

'Go on,' Mitchell urged.

'Grandfather will scale me alive when he finds out,' Aquatica continued, 'so I won't go home straight away. You don't mind if I stay here for a bit, do you?'

'Of course not,' Mitchell answered.

'Good,' Aquatica said, breaking into a smile. 'I prefer salty water myself, and lots of waves, but there are plenty of fish in the river, so I won't starve, and at least *you'll* be close by.'

'What did you want to tell me?' Mitchell pressed.

'Oh, well, the thing is,' Aquatica said importantly, 'I spied on Grandfather after he took your diamond, and I found out he was hiding the magic sapphire. Here.' She fiddled with the seaweed belt she was wearing, and held up a package tied to it. 'You can have *both* the diamond *and* the sapphire.'

Rhenyd dropped his quiver with a clatter, and Mitchell just stood there, his mouth opening and closing in amazement.

Sarah felt like she had been bowled over. 'This is incredible,' she breathed.

Next moment, Brodin was prancing about like a spring lamb shouting, 'Yippeeee!!'

Aquatica giggled. 'You look like a fish, Mitch.'

Mitchell gave his head a shake. 'It's just ... I didn't expect ...' His voice tailed away.

'Well, are you going to come and get the stones?' Aquatica said, waving the package teasingly.

Supporting his shoulder with one hand, Mitchell skidded down the bank into the water, and took the package from Aquatica. Then she flung her arms around his neck and planted a smacking kiss on his lips.

Chapter 34 – Unexpected Clue

Mitchell awoke abruptly the next morning, gasping as pain stabbed his shoulder. He quickly rolled off it and determined to ask Warvel for some healing ointment.

It was kind of nice to be back in the tree house.

'G'day,' he greeted a robin, which was using its beak to pull a long earthworm from the ground. 'Are you on the housekeeping team?'

The robin dipped its head in confirmation, swinging the worm from its beak.

'I suppose Sarah's gone to get breakfast,' Mitchell said, eyeing her unoccupied bed opposite. He got up, pulled on a fresh tunic and leggings, and wandered outside into the elves' assembly ground.

And there he stopped abruptly, faced with a wall of shaggy snufflelump rumps with long swishing tails.

'What are you all looking at?' he muttered.

Weaving between snufflelump legs, he found himself on the edge of a great gathering of elves, bears, skunks, otters, even unicorns, who all seemed to be listening to quiet voices coming from the centre of the clearing. A horned owl drifted sleepily down from the trees and landed on the slender back of a doe.

Elves edged apart, inviting Mitchell into the inner circle, and he stepped forward self-consciously. For the first time since he'd come to Wystovia he spotted an elf baby – a chubby, gurgling little thing being burped over its father's shoulder. And as Mitchell neared the centre of the crowd, he saw there were dozens of elf children, all wearing leggings, belted tunics and curly-toed ankle-boots.

Mitchell picked Brodin's face out from the other faces; Brodin's blue eyes met Mitchell's and he gave a roguish grin.

And now Mitchell saw what had drawn the crowd. Fyrddin, captain of the elven army, Warvel, his deputy, and Sarah were seated together, and cupped in Sarah's hands were the magic diamond and the magic sapphire, both of which so sparkled and pulsed with light that they were almost mesmerising to behold.

'Mitch, I hope you slept well,' Warvel said warmly. 'Come join us.' Mitchell returned the smile and settled himself on the grass beside a company of river rats. 'We've just been swapping stories with Sarah.'

An airy voice, almost indistinguishable from the breeze stirring the merrin leaves, spoke faintly in his ear. 'Would you care for a drink?' The voice belonged to a semi-transparent figure in a gauzy green gown.

Mitchell accepted a bark cup from the dryad with thanks.

'You two have absolutely stunned us, you know,' Fyrddin said, while Mitchell took a long draught of kipberry cordial. 'We had no idea that the dwarves had found the diamond, and Marinarvius would not admit the truth of the sapphire rumours.'

Mitchell wiped his mouth with his hand. 'Marinarvius was a moron. He thought we'd been sent by Vanrod. He said an elf told him not to trust us.'

Fyrddin's eyebrows went up and down in genuine perplexity. 'Did he now? I've no idea why he would say that.'

The other elves looked equally puzzled – all except the elf girl Elteace whose gaze dropped to her boots, but not before a guilty expression had given her away.

Mitchell ground the bark cup into the dirt, suddenly seething.

The little creep! I suppose she took our dragon skins and our unicorn tears too. We could have been killed by eagles. We could have been enbubbled for life.

Mitchell would have found it immensely satisfying to punch Elteace the way Elteace had punched him. When at last he refocused on the conversation Fyrddin was reaching into his pocket saying, 'Now that we are all here, I have a surprise to share.'

Straight away, Mitchell could see from Fyrddin's face that whatever he had been going to extract from his pocket was missing. Fyrddin's eyes roved over the assembly – a bear cub balancing on two paws, an antlered stag gazing back at him serenely, otters jostling good-naturedly for space – until his eyes lighted on a dwiggle seemingly absorbed in grooming her friend.

'Lightfingers.' Fyrddin's voice was deep and threatening.

The dwiggle lifted her head to look at him, a picture of innocence.

'Bring it back. It is *not* a toy … *Now!*'

The dwiggle capered forward, enjoying the attention she had attracted, and dropped a hand into her pouch.

Someone gave a yell of delight. Sarah clapped her hands over her mouth, and Mitchell gasped, 'Holy ravioli!' All thoughts of Elteace fled from his mind.

The dwiggle had produced a red gemstone that seemed to burn with an inner fire.

Most of the elves stood gawping at the magic ruby with unblinking, open-mouthed expressions. Brodin was wearing an incredulous joyful look on his face.

And then a tumult of cheers and bellows and roars and toots and squeaks broke around him, and Sarah was clapping with delight.

Lightfingers gave several bows, as if the applause was for her, and there was hugging, back slapping, stamping, jigging up and down, skipping, bucking, rolling on the ground, wheeling in the air, and all the elves were talking and none of them were listening.

Fyrddin took the ruby without delay, and the dwiggle reluctantly moved back out of the limelight.

When the crowd settled down, Mitchell breathed the question on everyone's lips: 'How did you get it?'

'Let me present the noblest of water rats – Rodenticus,' said Fyrddin, and a water rat stepped forward, standing about a foot tall on his hind legs. 'You may not think so to look at him, but this little fellow has more backbone than a dragon.'

239

Mitchell and Sarah said hello, and the rat twitched his whiskers most genteelly. When the rat turned, Mitchell observed that he had no tail.

Fyrddin went on, 'Our prior attempts to retrieve the ruby led us to suspect that Vanrod carried it *on* him, which made the task of stealing it a challenge. Rodenticus was adamant that it was *his* turn to beard the wizard in the den, so to speak. And here you see the result.'

Mitchell was already thrilling with the possibility of finding the emerald.

'Unbelievable!' Sarah exclaimed.

Fyrddin gave a short laugh. 'Believe it. Here, hold it. It's as real as the others.'

Fyrddin dropped the ruby into Sarah's hands along with the diamond and sapphire. Three Banishing Stones together.

Amid the laughter and chatter only Mitchell perceived something was wrong. He saw a vague, other-worldly look steal across Sarah's face, and seconds later her whole body broke into a violent quivering, like she was having some kind of seizure.

'*Sarah?*' Mitchell said, touching her forearm. 'Sarah.' He appealed to Fyrddin. 'Quick! Help her!'

But before Fyrddin could react, the stones tumbled from Sarah's hands and she came back to herself.

'Are you okay?' Fyrddin's wife Jevelle was crouching beside Sarah, her arm around Sarah's shoulders.

'It's … it's the stones,' Sarah faltered.

All eyes were on Fyrddin now as he picked up the three stones and abruptly entered a shivering trance-like state.

'Fyrddin!' Jevelle knocked the gems from her husband's hands, and relief broke across her face to see his blank look fade.

Fyrddin gazed piercingly at Sarah. 'Did you see the emerald too?'

Sarah nodded. 'It fell into water.'

'Mitch, *you* hold the stones,' Fyrddin told him.

Mitchell wasn't so sure he wanted to.

'Go on,' Fyrddin pressed.

Cradling the three Banishing Stones in his hands, Mitchell found himself looking at something that his eyes could not see: a vision had hijacked his mind, projecting the clearest picture of a forget-me-not blue sky, and a glimmering green gemstone arcing through it like a struck golf ball. And now the gemstone was dropping into the deeper greenery of a vast forest, plummeting through thick foliage, and splashing into a little round pool of water. The gemstone vanished beneath ripples.

Abruptly the vision dissolved, and Mitchell came back to reality.

The Banishing Stones were passed from one elf to another, while Mitchell sat in silence, recovering from his astonishment. Very soon the entire assembly was buzzing with questions and theories.

'This is a sign! The emerald is right here under our noses, hidden in this forest!' cried an elf whose voice rang with certainty. 'All we need to do is find the pool.'

Her fervour was infectious and another wave of jubilation and riotous noise swept the clearing. Young elf children caught each other by the hands and started whirling about in pairs. Even the noxies were full of bounce; a dwiggle-bub that tried to catch one promptly keeled over.

Caught up in the excitement Mitchell hugged his sister whose face was one enormous smile. They both knew what this meant – no more Vanrod, no more witches. The dwarves would be able escape from the mountain and go home.

Fyrddin rose to his feet. 'Troops, we mustn't waste another minute. Vanrod is likely to return as soon as he recovers. Scour every inch of this forest until we find the little pond or spring that hides the emerald!'

'Does that mean no school?' Brodin queried hopefully.

'Absolutely not,' declared an elf with her hair pulled back severely from her face and twisted in a hard knot.

Fyrddin was looking at the elf as if he did not agree. He opened his mouth to speak, but she beat him to it. 'There are plenty of soldiers, animals and birds to do the searching. I will not have my students running around the forest when they should be studying.'

'Very well, the children may only search *outside* of school hours,' Fyrddin conceded.

Despite the chorus of groans and objections from all the elf children, the meeting broke up in buoyant spirits. Mitchell did not doubt they would recover the last of the Banishing Stones.

Chapter 35 – No Stone Unturned

The days ahead were given over to emerald hunting, and Mitchell enjoyed exploring the many winding animal trails. One day, he and Sarah rose early and startled a herd of white-tailed deer grazing in a glade. Another day, they crept up on a unicorn foal suckling its mother.

'Come and see Pfenwyn Academy,' Brodin coaxed, after a week had slipped by. 'Fyrddin will make you enrol soon.'

Mitchell was horrified. 'Make us enrol in school? But aren't the lessons in elvish?'

'No. They're in the common tongue. Elvish is only used for formal things – like graduation.'

This was bad, bad news. Mitchell had just assumed that attending school with the elves would be out of the question.

Brodin led the way along a path that dipped into a hollow. The forest floor was dotted with colourful fungi, and young ferns caught underfoot, releasing a spicy scent.

'I can say five swear words in elvish,' Brodin boasted. 'Want to hear?'

'No,' Sarah answered decidedly. 'Hey, we saw your photo in Mrs Stockylegs' house. How come you grew up in Wipple and now you're living here?'

'Nosy, aren't you?' Brodin returned.

'I can mind my own business if you want,' Sarah said, with dignity. She fixed her eyes on the hummingbirds that hovered around the merrin flowers.

'I'm just teasing,' Brodin said with a chuckle. 'There's not much to tell really. Mrs Stockylegs found a tiny baby on her doorstep one morning. No note. Nothing. That was me.'

Sarah almost tripped over the twining merrin roots. 'Your parents left you on the *doorstep*?' She sounded appalled.

Brodin nodded. 'Mrs Stockylegs took me in and brought me up, until last year when she kicked me out.'

'Kicked you *out*?' Sarah sounded doubly appalled.

'Said I was too disobedient. Thought Fyrddin would knock some discipline into me. So here I am.'

'Did your parents ever come back?' Mitchell questioned. As he trudged along he was brushing his hand against the ferns, some of which were still wet with dew.

'No, I've never heard a peep out of them.' Brodin spoke matter-of-factly. 'Who needs parents, anyway? All my life I've had dwarves bossing me around. I hoped it might be better in the forest, but the elves are just the same. Fyrddin's the worst.'

'I miss *my* parents,' Sarah said quietly.

'Haven't you ever tried to find out about your parents?' Mitchell asked.

'Not really,' Brodin replied with a shrug. 'It's not like any other humans live in Wystovia.'

'Do humans ever *visit*?' Mitchell asked.

'Sometimes. Once a travelling circus stayed for a few days. And there are traders that take camels across the desert up north. And sometimes pirates dock in Deepwater Harbour.'

'Why didn't the dwarves send you to live with other humans?' Sarah asked.

'They didn't want to lose track of me, in case my parents ever came back again. I reckon my parents are pirates, and they'll take me away with them on their ship when I'm fourteen. Mrs Stockylegs said that would only happen over her dead body.' Brodin chuckled, as if he could imagine Mrs Stockylegs taking on a pirate or two.

Coming at last to a large grassy opening between the trees, a signpost announced 'Pfenwyn Academy for Elves and Brodin'. Beyond the sign, a score of young elves looked to be engaged in fierce battle, wielding wooden swords. As they nimbly danced around one another, a teacher was calling out a flurry of instructions. 'Block that overhand stroke. Good. Now thrust your blade into your opponent. Shield's too low, Therawys. That's right. No – don't mind what Tristor's doing. Mind what *you're* doing! Great backhand, Llysion. Try a side cut next. Nice. Now forehand. Good. Quentor – neat sidestep, but loosen your grip. It's too tight. Position your opponent with the sun in her eyes ...'

Mitchell began to feel hopeful. If this was school, then school was cool. He glanced at Sarah. She was biting her nails, probably worrying someone might get skewered.

'Sword fighting and archery are compulsory subjects,' Brodin said. 'I've got a *real* sword you know, not just a practice one.'

'Yeah?' Mitchell looked at Brodin with open envy, and Brodin seemed pleased with the effect his revelation had made.

Mitchell found himself bewildered by a series of whirling, slashing and stabbing strokes as swords locked and clashed. The fleet-footed elves seemed instinctively to know when to lunge and parry and jump. Mitchell was lost in admiration of their skill.

Further on, a dozen students were shooting arrows at wooden targets no bigger than saucers.

Thud! Thud! Thud! A cluster of arrow shafts protruded neatly around each bullseye. No matter where or how the archery students were positioned – on one knee, running past, or perched in a tree – 'Each arrow lands dead centre on target,' Mitchell observed in an awed voice.

'Mind you compensate for the wind,' the teacher was calling.

'They're not *always* perfect shots,' Brodin said mischievously. 'Watch this.' He tugged at a clump of tiny blue flowers sprouting nearby, then fished a dragon skin from his pocket, and, enveloping himself in it, disappeared.

It didn't take long for chaos to erupt. Arrows began flying in random directions, students ran screaming for cover and Mitchell and Sarah ducked behind a tree. Fortunately, the blunted training arrows weren't lethal. Still, one shaft planted itself in the backside of the teacher who demanded, 'What's going on?' He extracted the arrow with a none-too-pleased expression.

'Brodin! That was terrible,' Sarah chided as soon as the culprit materialised beside her. 'Someone could've been hurt.'

'How d'you do that?' Mitchell asked, choking back laughter.

Brodin pointed to another spray of blue flowers. 'Sprinkled crushed confusalus petals on the arrows.'

Mitchell had expected the journey to end at a bricks-and-mortar building. Instead, it turned out that classrooms were nothing more than rings of trees encircling carpets of decomposing leaves and rocks upholstered with velvety moss.

A history teacher was recounting the tale of a troll who gave a charm bracelet to a princess. He had to project his voice over the noise of robins twittering and scolding and flitting from limb to limb.

Abruptly he stopped speaking, looked up at the robins with a frown and loudly cleared his throat. 'Do you mind?' he demanded.

The robins fell silent.

'Thank you.'

As the teacher continued talking, a saucy robin fluttered above his head and something went *splat!* on his shoulder.

'I think they *do* mind,' Brodin whispered, with a giggle.

The teacher pretended not to notice, and carried on speaking. 'When the princess slipped the bracelet onto her wrist it put her under a powerful enchantment, an enchantment which made her fall madly in love with the troll. He asked her to marry him, and she said yes. Her parents were at their wits' end trying to convince her to break off the engagement. And that is how the saying "Beware of trolls bearing gifts" came about. You'll need to remember that for your exams.'

'The princess didn't marry the troll, did she?' Brodin asked, quite forgetting that he wasn't part of the class.

The teacher shook his head. 'She *almost* married him. The wedding day arrived. The princess was getting dressed for it, and one of her maids accidentally undid the clasp on the bracelet. The bracelet fell from the princess's arm and the enchantment was instantly broken.'

A little further on, a teacher was demonstrating the use of a goblin weapon that sat neatly in the palm of her hand and reminded Sarah of a light-dimmer switch. 'Turn the knob one way and your victim's mind starts to fog. Turn it back the other way and their mind recovers. Who would like to try?' Hands flew up in an instant.

'This way, to the book tree,' Brodin announced, drawing Mitchell away by the arm.

Moments later, Brodin dived into a hollow trunk, and Mitchell and Sarah followed. The book tree was lined with floor-to-ceiling bookshelves laden with books. Candles brightened the natural light pouring through the windows.

'This must be the biggest book in the world,' Mitchell said, stopping in front of a book which stood almost as tall as himself. He read the title. '*Basic Hygiene for Giants.*'

Sarah had picked up a book too, and had just begun to flick through its pages when she dropped it with a squeal.

Mitchell looked at her.

'Find a spider?' Brodin queried, bounding over as if to rescue a damsel in distress.

'The pictures move!' Sarah exclaimed.

'Oh.' Brodin sounded disappointed. 'What are you reading?' He stooped down and retrieved *The Art of Woodland Dance.* 'Well, *course* the pictures move. How else could you learn the steps?'

'Yeah, Sarah, what did you expect?' Mitchell echoed with a teasing grin.

Sarah gave him a withering look.

Brodin reopened the book. 'See here, first the fauns form a ring, then they hold hands, then they take a step to the left.'

Mitchell watched over Brodin's shoulder as the figures in the sketch kicked up their hoofs …

Inside another ring of trees, students were working with wood, whittling, sawing, sanding. Someone was carving a beautiful storage chest.

247

Mitchell picked up a toy boat and fingered it. 'D'you think I could make a cricket bat and a skateboard?' he whispered to Sarah.

She shrugged. 'I don't see why not.'

Brodin discreetly plugged a wooden piccolo with chewing gum before marching Mitchell and Sarah away.

The smell of something yummy wafted past Mitchell's nose, and now he saw they were making a beeline for a group of students bustling about stone ovens and wooden tables.

Two dozen muffins with steam still rising from them had been set out on a rack.

'Yum, kipberry muffins,' Brodin whispered. A moment later he had swiped one. 'Ah – ah – ahh!' He juggled the muffin from hand to hand.

Suddenly the whole cooking class was looking at him.

'Maybe you should *ask* in future,' the teacher said, with the ghost of a smirk.

***

One week stretched to two, two stretched to three, and still the emerald had not been found.

'It's like looking for a tick on a snufflelump,' Sarah whined, swiping aside the twining vines that encroached on the narrow trail.

A couple of metres to the left, Mitchell was keeping pace, kicking up leaves in frustration as he scanned the ground. A tiver, resplendent in green and crimson feathers, left off pecking for grubs and hurried away.

'D'you reckon Vanrod's better yet?' Mitchell asked.

'Probably,' Sarah said gloomily. She looked up at the dwiggles jabbering and squealing as they darted along the limbs of the merrin trees. 'They never shut up, do they?'

Ordinarily the noise didn't bother Mitchell, but today everything was grating on his nerves, including the dwiggle skipping along in front, which kept stopping and turning, waiting for him to catch up as though it considered he was moving too slowly.

Yet he could not have asked for a more glorious day. There were dragonflies zipping around in pockets of sunshine, blossoms spilling down from the merrin trees, and playful breezes whisking subtle perfumes about.

'I keep thinking about that vision,' Sarah confided. 'I reckon we might all be wasting our time.'

'What d'you mean?'

'Well,' Sarah said, hesitantly, 'the forest could've changed heaps since the day the emerald disappeared, couldn't it? The pool might've dried up, or a tree might've fallen across it, or bushes might've grown over it –'

'Great! Just great!' Mitchell burst out, stopping in his tracks. 'If you're right, the emerald could be buried *any*where. We could spend all *year* digging and never –'

Mitchell broke off. A movement just on the edge of his vision caused him to look around. Winding through the trees towards them, he made out Elteace.

Sarah had seen her too.

'Come looking for a punching bag, has she?' Mitchell huffed.

'Shhh! She can hear you, remember?' Sarah said, her voice fading to the merest whisper.

The elf girl was drawing nearer. Mitchell shuffled closer to his sister, ready to defend her, and himself, if need be.

'I think I know where the emerald is,' Elteace said, as she advanced.

Scowling, Sarah crossed her arms. 'What's this? Some kind of trick?'

Elteace halted and locked eyes with Sarah. 'Listen, I'm sorry I gave that note to Marinarvius. When you brought us two Banishing Stones, I felt really bad.'

'So where d'you think the emerald is?' Mitchell asked, maintaining a sceptical expression.

'Well, when Sarah said that the Fragrant Forest could've changed a lot since the Banishing Stones disappeared, it made me think of *another* forest in Wystovia that's changed *heaps* since the stones disappeared.'

'Another forest? What other forest,' Mitchell asked.

It was Sarah who answered his question. 'The Dead Wood,' she breathed, her face suddenly brightening.

Elteace nodded. 'Dad once told me that the Dead Wood used to be as green as the Fragrant Forest. I'll bet the pool we've all been looking for is *there*, not here.'

Mitchell could feel his pulse quickening at this new possibility. 'Quick! We've got to tell Fyrddin. Hurry!'

Chapter 36 – Banished

Within the hour, Fyrddin dispatched the Special Recovery Team to the Dead Wood.

'Now all we have to do is wait,' Mitchell said complacently.

Sarah felt that waiting was the hardest thing of all. Would the emerald be found? Or would Vanrod return first?

A whole week dragged by, and Sarah was in an agony of suspense. She could hardly eat, she barely slept, she could not sit still.

Mitchell, on the other hand, found plenty of diversions. He learned to start a fire with flint and steel, he tried his hand at catching and smoking fish, and he even had a go at making beeswax candles.

'I'll just *die* if those elves don't return soon,' Sarah groaned, tossing another twig into the Crystal River as she paced the bank.

Both Mitchell, who was attempting to sew a pair of pyjamas, and Brodin, who was standing waist-deep at the river's edge, clasping a tiger cub, ignored her. The laughter of little elves playing nearby, hidden from sight by the trees, mingled with the chatter of the river and the chorus of birds.

Sarah didn't like being ignored. She looked critically at Mitchell's pyjamas. 'You know one leg's longer than the other, don't you?'

Mitchell's mouth curved in a half-smile. 'I'm setting a new trend.'

Sarah had never seen such untidy stitching. 'They're gonna fall apart as soon as you wash them,' she predicted.

'Then I won't wash them,' Mitchell said, still unruffled.

The elf infants had broken into song, the tune of which sounded vaguely familiar. Sarah listened closely to the words:

'Ring-a-ring-a-roses,

251

Watch your little toesies,
A noxie! A noxie!
We all fall down.'

'I don't know why Fyrddin isn't making *you* go to school,' grumbled Brodin. The tubby little tiger cub shrieked piteously as he plunged it into the water.

'Yeah, well, don't remind him,' Mitchell shot back. 'Sarah's the brainiac, not me.'

With a swift movement that made Brodin cry out, the cub swiped Brodin with its claws.

Sarah rounded on Brodin. 'Leave the poor thing alone. He'll learn to swim when he's –'

Distant shouts distracted her, and she looked around.

'They've returned!' someone hollered. 'The SRT's back!'

Mitchell flung down his pyjamas and was on his feet in a flash, but Sarah was already racing ahead as if her feet had wings, joining the rush towards the elves' assembly ground.

As she ran, she could hear applause, yells of delight, and children hooting, and her heart gave a great leap.

She pried her way through the press of elves and deer and bears.

And there was Gwynia, from the Special Recovery Team, holding high a stunning green stone for all to admire. 'The little spring guarded its secret well,' she said, smiling.

Sarah's heart flooded with triumph. She didn't know whether to laugh or cry or sing. Before she had quite decided, her feet started to jump up and down on springs of joy.

A skunk was tearing up and down a merrin trunk in a transport of excitement.

'Woohooo!' Mitchell had come up beside her, a vast grin stretching across his face. Sarah high-fived him.

The faces of the forest dwellers conveyed a mix of emotions: some wildly happy, some exultant, some dazed-looking or even blank with shock that the four stones had finally been reunited. Brodin had broken into a victory boogie. Fyrddin, who had hold of the other three Banishing Stones, beamed as he congratulated the

Special Recovery Team. Warvel was hugging his sister Aolyn, who was still carting around the owl chick, which seemed much perkier now and was nibbling her fingers. Elteace had turned up, with her mother and younger brother, and although she wasn't exactly smiling, she didn't look *un*happy either.

'That's brilliant!' an elf boy in glasses exclaimed. 'Just brilliant!'

'Elteace is the one who's brilliant. It was *her* theory that proved to be correct,' said Jevelle, resting a hand on Elteace's shoulder.

'The time to act is now,' Fyrddin announced in a clear, carrying voice. 'I think we all agree that Vanrod, his dragons and his eagles should be banished –'

His words were drowned by elves calling out in the affirmative.

'– as well as the witches and the wolves,' Fyrddin pressed on, raising his voice to be heard.

The clamour increased. Even more heads were nodding. It seemed like everyone was in agreement.

'No!' Sarah's voice stood out from the rest. 'No!' she repeated vehemently.

Every head swivelled towards her, a few throwing disagreeable looks her way.

'What's up with *you*?' Mitchell muttered, shrinking with embarrassment.

Fyrddin's eyebrows had risen in puzzlement; he waited for Sarah to explain and she met his gaze unflinchingly.

'There's one little witch girl who is kind, and I don't think we should banish her.'

At this there was an immediate, predictable outcry.

'The witches have done despicable things in Wystovia. We don't want *any* of them.'

'Send them all away.'

'They can't be trusted. We've learnt *that* the hard way.'

One voice was more passionate than the rest. Whose was it? Sarah's eyes sifted through the faces until they lighted upon Elteace's mother.

Sarah was tempted to let the matter drop. She had no desire to make herself unpopular, and clearly she alone felt that it wasn't fair to treat the kind witch girl the same as the others. Yet something in Sarah's character – perhaps a strong sense of justice – compelled her to speak out. 'She helped a baby deer that got hurt when the witches attacked the forest ... and she gave us a tuning fork that scared off the bats ... and I saw her feed a little bear in a cage in Wartville. Doesn't anyone know who I mean? She's shorter than me ... really ugly ... with a mole on her nose ... and a long, pointy chin ... and hair that's all messy and greasy.'

'They all look the same to me,' someone muttered.

Only Rhenyd, from the Special Recovery Team, was nodding his head. 'The child is called Stella.' Hundreds of pairs of eyes swung his way. 'Stella came to my notice when the ravens caught a robin flying over Wartville and she released it. In punishment, she was whipped with magic lashes. I think it was she who helped the bear cub escape – she's being held in Wartville dungeon.'

'Mightn't it be better to banish her with the rest, just in case she turns bad when she grows up?' the bespectacled elf boy suggested.

There were noises and gestures of support.

Concern creased Fyrddin's forehead. 'It's impossible to know what someone *might* do in the future, but on the basis of the child's past behaviour, we have no grounds to condemn her.' He turned to his wife. 'Shall we bring her to the forest? Teach her other ways than Wartville ways?'

The suggestion was met with a hail of protests.

'That's preposterous!'

'Outrageous!'

'Yuk! No way! I don't want that freak show living here!' Brodin declared, pulling an unpleasant face.

Jevelle ignored them all, and nodded at her husband. 'If she will come.'

'Surely you're not serious!' Elteace's mother exploded.

Sarah wanted to shrink from the reproachful glares.

'You've set the wolf among the dwiggles now,' Aolyn whispered in her ear.

Fyrddin held up his hand for quiet. 'It's only fair to give the child a chance,' he responded evenly. 'She's only young.'

There were muted rumblings, but in the end the elves bowed to Fyrddin's authority.

Sarah suspected many of the elves would never talk to her again, but then Aolyn whispered in her ear, 'That took moral courage to speak out. Well done.'

Sarah lifted her chin. It was true – it *had* taken courage; not the same kind of courage Mitchell showed in the face of dragons, but courage nonetheless.

'So,' continued Fyrddin, 'it is decided. And I don't think anyone will object if Mitch and Sarah do the honours' – he offered the Banishing Stones to Mitchell – 'since they played a pivotal role in bringing the stones together.'

Mitchell looked at Fyrddin in pop-eyed amazement.

Sarah shuffled a little uncomfortably; she was sure *plenty* of elves would like to object.

'Just tell the stones to banish Vanrod and his dragons and his eagles,' Fyrddin prompted.

Mitchell accepted the stones with a grimace, as if he expected to be overcome by another vision, and the front row of the assembly shuffled back a little.

And now the chatter died away and everyone stood, formal and silent. It seemed like the appropriate thing to do; somehow the deep magic in the Banishing Stones deserved to be acknowledged.

Mitchell dropped his gaze to the stones, which were shot with coloured light, and he took a deep breath.

'You can do it,' Fyrddin said.

The crowd shifted restlessly; Sarah could sense the mounting anticipation.

This was it then. The moment they had all been waiting for. Sarah felt a shiver of excitement run up and down her spine.

'Banish Vanrod and his dragons and his eagles,' Mitchell said loudly.

The magic took immediate effect. The ground shook and a piercing white light burst from the stones, a light so bright it stabbed Sarah's eyes; she hid her face in her hands for a moment.

Far away, in the Midway Mountains, Vanrod vanished from his cave, and the dragons and eagles vanished along with him. Although the forest-dwellers could see nothing of this, they knew it to be true and stood in complete and utter silence.

Then they could contain themselves no longer, and the forest resounded with cheering, screeching, clapping, bellowing, twittering, and roaring; an elf danced with her baby in her arms; the dwiggles were pinging like popcorn; even the merrin trees brushed branches together in applause.

When the gleeful madness subsided, Mitchell handed the stones to Sarah. She could hear their humming now, feel them vibrating in her palms. A tingle of excitement ran through her all way to her toes.

'Go ahead,' Fyrddin said with a supportive nod. 'Tell the stones to banish all the wolves and all the witches except for Stella.'

Warvel was beaming encouragement.

Speaking in a clear voice, Sarah said, 'Banish all the wolves, and all the witches except for Stella.'

Again the stones exploded with light and the earth quaked. A riot of renewed cheering, stomping, pawing, trumpeting and fluttering followed.

Sarah looked down at her hands. The Banishing Stones had ceased to tremble; they had lost their inner fire. Their work was done.

'So that's that then,' Fyrddin said, when most of the noise subsided. 'Oh, except there's still one *very* important matter to resolve.'

Everyone looked at him, their faces spilling over with happiness. All the birds in the forest had burst into song

'What important matter?' Jevelle asked.

'I think we should banish Mitch and Sarah, too, don't you? After all, *they* don't belong here do they?'

His words fell into a resounding silence.

Sarah stared at Fyrddin. *Surely he can't be serious? After everything Mitch and I have been through ...* Her insides began to twist and knot with feelings of betrayal, resentment and hurt.

She glanced at her brother; the joy of just minutes ago had been wiped from his face. Her eyes swept pleadingly over the crowd. Jevelle looked astounded and Warvel seemed distressed, yet neither was prepared to publicly challenge Fyrddin.

'You ... No ... That ...' Brodin spluttered, clearly struggling for words to express his indignation. There was a growl, low and threatening; a white tiger did not approve either, and it showed from the peaks of his pricked ears to the tip of his twitching tail. Sarah felt a rush of gratitude towards them both.

'Relax, friend,' Fyrddin said, addressing the tiger. 'Mitch and Sarah *want* to go home, to return to their world, and the Banishing Stones can take them there.'

Sarah felt like she had been struck by a freight train.

Go home? Was it possible?

She scoured the cobwebs of her memory for what Fyrddin had told her about the Banishing Stones.

Fyrddin seemed to guess what she was thinking. 'Don't you remember that I told you the Banishing Stones give us power to expel anyone we want from our borders, back to wherever they came from?'

Back to wherever they came from!

Sarah swallowed and found her voice. '*Really?*'

Mitchell's face was breaking into a hesitant smile, and the clearing began to swell with voices talking at once, some in the common tongue, some in elvish.

Fyrddin waited for quiet before he resumed. 'Moreover, I propose that Mitch and Sarah take the Banishing Stones *with* them – that Mitch and Sarah banish themselves.'

The faces that looked back at him were mystified. A bear scratched the fur around its neck, as if it were thinking hard, then shook its head as if it couldn't make sense of Fyrddin's suggestion.

'You want Mitch and Sarah to take the stones *out of our world?*' an elf clarified. 'You don't want us to keep the stones *here* in the forest?'

'It's a radical idea, I know,' said Fyrddin, 'but let me explain my reasoning. You recall that the last time all four Banishing Stones were together, Wystovia was torn apart by civil war because the races could not agree on who should guard the stones. That dispute was never resolved, so what's to stop another war starting all over again? Now if, as I propose, Mitch and Sarah were to take the stones *away*, then arguments would be pointless. When the stones are needed in future, they'll start flashing, and Mitch and Sarah can unbanish themselves and return the stones to Wystovia. That is' – Fyrddin turned his gaze on Mitchell and Sarah – 'if they would be happy to serve us in this manner?'

You could have heard a ripe kipberry drop from the bushes. Everyone was thinking hard, you could see it on their faces, see them working through the merits of Fyrddin's suggestion. Then a chant started up – was that Brodin's fervent voice?

'Stone bearers, stone bearers, stone bearers!'

The call was taken up by others, louder and louder.

'Stone bearers, stone bearers, stone bearers!'

Even the dwiggles showed their approval by capering around throwing handfuls of leaves and twigs into the air.

Mitchell turned to his sister, eyes alight. 'Well?'

'Stone bearers, stone bearers, stone bearers!'

Sarah could only nod her head and compress her lips tightly; she didn't trust her voice. They were going home, and the possibility that one day they might pop back to Wystovia was the icing on the cake.

'We'll do it!' Mitchell added his voice to the confusion. 'WE'LL DO IT!' he shouted.

Cheers erupted, and Warvel was pumping Sarah's hand. 'I know we can trust you,' was all he said.

When the noise faded, Fyrddin waved Mitchell and Sarah away. 'Go and get changed out of those embarrassing tights,' he said, with a smile hovering around his mouth.

Sarah felt so light and trembly with excitement that she seemed to float all the way to the tree-house. It took her several attempts before she managed to put her t-shirt and shorts on the correct way.

Mitchell gave her an about-time-too look when she finally announced, 'I'm ready.'

And now, as they picked their way, barefoot, back to the centre of the gathering, animals, dryads and elves surged closer to bid farewell.

'I'll show you Penangalus next time you come,' Brodin promised.

Sarah felt a deep shiver of gladness. *Next time.*

'Maybe you'll have found your parents by then,' Mitchell said hopefully.

Brodin shrugged. 'Maybe.'

Jevelle gave Sarah an affectionate hug, and Sarah's eyes glazed with tears she had been trying to repress.

'Thanks for lending us the clothes and everything,' Sarah said as she hugged Jevelle back.

'Oh, that's nothing. Now take good care of yourselves,' Jevelle instructed in her motherly way.

'Come back soon,' Aolyn ordered, and the owl chick in her hand peeped softly.

Then there were more hugs, handshakes, hearty back slaps, and friendly licks.

Not everyone hates me, Sarah reflected happily. She stretched out her hand to a unicorn. It sniffed her hand cautiously before allowing her to rub its warm, silken muzzle and stroke its beautiful mane.

When the goodbyes had been said, Fyrddin blew a leaf whistle to call for attention, and said, 'Sarah, are you ready?'

Sarah clasped the four Banishing Stones in her trembling hands, conscious that all eyes were upon her. And now, quite suddenly, she found herself beset with doubts. What if the stones didn't work between worlds? What if they didn't send her home? She just knew she wouldn't be able to bear the disappointment.

'Hurry up, then,' Mitchell urged.

And so Sarah swallowed hard and spoke the terrifying words – 'Banish Mitch and me.'

Chapter 37 – Secrets

The last thing Mitchell glimpsed, before his vision went fuzzy, was a snufflelump rearing onto its substantial hind legs and elves ducking for cover. He felt a peculiar squeezing, pulling sensation all over, not painful, just weird, and moments later, a vast blue ocean surged into view.

And there he stood, on the very same rock where his adventure began, with salt spray dashing his shins and a thin layer of cool water swelling around his toes before the sea sucked it away again.

Beside him, Sarah was gazing wordlessly about.

The beach seemed at once familiar and foreign, as if he was a shipwreck survivor returning home after years of being lost. Wystovia might have been a mere flight of fancy, except for the gemstones in Sarah's hands.

Something wet glided down Mitchell's cheeks, and, surprised to find that it was tears, he smartly brushed them away. He could have stood there for ages, letting everything that had happened sink in …

'Let's go,' Sarah said, tugging his arm. 'I don't know how we're going to get home.'

Mitchell and Sarah found their towels, very surprisingly, lying a few feet away.

'Here, take these and wrap them in your towel,' Sarah said, handing him the ruby and the diamond. 'We'll have to keep the stones hidden. No one'll believe us – they'll think we've stolen them.'

Once they had concealed the Banishing Stones in their towels, Mitchell and Sarah headed in the direction of the caravan park, across the rock shelf, across the warm sand, past children splashing in the surf, past teens soaking up sunshine and music, past parents keeping a watchful eye on toddlers.

It felt bizarre to be surrounded by ordinary beachgoers – holidaymakers working sun-cream into their shoulders. Mitchell felt an impulse to run along the sand shouting, 'Dragons are real! Elves are real! Mermaids are real! Magic is real!' That would shock them. He guessed that if Sarah knew what he was thinking, she would run in the opposite direction.

'There's probably a police station in town we can ring home from,' Sarah was saying. 'But we're going to need a story, to explain –'

She stopped short, staring a little way ahead. Following her gaze, Mitchell's eyes widened in disbelief, and he halted too. There was their mother, lounging at her ease on a foldout beach chair, reading a book. Beside her, on another beach chair, Aunt Alison was strumming a ukulele, and in front of them both, their cousin Rufus was building a sandcastle.

Rufus! Mitchell had completely forgotten about his little cousin.

'Why are they … why don't they …? Sarah couldn't get her question out, but Mitchell guessed what she meant.

'Looks like they haven't even missed us,' Mitchell answered thoughtfully. 'Time must go slower in our world. I've read about that kind of thing.'

'No!' Sarah looked incredulous. 'That can't happen, can it? Not *really?*'

Mitchell shrugged.

Sarah fired up with indignation. 'You mean, I've been worrying *all* this time about Mum and Dad worrying about us, for *nothing?*'

'Just act cool, and see what Mum says,' Mitchell advised. 'Come on.'

Rufus lifted his head when Mitchell's shadow fell over the conch resting by his side. 'How did you disappear like that?' he demanded, getting hurriedly to his feet. His pudgy face looked a little scared as well as resentful.

Aunt Alison stopped her tuneless strumming and frowned behind her sunglasses.

'I was wondering when you'd show up,' Mrs Weaver said from under her big floppy hat. 'I was starting to get a bit worried.' She closed her book, using her finger as a bookmark. 'You really upset Rufus, you know. It was unkind to just go off without him like that. I *did* expect better of you.'

'Sorry, Rufus,' Sarah said contritely.

'Yeah, sorry, Rufus,' Mitchell echoed.

Before their mother could embark on a lecture, they were down on the sand with their arms flung about her.

'It won't happen again,' Sarah's muffled voice promised.

'Well, I hope not,' Mrs Weaver responded, clearly unprepared for this sudden display of affection. She hugged her children back.

'So, where *did* you guys disappear to?' Aunt Alison queried as the hug broke up. 'I had a quick scout around when Rufus told me you'd just melted into the ether.' She winked at Sarah. 'Such a vivid imagination, what with gremlins under the bed and ghosties in the attic.'

Rufus puffed up with fury. 'They *did* just vanish! They *did*! I *saw* them!' He stomped his porky foot on the sand.

Mitchell felt the eyes of his mother and his aunt upon him. He knew he had to come up with *some* explanation. 'Oh, we just meant to walk as far as the rock-pools, but we ended up going a lot further,' Mitchell answered in his most casual, mature manner.

Rufus pushed out his bottom lip, glaring up at Mitchell with a look of fury.

'Hmmm, well, don't wander so far again,' Mrs Weaver chided. 'I wouldn't like you to get into any kind of trouble.'

'We won't,' Sarah promised, slipping a hand into her mother's.

'But ... you ... they're *lying,* Mum!' Rufus exploded. 'They're *lying*!'

'Rufy-boy.' His mother spoke gently to him. 'Come here.'

Rufus stumped over to her.

Aunt Alison looked at him fondly for a moment, then spat on her hand and used the spit to slick down his hair. As she did so, she spoke coaxingly. 'That's not nice, is it, to say that about your cousins? Especially when they've apologised. Forgive and forget, and play nicely. How 'bout you show them that super-duper shell you found?'

Mitchell winced as he guessed how Rufus must feel not being believed. Recent experience had shown him what *that* was like.

Deciding to sulk, Rufus stomped off down the beach by himself with his arms crossed and his shoulders hunched.

'He's just having a little tanty. He'll get over it,' Aunt Alison said. 'Anyone want to read *Ukulele for Dummies*? – No? – Then, if you can amuse yourselves without me for a bit, I'll just carry on practising.'

Aunt Alison recommenced her strumming, and Mitchell glanced around. No wonder the other beachgoers had left a large gap around her. He wondered how his mum could concentrate to read.

'Mum, have you got change on you for an ice-cream?' Mitchell asked quickly.

'Ice-cream? I'd rather you ate a banana or –' Mrs Weaver began.

'Fetch me a double scoop waffle cone, Mitch,' Aunt Alison cut in. 'One of those ones dipped in chocolate.'

Mrs Weaver shook her head but caved in.

'Sarah, mind my towel,' Mitchell said, giving his sister a significant look. Then, jiggling coins around in his hand, he chased after his cousin.

'Hey Rufus, want an ice cream?'

Rufus looked around at Mitchell with a hard glare.

'Come on,' Mitchell insisted. 'There's a van just up here. And then I'll play cricket with you, if you want.'

Rufus appeared to soften. 'Can I bat?' he asked.

'Sure,' Mitchell answered.

Chapter 38 – Fairytale Ending

Something strange was going on, Stella was sure of it, and it made her feel uneasy.

For one thing, it had been hours since Cruella the gaoler had last stopped by to taunt the prisoners. This seemed most out of character.

Then there was the mysterious disappearance of the old witch two cells away. As soon as a fresh slice of bread had appeared on Stella's magical plate, Stella had torn the bread in two, calling out, 'Hazar, lunch is ready.' But Hazar had not responded with her usual, 'Throw it here, then.' She hadn't responded at all. And when Stella stared hard into the shadows, Hazar was nowhere to be seen.

Something else was missing, too. Where were the noises that usually floated from the street into her cell through the tiny vent high in the wall; the heated arguments and cackling laughter?

Yes, Stella was convinced something was brewing, and it put her into a state of nervous apprehension.

Nothing could have prepared her for the sight that roused her some hours later: three silvery lights, like miniature glimmering stars, floating along the dungeon corridor, and three tall elves following soundlessly in their wake.

Stella felt her forehead. Had she sunk into delirium? No, there was no fever. Perhaps being imprisoned had finally reduced her to insanity.

'Don't be afraid,' said one of the elves, passing Stella a merrin fruit through the bars. 'We'll have you out of here in a twinkling.'

Stella could feel the weight of the merrin fruit in her hand and smell its ripe sweetness, yet still she sat there, in a kind of daze, gazing out through the bars.

Only the echoing racket of axes smashing locks brought Stella to her senses. Incomprehensible as this all seemed, it was no hallucination.

'Eat up, then,' another elf told her. 'You'll need your strength.' Reassured by his friendly tone, Stella peeled the merrin fruit and tucked in, slurping up the sticky juice dribbling down her wrists.

There were merrin nuts too, and Stella cracked them open between the palms of her hands by applying a little pressure. The nut meat was sweet and crunchy.

And now the door to her cell swung open.

'Out you come,' the elf said pleasantly, before moving on to free another prisoner.

Tentatively, Stella stepped into the corridor.

'Help me,' pleaded a faint voice.

Stella immediately began squinting through the dimness into first one cell and then another, looking for the owner of the voice.

'Help,' called the voice again, closer now, and an emaciated-looking faun took shape out of the gloom. 'I find I am unable to walk without assistance,' he said, apologetically.

'That's okay. I'm pretty strong,' Stella responded. She hoisted him up and slipped an arm around his hairy waist. 'This way.' And she guided him towards the narrow flight of stairs leading out of the dungeon.

Clip ... clop ... clip ... clop went his hooves on the stone floor as he tottered slowly along.

Stella soon discovered she wasn't nearly as strong as she had supposed, for her long confinement and poor diet had sapped most of her strength. The steep stairs took quite an effort to negotiate, supporting the faun, and it was some minutes before they gained the top and emerged, blinking, into lovely sunshine.

Stella glanced up and down the street. Where was the smog that usually clogged the air? A black cat perched on a first-floor window sill gazed at her with insolent green eyes, but there wasn't a single witch to be seen. It was astounding.

266

Finding the least filthy patch of cobblestones she could, Stella eased the faun down to a sitting position. 'Thank you, thank you indeed,' he murmured.

Two elves joined them. 'I'll take over from here,' the male elf said.

As he crouched down beside the faun, and pulled a flask from his belt, the female elf addressed Stella. 'Hello. You must be Stella. My name is Jevelle. You're probably wondering what's going on?'

Stella nodded. Was she ever wondering!

In a few words, Jevelle explained that the Banishing Stones had been found and the witches had been banished.

'Do you want to sit down, child?' Jevelle said hastily. 'You're looking a little pale.'

Stella sat before she collapsed, completely overwhelmed. Jevelle squatted down beside her.

'But ... I ... what about *me*?' Stella managed to say after a moment.

'That depends entirely on you,' Jevelle answered.

Jevelle put a series of questions to Stella: questions about her imprisonment, her family, her life in Wartville. As Stella answered, she could feel the elf's steady indigo eyes appraising her, nice eyes, concerned eyes.

When Jevelle ran out of questions, she began to tell Stella what it was like living in the Fragrant Forest. She spoke about the island of Penangalus where the elf children live, and Pfenwyn Academy where the elf children study. Stella heard the elf out in attentive silence, although in the back of her mind she wondered why the elf would be telling her all this.

She found out soon enough.

'Stella, we would like to offer you a home in the Fragrant Forest,' Jevelle concluded.

Stella was so overpowered with amazement she couldn't move, couldn't speak.

'I know it's rather irregular,' Jevelle went on, 'but I think you would be happy living amongst us.'

'You want *me* to come and live with the elves?' Stella finally managed to stammer.

Jevelle nodded. 'Only if you'd like to.'

Stella felt her throat tighten. Oh wouldn't she? It seemed too good to be true. A beautiful green forest. All sorts of wonderful birds and animals and flowers.

She yearned to say 'Yes!' … but there was one obstacle.

'Can I take Twiggy?' Stella asked, her voice husky with emotion. Then, in response to Jevelle's look of incomprehension, Stella rephrased the question. 'Can I take my broomstick?'

Jevelle nodded. 'Of course.'

Then another thought struck Stella. 'Can I take my wand?'

Jevelle considered for a moment before replying. 'If you promise to use it only for good.'

'I promise.'

The gargoyle over the dungeon doorway twisted its mouth into a grotesque scowl.

'I don't suppose you can grow a tail on a rat?' Jevelle inquired, as if by afterthought.

'Rat tails are easy,' Stella assured her.

'That's excellent!' Jevelle looked extremely pleased. 'Our medicine can heal damaged tissue, regrow skin, and mend broken bones, but entirely new rat tails are beyond us. Oh, one more thing. Everyone in the forest has a job to do, so you will be expected to contribute in some way too.'

Uh-oh! Alarm bells pealed in Stella's head. Would she be forced to cook and clean? She listened in trepidation as Jevelle went on to say, 'We've been searching for someone to take on a *very* special responsibility and so far no one has been found who quite suits the work as I think *you* might. You see, we have five dragon eggs that are close to hatching, and baby dragons could get into all sorts of scrapes without a mother or father looking out for them. We need someone to care for the hatchlings, someone to feed them and teach them to fly, someone to keep an eye out that they don't get hurt or lost. Do you think you would enjoy taking on this important role?'

'*Me?*' Stella gasped. 'Why *me?*'

Jevelle laughed kindly. 'Because, my child, you obviously love animals.'

My child.

Stella, who had never felt like anybody's child, savoured Jevelle's words like a tasty morsel.

'You are also an expert flyer, and we want our dragons to learn from the best. Moreover, you have the power to shape-shift into a dragon yourself, which could prove useful when bringing a wayward youngster into line.'

As Jevelle spoke, Stella envisioned herself cruising a few feet above the merrin trees on Twiggy, with five dragon fledglings in tow flapping and panting, trying to keep up.

'The work won't be easy but we would all support you,' Jevelle added, as if Stella needed convincing.

Stella felt just as if she had toppled into a fairy story, just as if she was about to embark on her Happily Ever After. Too overcome to speak, she nodded with enthusiasm and her black eyes shone.

***

Late the next evening, Rodenticus completed the rounds of his burrow and satisfied himself that all his little ratlings were snug asleep in bed. Then he wandered outside and gazed up at the starry sky, hugging his fine new tail. It came as no surprise to him to see both moons wearing broad smiles, for surely *all* the world was happy tonight.

The large moon happened to be smiling upon the joyful spectacle of fireworks whizzing and exploding and tumbling like shimmering gems over Wipple. The dwarves who had been enslaved in the mountains were now reunited with their families and celebrating their freedom.

The small moon, likewise, was captivated by a very pretty scene it hadn't enjoyed for a long time: pods of noisy merchildren romping in the churning surf of the Stormy Sea.

But happiest of all was the merrin tree watching over Stella as she slept nestled between a dappled baby deer and a fuzzy bear cub.

'It's great you came to visit, Peter,' Stella mumbled in her sleep, 'but I'm not coming to Neverland. I like it way better here.'